The Nightingales of Troy

The NIGHTINGALES *of* TROY

STORIES *of* ONE FAMILY'S CENTURY

ALICE FULTON

W. W. NORTON & COMPANY

New York   London

For information about permission to reproduce
selections from this book, write to Permissions,
W. W. Norton & Company, Inc.,
500 Fifth Avenue, New York, NY 10110

For information about special discounts for bulk purchases,
please contact W. W. Norton Special Sales at
specialsales@wwnorton.com or 800-233-4830

Manufacturing by The Haddon Craftsmen, Inc.
Book design by JAM Design
Production manager: Anna Oler

Library of Congress Cataloging-in-Publication Data

Fulton, Alice, date.
The nightingales of Troy : stories of one
family's century / Alice Fulton. — 1st ed.
p. cm.
Includes bibliographical references.
ISBN 978-0-393-04887-2 (hardcover)
1. Women—Fiction. 2. Troy (N.Y.)—Fiction. 3. United States—Social
life and customs—20th century—Fiction. 4. Domestic fiction. I.
Title.
PS3556.U515N54 2008
813'.54—dc22

2008013206

W. W. Norton & Company, Inc.
500 Fifth Avenue, New York, N.Y. 10110
www.wwnorton.com

W. W. Norton & Company Ltd.
Castle House, 75/76 Wells Street, London W1T 3QT

1 2 3 4 5 6 7 8 9 0

F

for HANK

Contents

The Nightingales of Troy

Happy Dust

Mamie Flynn Garrahan

I N THE TWENTIETH century I believe there are no saints left, but our farm on Bog Road had not yet entered the twentieth century. At that time, around 1908 it would be, I had a secret I could tell to no one, least of all a saint or an arsenic-eater. In my experience, it is better to keep away from saints unless you have business with them. The same backbone that makes them holy virtuosos makes them eager to mind other people's p's and q's. But some of the saints I knew were family, and this made them hard to fend off. Don't think I am speaking of my sister-in-law, Kitty. She was not a saint but a lost soul.

It was through Kitty that I first got wind of the spiritual genius down the road. My sister-in-law had mixed up a batch of French chalk and gumwater colored with Prussian blue and was using this to fashion veins on her face. I was washing the bedroom windows. As she painted, Kitty let it slip that she'd brought some extra milk from our dairy over to St. Cieran's Home. I knew the history of this "extra milk." And I knew only a lost soul would give it to an orphanage. That part of her saga rang true.

While searching for a foundling to take the milk, Kitty said she'd wandered into St. Cieran's garden. It was full of crispy white flowers, and in the midst of these blooms, a nun was standing with her arms outstretched "like an oaken figure on a cross," Kitty said. The nun had her back to Kitty, who was about to vamoose when the sister fell to her knees, kissed the earth, and commenced to speaking Latin.

I put no stock in this at first because Kitty had very refined nerves. I'd sized her up the minute I saw her alighting from our dairy wagon in full feather and needletoed kid shoes. My brother-in-law, Bill Garrahan, was holding a parasol dripping fringe like a horse's fly sheet over her head with one hand and steering her around cowflops with the other. My husband Joe tagged behind, lugging her trunks and looking dumbstruck. Oh Mary! I thought, what kind of rigamarole is this? Why would a fine tall man with Bill's black curls and his eyes like bachelor buttons hitch up with such a helplessness?

"Enchanted," Kitty said in that voice you'd need an ear trumpet to capture. She extended her hand in glove to me in my leaky shoes and dress so mended it fell apart in the wash. I shook it thinking *this girl's a lost soul.*

When we moved to the farm, I was a young woman of twenty, hardy though never comely, with lanky dark hair grabbed back in a bun. They called me Mamie Come Running because if anyone needed help, I was the one that would go and do. Now, at twenty-six, I was chapped and thoroughly sweated from the care of four children and the day-in day-out labor of the place. The washing and mangling, blacking and beating, scrubbing and baking, the making of soap and babies had taken all the calorie out of me.

I was thin as a cat's whisker. I had a hacking cough and pallor. My face had taken on shadows. Though I was in a bad state of wilt, I couldn't admit it. In 1908, a wasting disease was a blot on the family name.

Kitty's delicate ways had me all the more overtasked. She was supposed to do the sewing, but left to herself she'd make only belle-of-the-ball garments and nothing for everyday. And everyday was all there was on the farm. Our little brick house was neat as the Dewey decimal system but meager and common as could be. We had windows but no curtains, rooms but no closets, walls but no wallpaper. It was mostly brown and coarse, and Kitty shed tears when she saw it. She and Bill lived on the second floor. We took our meals together, and I soon discovered she could make a cup of tea at most. She'd drink it in little sips while Joe and Bill poured their coffee into their saucers and slurped. I don't know what she thought of them. She had that way of soft-soaping a man till he felt he was her all-in-all no matter what was in her head.

Her with her milk baths, saying we were a dairy and could afford the waste. We could not. One quart, sufficient for a sponge-down, was what we settled on. Then she wanted to sell the used milk to the poorhouse at a reduction. It doesn't take a wizard to figure what she gave the orphans. She and Bill had a childless marriage. If I was called to help Doc Muswell with a delivery, I'd return to a bedlam of bawling infants, for Kitty was no good with them.

Now that I was expecting again, I wished we could pack up our home and roll it down Bog Road to Watervliet on a barrow. I would have liked to pull a shade on the past and have this baby in town. I had a superstition that a child's birth predicted the course its life would take. And I was determined that my fifth would be welcomed in perfect circumstances, without any forceps or cows in the house.

It was this intention that led me to take things up with Katherine Tekakwitha, the Lily of the Mohawks. Kitty begged to join my pilgrimage, and in September we boarded a steamer for Albany, followed by a train bound for the Shrine of Our Lady of Martyrs in Auriesville. I had baby Dorothy in my arms, and the three runabout children, Edna, Charlotte, and my Joseph, clinging to my skirts.

The train left us off, dusty as coalmen, at the foot of the Hill of Torture. This long path wound grandly up through massive gates and meadows toward the sky. I suspected many pilgrims from the city never knew there could be such earth on earth. I shaded my eyes and gave the crowd a once-over but saw no sign of Sister Immaculata or Sister Adelaide. These relative nuns from New Jersey were meeting us and returning to the farm for their annual home visit.

Kitty put down our market basket and fanned herself with a holy card. I tried to keep baby Dorothy from grabbing it. "What are you going to pray for, Mamie?" she asked.

"That the nuns won't stay more than three nights," I told her. They had requested courtesy at St. Cieran's Home since their Rule required them to sleep in a convent. But Yours Truly would have to feed and entertain them. How to do that was the puzzle. I only knew they liked looking at the Sears catalogue to see how many things there were in the world they didn't want.

"You'll never guess what I'm going to pray for." Kitty gnawed delicately at the holy card. "But do try."

"A magic lantern and a switch of store-bought hair." That was what she'd told me last night. Feeling a cough coming on, I set baby Dorothy down and fished a clean handkerchief from my shirtwaist.

"No. Something ever so much more important."

The cough changed its mind and I was grateful. "You wouldn't be wanting a little fountain in your room that shoots perfume before falling back into a marble basin, or white satin slippers, exquisitely fitted, that do not button or lace but are cunningly sewn on in the morning and ripped off at night? You wouldn't be praying that your name become Fannie Wellbeloved, Annabel Lee, Clara Lazarus, or Evelyn Friend?" Kitty's pipe dreams were famous to me.

"Dare I speak my heart aloud?" Kitty asked. "I'm praying to be accepted as a nontuition scholar at the Troy School of Arts and Crafts." She gave me a cow-eyed confiding look.

"That saloon run by teachers excommunicated from the Emma Willard School?"

"Darling Mamie." It was a sweltering day, and the party next to us had a coverlet fixed to four broomsticks raised above their hats as a canopy. "I wish I'd brought my sundown," Kitty said. Reaching into her purse, she found a little pocket mirror, a jar of finely powdered starch and orris root, and began dusting herself. "This weather is a persecution, is it not? I'm dying, I'm dying, I'm dead."

"You'll be a beautiful corpse," I told her. And she perked up. If she wasn't bleaching her freckles with borax in rose water, she was applying solutions of corrosive sublimate, prussic acid, and caustic potash to her complexion. There was a tin of Poudre Rajeunissante containing ratsbane in her room, for Kitty had been an arsenic-eater since the age of seventeen. She stayed pretty nimble despite this habit. But she'd experience the fatal symptoms and be carried off should she stop. Once begun, an arsenic-eater is tied to that unnatural diet all her days. I never let the children visit her upstairs for fear they'd get into her poisons and destroy their lives.

I followed her eyes to six-year-old Charlotte. She was standing with her arms spread like wings and her head wrenched back toward the sky.

"That's cross prayers," Edna told us. "Sister Honoraria showed her." Edna was my eldest, an independent girl of eight years.

"The nun in the garden, I'll warrant," Kitty whispered. "That child has the most charming buck teeth."

The Hill of Torture was lined with peddlers pitching miraculous medals and phony relics, and I just then spotted our Brides of Christ standing in full poverty by a vendor's cart. Nuns had such dignity and difference, I always thought they should be introduced by a loud gust of trumpets. By the same token, ours were something of a Mutt and Jeff. Sister Immaculata was stately as a steeple, while Adelaide was jolly and stocky. Each had her hand concealed up its opposite batwing sleeve, and no hucksters were rushing them. Those men knew better than to pester a nun. I ran over to grab the little black satchels leaning against their hems.

"Good day, my dears. God be with you," Sister Immaculata said. The woman had a voice in her like a velvet counterpane. Adelaide was making an ado over the kiddies.

We saw the procession forming then for the march up the Hill of Torture to the park where Katherine Tekakwitha had been born and saints had been martyred in days of old. We fell in with the other parishioners on the upwards trudge, saying the rosary and singing *Aves* aloud. Before long, we were wiping the dust off our eyes with holy water passed hand to hand.

Everyone had been fasting since midnight, and I'd all but lost interest in human sacrifice by the time we got to the top. The nuns were still full of tallyho, of course. The procession followed a dirt path through the Seven Dolors and the Stations of the Cross to the Martyrs' Chapel. This was a rough-hewn log pavilion, open on all sides so overflowing pilgrims could hear Mass from the lawn—though being with two Mercy Sisters guaranteed us seats inside. Baby Dorothy was asleep, my Joseph was hoping for a sermon full of tomahawks, and the girls were busy with the pictures in my missal. Seeing as I could not confess my ill health to anyone alive, I roosted on the kneeler, eager to air my secret shame and heart's desire before God's saints.

I knew Katherine Tekakwitha, the Lily of the Mohawks, had recovered from smallpox. She had been an orphan. And she had been Godly without being martyred. I respected her for that. My prayer went: If I was not worn out by the white plague, I would not worry about adding again to our household. But as I am poorly, I am sincerely sorry for it. I cannot go to a resort where the air is Adirondack and sleep on a screened-in porch. But help me be fit enough to give the child its life. Give me gumption. My spirit is gaunt. I told Katherine that if I died, my children would be half-orphans, halfway to St. Cieran's Home. As an orphan herself, she'd know that when a mother goes to bed and dies, her little children stand crying because no one is minding them. The father might try, but he is too discouraged and new to the work to be useful.

Since a feeble mother will have a weak infant, I prayed mine would not be a blue baby or an idiot. Let it be born modern, a twentieth-century child, with no muck or mire, no caul or purple mother's marks upon it, I prayed. Lily of the Mohawks, I said, let this baby have a decent, not a blind-alley life. I would not mind this baby being a saint, but I would not like it to be a martyr or a lost soul. A saint wasn't much of a livelihood, but it was better than farming. Farm life was what I did not want for the baby most of all. Last, I prayed it would be an ordinary child and have happy luck all its days.

I got so caught up I hardly noticed the incense and adoration. The next thing I knew, we'd genuflected and were out on the grass again. I spread the cloth and unpacked the bill of fare. I always cooked day and night before the Sisters visited, and then they'd peck away with their puny appetites, selecting a tidbit here, a morsel there. I'd made a round of beef, fricasseed chicken, potato salad, picalilli, chili sauce, and rhubarb pie, all the same. I knew from last time they would not touch my home-made root beer because of the word "beer."

"Mother, is Sister Immaculata a saint?" Charlotte asked. She and Edna were braiding each other's brown straight hair. The sky had turned dreary, and the trees looked boisterous.

"A saint has to be dead, I guess." I handed Sister Immaculata a corned beef sandwich and began helping everyone to salad. I didn't know what to say.

"Sister Honoraria is a saint," Charlotte went on. "She was

struck twice by lightning, and now if someone sticks pins in her, it doesn't matter, for she don't feel it." I thought this must be a great gift to a Sister. I knew from washing our relatives' habits that nuns were mostly held together with pins.

"Some religious women fancy they are specially singled out for miracles," Sister Immaculata said, brushing crumbs off her worsted skirt.

I'd seen lightning split a crystal dish without a shatter. I'd seen it roll itself up in a ball before exploding. And I believed it could strike twice if it had a mind to. There were but two things I feared: lightning and a dark cellar.

"Sister Honoraria is Charlotte's teacher," I explained. St. Cieran's was the nearest school. The children went there to be educated with the orphans.

"The Presentation nuns are all very well," Sister Immaculata said. Veils were flapping, and I had to hold on to my hat.

"Their order is enclosed, and a few decades older in the faith than ours," Sister Adelaide allowed.

I told Charlotte and Edna, who were dandy helpers, to get a move on and find their little brother. He'd gone to watch some boys carve a cross in a tree, and now with a storm brewing, I'd lost sight of him.

"Mamie, I couldn't broach this with the children here," Sister Immaculata said as soon as the girls were gone. "But it is my duty to warn you." She fingered her beads. Kitty leaned forward, egging her on. "It's passing strange how some vowed women believe they're doing God a great favor instead of thinking the world well lost."

"Obedience comes more readily to some than others," Adelaide explained.

"There have been allegations concerning Sister Honoraria," continued Immaculata.

"Concerning her past," said Adelaide.

"Don't be grabbing Sister's spectacles," I told baby Dorothy.

"It is said that Sister Honoraria was called back from a foreign mission, and that she engages in excessive penitential practices." Here Immaculata touched the big black crucifix shoved under her belt. "What's more, this Sister's conduct with a priest was deemed . . ." She paused and puckered her lips. "Familiar. He was observed to impiously venture to touch her hand."

"It is said," Adelaide put in.

"You mean there was a scandal, Maggie?" The shock made me forget and call Sister Immaculata by her Christian name.

Kitty was in her glory. I could feel her nerves shaking next to me. "The nun in the garden," she said.

The girls came skipping over then, dragging my Joseph behind them, and we had to shush. There was no more talk of Sister Honoraria, though Kitty kept trying to sneak up on the subject. The storm held off, and we spent the rest of the afternoon strolling the grounds, greeting old cronies, and telling each other what a grand time we were having in this heaven on earth before the sun got low and the train left for home.

The nuns came and went without any uproar, and it must have been a week after their visit that Edna raced home in a great state of emergency. I was putting sheets out to dry on the lines and hedges when she skidded into the yard, out of breath, yelling Mother Come Running! Sister has fallen! "Sister is down?" I said, stopping my work to listen. When I'd heard enough, I left the little ones with Kitty and took off down Bog Road at a good clip.

Once we got to St. Cieran's, Edna led me through the high brick gates into a big garden patch out back. There was Sister lying down in the dirt. A blunt knife and a jar of water were on the ground nearby. She looked dazed but awake. "Was I struck by lightning?" she said, looking up at me with great gray eyes.

I knew I had to get her out of that sun posthaste, but she

proved hard to move as a trolley off its track. As I tried to raise her, I noticed an open can of gummy brown perfumy stuff fastened to her belt. When I saw her bare feet, I thought this Sister is a rugged little number—light yet durable, scanty yet galvanized. Once I got her up, Edna wedged herself under one arm, I got under the other, and we limped toward the convent.

As we stepped into the cool gloom of the place, I was struck by its smell of starched linen and dusty paraffin. Though it was a hotter-than-blazes Indian summer day, some frosty twilight poured from the high windows. Sister Honoraria (for she was our fallen nun) said the others were at prayers and must not be disturbed on her account. "Let me take up my cross," she said, "or I will never have my crown." She directed us through waxed amber corridors, up an oak stairway to the nuns' dormitory.

The Sisters' beds were separated by sheets hung from poles to make cells the size of small box stalls, maybe six feet square. We entered Sister's alcove through a curtain and laid her down on her iron cot. The place was dark as an icehouse. It took a while to make out the white wooden box, straight plain chair, washstand, soap dish, and tin cup that were the furnishings. I told Edna to go rescue the kids from Kitty and ask Papa to fetch Doc Muswell.

I then set about pulling the heavy togs off Sister. She spoke of this and that she had to do, but I said the doctor was coming, and she was too listless to argue. When I unfastened the strings of her headpiece, I was surprised to find that the starched bonnet had prickers on its inside. I saw they'd left marks on the skin and stubby scalp of her. Under her habit was a muslin gown big as a croup tent, and as I wrassled with her outer outfit, this undergarment pulled in such a way that I glimpsed a scar, livid and cross-shaped, on her ribs. "You got a bad cut there, Sister," I said, just to keep the conversation going.

"Here cut and here burn, but spare me in eternity," she said.

"How'd you get a cut like that?" I had lockjaw on my mind.

"No doubt you've heard tales," she said. "People, even good people, are given to falsehood and exaggeration. And yet I would do wrong to say I did no wrong." She asked about the can that had been fastened at her waist, and I said I'd put it out of the way, under the cot.

"If I had walked too heavily, or used my eyes with liberty, or kissed an infant for its beauty . . . for these sins, I might be forgiven," she continued.

"Nobody's perfect," I said.

"Perfection is a nun's purpose," she replied. "She must wash the taste of the world from her mouth with carbolic and sleep on thorns lest she sleep too well. If the chapel is cozy, let her kneel in snow. If for an instant she forgets Christ's suffering, let her take switches to her shoulders, brand herself with faggots, wear an iron chain about her waist."

I was beginning to think this Sister was a deep customer. "The worst sin is shiftlessness," I said. "It's better to shuck your blues and shake a leg."

"Perhaps tales have reached you. Vile accusations have been made," she said, "concerning the orphans. That I had them kneel like dogs and used their backs as writing desks, when in fact they are raised most tenderly."

"That I didn't know," I said.

"I was torn by a confliction of duty—" and she would have gone on but we heard footsteps. There came a light scratching of fingernails on the curtains, and Doc Muswell entered, along with the Mother Superior or some other bigwig, by the look of her.

In his single-breasted Prince Albert suit, I'd call Doc Muswell pretty nobby-looking for a country sawbones. Before I married, I'd worked as his housekeeper and assistant, so we were old pals.

I knew his wife to be a malingerer, and he knew I had a wasting disease. He had trained me as his nurse, and many's the time I'd saved him the weary night work of delivering infants. As he saw it, childbirth was long hours for short wages.

"Does Sister suffer from any known disease?" he asked the Superior nun.

"Only the disease of scrupulosity," she answered back. She told him to report to her before he left and excused herself.

Once he'd overlooked the situation carefully, Doc asked Sister if she knew the day and place she was. She said, "I thought I was on the Ganges plain between Patna and Benares, but now I see I'm in Watervliet."

"That's right, Sister," I said, to encourage her. I didn't know where the Ganges plain was located. Somewhere near the road to Damascus most likely.

Doc Muswell took out his stethoscope, and I thought he'd see her scar, but he turned his head to one side and listened without looking, as doctors did in the presence of modesty back then. "You have heatstroke, Sister," he told her. "Forgive me for saying so, but you are chronically overdressed for garden work."

"Your rebuke is well-taken, Doctor. The great discovery is in the heavens above us, not the garden below." She liked to browbeat herself. I'd seen that instantly.

"Well, Doc," I said in her defense, "Sister's skirt, sleeves, and veil were pinned up, under, and back when she had this spell."

"In accordance with Protocol Number 17," said she.

The words no sooner left her lips than her breathing told us she was asleep. Doc Muswell asked me to stay awhile and see she drank all of the potion he'd leave. He inquired after my own health, and I told him I was expecting.

"The married woman's disease," he said. When I confessed to coughing blood, he shook his head. "Mamie, it's as I've said. You'll have to get by on one lung the rest of your life."

Then he took a packet from his bag and pressed it into my

hand. "As a sedative for coughs, this is five times stronger than morphine," he said. By the lion and globe on the label, I recognized it as Bayer Heroin Powder. "Use it sparingly, and you won't become habituated. You will have call for it, I think." I was grateful as this medicine was very dear, and the more costly the cure, the more effective. "With your constitution, you'd do well to avoid stimulating food and drink, heat and cold, singing, hallooing, and declamation." So saying, he donned his hat and took his leave.

Sister opened her eyes then, and I fed her the potion he'd left. She was looking more chipper. "I could not but overhear your conversation," she said. "You are in a delicate condition. I have a remedy that will damp the fires of bodily mechanism and shallow the breath, resting your inflamed lung and encouraging the cavities to close."

Nothing could be more powerful than the nostrum of a consecrated virgin. This I knew.

"It is Indian Perfection Medicine. Take it when your time comes, and the pain will not threaten you," she said.

Hearing this, my heart soared, for I knew Katherine Tekakwitha had answered my prayer. I figured Sister got the recipe from a Mohawk maiden with a difficult vocation, and I thanked her feelingly.

"There is no need to thank me," she said. "There is a giving that does not impoverish and a withholding that does not enrich. I have but one request."

Nuns always want some little selfless thing in exchange for their favors, I find. God's the same way when you think about it.

"Everything in the convent is ours, not mine. To give property without permission is a form of theft. I have been chastised in the past for giving to the indigent. I have been called more of a chemist than a Sister, more nurse than nun. I battle for obedience. Yet St. Dominic said he would sooner cut up the rule book than let it be a burden to one's conscience. I have taken you into my confidence. I ask only that you hold my words in trust."

"You mean keep mum?"

She nodded, and I didn't stop to dicker. Give me that remedy! was how I felt. She told me the way to the convent's medicine closet, a large room in the cellar that would be open at this hour.

"What if I meet up with one of your sidekicks?" I wondered.

"If questioned, you must tell the truth," she said firmly. "Tell the truth, and say St. Gregory the Great directed us to dispense to all sufferers that which they need."

I set off for the medicine room on a trail that twisted through corridors of mostly closed doors. The worst of it was windows now and then threw rays on big framed pictures whose sudden faces scared the daylights out of me. All along, I worried some nun would creep up on the balls of her feet in high perfection behind me and ask my business. I had to keep thinking of the baby and of all the cures I'd tried to no avail. When I got to the convent's depths, which were dim and dank as a root cellar, I wished especially for a lamp. But I remembered "Tekakwitha" meant "she who cuts the way before her" and felt steadier. At long last, I arrived at the third left-hand door of the west wing. In the sincere hope that I had not gone off course, I stopped and turned the knob.

My eyes had a tolerance for darkness by now. I could make out a long table of ledgers and accounts, along with stacks of labels, stamps, and envelopes. It looked like a tidy business for the Sisters, and I wished them well. To my left, I saw shelves holding small white cakes and bottles. Seizing one, I read the Indian Perfection label thrice. I'd already knotted the Bayer Heroin in my apron corner, and now I rolled the remedy in this garment and tucked the hem at my waist. It was high time, too, for a bell was tolling. And since early and provident fear is the mother of safety, and I'd as lief have my wolf teeth pulled as be caught red-handed, I fled.

⁓

That fall was damp as a gravedigger's skin. By November I'd developed a hectic fever that left pink circles in my cheeks. Before the winter zeros struck, I thought I'd better mend my lacy lung with Sister's remedy. Whether it was her medicine or the disease itself, by some means I was lifted into the high altitudes of hope and held there. I somehow kept my cheer, and in April the last shrouds of snow melted. Though I was large as Jumbo by then, the work of the farm would not allow me to remove myself from view as some think prudent.

One Saturday, having finished the morning chores and served a bountiful hot lunch, I was on my knees scrubbing the kitchen oilcloth and thinking about Kitty. That one isn't one to make love to the corners! I was thinking. Why, I've seen her grab a pair of silk drawers and begin dusting if she heard a neighbor on the steps. When I opened her trunk to get fresh linen, a swarm of mothmillers flew out, and we had to fumigate. Such were my thoughts when I felt the first pain. I didn't trust it since the baby had been incubating only eight months by my reckoning. And even if it was not a false alarm, it takes time for pain to work itself into a birth. Joe and Bill were leaving for town, but reasoning thus, I said nothing.

Every week they went into Watervliet to buy our groceries at Dufrane's Market. While the clerk was making up the order, they'd go across the street to Sherlock's Grill. Once they'd left, I noticed the pains were coming closer. Mamie, I said, this baby is going places. I stopped scrubbing the floor and began scouring buckets and bowls. I pumped water for boiling and placed torn strips of cloth in the oven to bake clean. A woman in labor should have plenty fixed for others to eat, yet I was caught short. I could only put a big plate of bread and butter on the table.

In our bedroom off the parlor, I set out the spotless containers along with a bar of carbolic. I tied a twisted towel around the headboard rails and fastened two more, like reins, at the foot. Then I covered the room and the bed with old issues of the *Troy Record*. Some expectant mothers put their own laying-out clothes in a bottom drawer, but my warm hopes would not allow this. I was thinking of the here and now, not the always was and will be. If you go to bed, the infant sleeps and you have to start again. So I kept pacing.

After the third birth, things get riskier. I tried to keep my mind on the happy deliveries and forget the poor devils I had seen. I would not think of the abnormal presentations, hemorrhages, obstructions, retained afterbirths, blood poisonings, convulsions, milk legs, and childbed fevers. Working for Doc Muswell, I'd seen prolapsed women full of ironmongery, pessaries to hold their insides in. Childbirth left them wearing these "threshing machines" only hoop skirts could hide. Such trials swept through my mind in Kinetoscopic flashes. Yet those poor devils did not have Sister's remedy. This I knew.

The children were outside playing pirate, and I called Edna in. "You're a young miss now," I told her. She was all of nine. "You can be your mother's helper." I asked her to go upstairs and alert Kitty, who soon appeared and settled herself on the divan like a brooding hen. When a pain came, I shushed, and when it let up, I started bossing the job again. All along I was trying to gauge the labor's progress, whether I was at the dime, nickel, quarter, half-dollar, or teacup stage. At the teacup stage, I would be "fully delighted," as Doc Muswell said. I figured I was halfway there.

It was twilight, and I was lying down to catch my breath, when Kitty began hollering from the yard. Mamie Come Running! she said. The team is back! Rushing out, I saw the wagon and lathered horses but no sign of Joe or Bill. By the ropes of green froth dribbling from their bits, I could see Ned and Susie had grabbed a bite to eat. "We'll have to unhitch the horses," I told her.

"They are such great brutes, Mamie. Do let's leave them as they are. But what of William and Joe? Do you suppose they were thrown and are even now lying in some dark spot?"

"Joe and Bill are skillful whips," I said. "If they got thrown, then they must foot it." I knew those brothers were not brawling or visiting sweethearts. *Nothing ventured, nothing lost*, that was the Garrahan motto.

I watered and unharnessed the horses without coming to harm, and when I returned, Kitty was strewn across my news-papered bed in an attitude of weeping. "Perhaps the dainty waist and deep full inspirations of some Watervliet wanton have commanded William's admiration," she said. I could hear Edna trying to convince my Joseph and baby Dorothy it was bedtime. Charlotte was singing them a little song. I scrubbed the horse dirt off and lit the oil lamps. Then I lay down on the divan. Now that the pain was mustering, I wondered out loud if I'd have enough of Sister's remedy.

"Mother, if you needed more, we could have made it ourselves," Edna piped up. Having settled the little ones, she and Charlotte were giving me big looks. I only half listened as she prattled about *Papaver somniferum* and lancing the pods so sticky flower milk oozed out. She spoke of scraping, drying, beating, molding, boiling, skimming, and straining, but it wasn't till she mentioned covering the cakes with white poppy petals that I sat up and attended. The word "poppy" had roused me.

"Is this what Sister was doing when she took that bad turn?"

"Yes, and I was helping her," said Edna with a proud little smile.

"You were helping her harvest opium," I said. I got up and stood with arms akimbo, thinking. If Sister's remedy was mostly opium, like Black Drop or Laudanum, I might have become a dope fiend. Hoarding the medicine for tonight's baby was all that saved me. Now I had to weigh the danger of opium against the danger of pain. Most of all, I wanted this baby to be protected by the power of good. And I thought Sister Honoraria was a good woman, even if she was a bad nun. As I stood thinking, my waters broke.

I marched into the bedroom where Kitty was sleeping. "See here, Clara Lazarus," I said. "It's time to rise from the dead. I need streetcar courtesy. I have to push this baby out."

"Oh, Mamie, I am a wretch. Forgive me," she said. I lay down in a sweat and would have taken Sister's medicine, opium or no, but I could not afford to be dopey until the doctor got here. It must have been near midnight. I sent Joe wireless messages in my mind: Come home, come home.

Charlotte brought me a saucer of dark fruit. "What have we here?" I gasped.

"Kitty says they are little black-coated workers." She looked at me with her bashful, born-yesterday eyes. I set the prunes down carefully and told her to fetch the blessed candle from the parlor.

My mother, Peg Flynn, had unfastened every knot or button, door or stall, while I was having baby Dorothy. She supposed so much opening would help the infant enter the world. Thanks to her, baby Dorothy was welcomed into a household of men with their garments falling off and an old bossy in the kitchen. I wanted this child to be born newfangled and free of Irish hoodoo. But I'd kept a copy of a prayer my mother had recited, and I asked Edna to fetch it from the dresser's depths. It was written on vellum older than Plymouth Rock. I used the oil lamp to light the candle and read the words to myself: "Anne bore Mary; Mary, Christ Our Savior; Elizabeth, John the Baptist. So may this woman, saved in the name of Our Lord Jesus

Christ, bear the child in her womb, be it male or female. Come forth." That's how it went. It ended with Latin words written so they'd read the same in any direction:

```
S  A  T  O  R
A  R  E  P  O
T  E  N  E  T
O  P  E  R  A
R  O  T  A  S
```

Though she was no scholar, my mother, Peg Flynn, said the Latin meant "I creep toward the sower and holder of the workings and the wheels." I placed the paper on my big belly and asked Edna if she could see to read it. With a little prompting, she soon had it down pat. I told her I wanted her to recite the list of holy births in a saintly voice while Charlotte held the candle aloft. My lambs looked scared in the shaky light, but Edna set her balky tongue to the task. " 'Anne bore Mary—' " she began.

She got no further because Charlotte yelled, Papa's home! just then, and the spell was broken. A moment later, Joe was standing at the bedroom door. He had mea culpa written all over him, but I was happy to see him in good health. "How are you, Mamie?" he said, with hat in hand.

"I am fully delighted," I replied. His face was barn-red, and he looked more at a loss for words than always. "Where are the groceries, Joe?" I asked.

"I guess we lost track of time in the grill, and the team got tired of waiting for us."

He was standing like somebody rusted in place, and I told him he'd better go after Doc Muswell. "If he's out on a call, don't write CHILDBIRTH on the slate or he'll mosey along. Write FULLY DELIGHTED," I said. Joe repeated this. "You heard," I said.

After he left, I started to cough. Then, my stars! The pain changed in character. I thought I had a lightning bolt lodged in my spine, though I couldn't let on with the children near. I had been leaning on Sister's remedy to see me through. And if that failed, Doc's Heroin. But how could I bear down if I was doped? I needed all my wits. And what if those medicines fatally depressed the baby? Once a heavy thought has a grip, it is hard to dispel. I knew labor proceeded at a pace and mine was stalled. I felt my efforts coming to naught. This is the reckoning, I felt. I'm flagging, I'm past repair. I'm at the last gasp. Soon I will not want my body or the breath I breathe. This is the end of the world.

"Go get Kitty," I told Edna, who was standing by. My sister-in-law had been delicately raised, that was evident. She was genteel and artistic, though the man in the moon would make a better midwife. The children could do worse in a stepmother, I thought. She came in, and I showed her and Edna the basin on the chair for bathing baby, the penny and binding for its navel, the boiled scissors, baby clothes, and diapers.

"Mamie darling, don't be blue," Kitty said, in her namby-pamby way. "You must use the happy dust the doctor gave you. It is much favored as a stimulant, I've heard."

"You're a good sister, Kit," I told her. "If the baby's a boy, I want him to be called James, after my brother. And if it's a girl, you can call her Annabel Lee."

"Stop it, Mamie," Kitty said. "You're frightening me." Her hands were shaking like a palsy victim's.

"Ma, are you dying?" Edna asked, and Charlotte started to cry.

I'd seen women lose heart and die of exhaustion. I'd seen them die with babies half in and half out. They died because they were frightened. I fully understood it. But seeing those little girls with the solemn waif look already on them, staring at their mother like she was a hobgoblin, I came to my senses. I realized nobody was going to help me. I was it all. And I told myself to get cracking.

"Don't be crying," I said. "Your mother is a fighter. How can I die when there's a baby coming?" Course I can grunt it out, I told myself. God send me a pauper's low Mass funeral with no solemn requiem sung by three priests if I cannot. And I pulled on the towels I'd rigged, and I bore down.

Suddenly it seemed my little shut-in had been cooped up long enough. Suddenly it wanted liberty. It was coming like a locomotive headlight. It was coming quick as scat. God Almighty! Now this baby was helping. Now this baby wanted to be born. " 'Anne bore Mary—' " I kept praying, for that was the one phrase I could recall. The pain waxed as it waned, with no pause, and I let the head creep slowly into my hands, though Immaculate Mary, it must be easier to thread camels through needles. The head, the shoulders, then the rest!

I caught the baby and laid it on my stomach. It lay there like a red frog, belly down. I rubbed its back to make it breathe. I held it upside down and patted the soles of its feet. I wiped the blood out of its mouth and blew on it. I dunked it in water. At last I tossed a pinch of Doc's powder over its head and dabbed Sister's soporific of vegetable origin behind its ears. It gasped and was alive. May God protect the child!

After I'd cut the cord and had the afterbirth, I got up and cleaned the room of gore. Kitty brought in my Joseph and baby Dorothy. "Meet Annabel Lee," she said. I was imagining what Joe would think of this name. Annabel Lee Garrahan? Sounds like a lost soul, he'd say.

"You know, Kit, now that I see her, she looks more like she should be called Anne." I had it in mind to name her after Anne who bore Mary. And Anne Sullivan who taught Helen Keller to read. And Anne of Green Gables, an orphan of renown.

"Anne is the perfect name," Kitty said. "Though I will always think of her as Annabel Lee." She said her William would take my Joseph fishing later, and I told her to thank him. "Am I truly a good sister, Mame?" she asked.

"You are one of a kind," I said.

About thirty minutes later, Doc Muswell and Joe arrived. Joe's face lit up like a jack-lantern when he saw the baby. Jiminy Crickets! was all he could say. And he took her to the window to get a better look.

Doc Muswell, meanwhile, had walked right past the bedroom door toward Kitty. I figured she must have arranged herself on the divan in a pose she called a "tableau vivant." "What the deuce is wrong with the girl?" I heard Doc say.

"Oh, Doctor, I'm dying, I'm dying, I'm dead," said Kitty.

"That's impossible, my dear. Mamie would not allow it," said Doc.

Our little bedroom would soon be as full as the St. Louis Exposition with neighbors, nuns, orphans, and my mother, Peg Flynn. And I would be unruffled, as if the whole matter had been an everyday affair. Only to myself would I admit there should be singing crowds and a parade. Like every new mother I thought there should be aerial fascinations—gyrating star mines, electric flowers, and Catherine wheels—to celebrate this birth. For it had been as pretty a fight as any sportsman could wish to see. And since my children now numbered five, I would have liked a display of five balloons from each of which depended a single star that changed its color as it burned.

Just then I heard a bird with a voice so rare it sounded like it had studied at a conservatory. The sun was coaxing the first dusty colors from the ground, and I lay there thinking it had been an ideal birth, after all. Everything went smooth as glycerin, I thought. I looked at the children dozing on the floor

with their stocking feet flung over each other, and our Annie in
Joe's arms, and I thought perfection is not what you imagine.
Happiness is nothing but God's presence in the silence of the
nerves. And though my children were sleeping the sleep of the
just, I half believed my unvoiced thoughts would reach them
across that room full of twentieth-century light.

Queen Wintergreen

Peg Flynn

P EG FLYNN WAS on her knees in the front yard, picking
dandelions for wine, when she spotted a snowy mystery
on the ground. Jarvis Fitzgerald's sight was surer than her
own. Yet she had to call his attention to the crumpled whiteness.
Jarvis picked it up and settled spectacles on his face. Although
the day was warm at eight a.m., he wore his best heavy coat
with no tatters at the cuffs and a vest smooth as a new sail. There
must be some high fussing on him to send him into his holiday
clothes, she thought. I suppose he thinks we're keeping company. But it must be a brother and sister state of affairs at our
age.

He curled the wire spectacles like tiny ram's horns around his
ears and read the white circular aloud: "'Americans who believe
in the demands of Ireland that they be allowed to govern themselves will hold a meeting the night of July 1, 1919, at St.
Comin's Hall.'"

Peg Flynn didn't listen. He is here again, as he is every morning, she thought. He is here, reading to me with the vast gaze in
his granite-blue eyes. Since the girls in her hamlet weren't sent

to school, she'd never learned to read. Was it just three years since her husband Michael had read to her the accounts of the Irish and the Strangers? Although she was tired of the Troubles, she would have liked to read on her own about the girls of the city fighting shoulder to shoulder with the boys.

Jarvis braced his feet apart like a horse in rough country as he concluded, " '. . . so cognizant of their rights, and so determined to remain what God made them—a distinct and independent nation.' " He folded the flyer and put down the sack he'd been holding for her. "Except for the shoes on your feet, you could be a pilgrim circling the stone beds of St. Patrick's Purgatory," he said. "Get yourself up from the dirt, and we'll have a word."

Her straightening was hampered by the arthritis, the shingles, and the bee buzz in her head. These days she had no pluck in her limbs to walk without a hard blackthorn stick. The heat weighed like a basket of wet seaweed on her back. Peg Flynn had never lived far from water. First the sea, so full of itself, now the state waterway, calm and contained as a pint of bitter behind their house. Addled, she'd lately mistaken this canal for Irish water.

"Dandelion wine, is it?" Jarvis said, steadying her elbow.

"I'll hold in big esteem the man that gets a great country to take the pledge."

She knew the tale of the king who had another head darned with blond wool inside his skull. All her life she'd felt there was another, arguing head sewn within her own. And lately she'd begun to see glowing stitches on the outside of things. There was a wreath of rubbery shimmer around each yellow flower, and Port Schuyler, New York, had taken on the cloud colors of Ireland. America, once so brashly bright, was getting dim as a chapel.

They sat on the stoop. Peg separated the roots from the greens in her apron, and Jarvis began to fill his pipe. "On my soul, if it's not good to yourself you are," she said. He hesitated.

"The appearance of desire is on your face. Go on, put fire to your pipe." But he planked it down on the step.

At this hour the kitchen was full of her son's family launching themselves on another day of dust. It hadn't rained in over a month. With so many bodies inside, the house would be close and hot. And her son's wife, Dolly, had nerves. Still, Peg felt sorry for Jarvis, who had no people. She could well imagine his rented room with its cracked shaving mug and yellowed brush, the pictures of Thomas Ashe and the heroes of 1916 on the walls.

"I'd say come in, but the children would be in a hundred pieces around us," she told him.

"How are you this morning, Peg Flynn?" he said, and he wasn't one for pleasantries. She had sized him up as a direct man with no mischief in him. Straight as the hands on a clock.

"Ailing I am, and wasting. It's a grief to be old."

"And a sorrow." He glanced at her. "But you've still got a fine physique. Will you be at the freedom meeting tonight?" He gestured with the circular.

"Oh, it's the Cause you've come for, is it?" There's little taste of Irish in his language, she thought. If I said some, he wouldn't know but it was Latin I spoke.

Jarvis hooked a thumb in each lapel. "I have more than the one Cause today. But every Irishman wants her to remain a distinct and independent nation. This notice is signed by the men and the Fathers. I know you'll take an interest in their manly and dignified stand."

She secretly believed that Ireland was a bad luck country, where people were sent to dine on rocks and hope. As a girl she'd looked at the messy stone fences full of voids and thought they should turn the place into a tombstone quarry. She'd stood on the Point to watch the ships coming home in a lather, the ghost of a mountain in every wave.

"I wish them well, indeed I do. But a woman isn't welcome

when the talk is of the Troubles. A woman has no vote nor did she ever."

She watched a rivulet of sweat run down his neck, which was long and clean as a gander's. He laced his fingers together over his vest. "Now Peg, if women got the vote the Blessed Mother would blush."

"It's only a man who'd think that Mary Mother of Sorrows would care at all about such a thing after losing the idol of her heart." There was a spark on his small finger. A diamond pinkie ring. Holiday clothes! Isn't that the spit for the venison and the deer not yet killed, thought the head inside her own.

"If Irish freedom don't interest you, there's another wonder in town you'll want to see. The flying boat is coming. It gave an exhibition and raced with a train, and tonight it stops in the water." He fiddled with his watch chain. "Will you come along with me to see it?"

A flying boat! exclaimed the royal voice inside. What would such a thing resemble at the departing of day for night? Would it have the two sails set and a nice following wind? Would it have wings? " 'Come along,' he says to a woman with the gait of a foundered horse," she said.

There was a small gap in his smile so you could tell it was not store-bought. She was reminded of the spaces her son Jim, a train conductor, punched in tickets. Jarvis took the flat cap off his head and revolved it in his hands. She'd wondered whether he had hair underneath, but there it was, calm as carded wool. "Peg, we understand each other. You're a bold woman, and I like that. As for myself, I don't spit or wipe my mouth on my sleeve. It would be an honor and a pleasure—"

"Not to come before you in your speech, but can I fetch you a cup of cold milk? I'm sure that's what you're after asking."

Jarvis paused. His collar had dug a ring into his neck, and he touched the red brand. "Like I said, you're a woman full of sport, and I get a fit on my heart when I think of you." He tapped his toe on each word. "It would be an honor and a pleasure if you'd consider this an offer of matrimony. I've been meaning this while back to ask you."

Thank the Lord for faces to cover what you felt, though it caper behind the smile or frown, she thought. A vain bit of her warmed to think of Jarvis's words. It was a triumph to be proposed to at the age of sixty-five by a man not given to drinking or fisticuffs, neither God-beset nor from a family of soupers—those who'd turned in their religion for broth during the famine years—a man, what's more, without the ringworm or the twitch, neither a brute nor a murderer. A fine physique he'd said. He must be touched in the head to want me, she thought and thought, I'll not have him anyway. Don't be a gloat, she told her triumphant self and felt shamed in advance at the scandal. The scorn of the world her wedding would bring upon her family!

And she wasn't about to give up her pleasures. She had a clay pipe to smoke on the sly and no wish to serve a husband like a Christ on earth. A wife must sit to the side of the fire and let her husband warm his vamps in front. She could still hear her children cry "Oh Ma, Daddy is coming and Mamie has taken his newspaper!" In the pinch times, she'd said she'd already eaten so Michael could have his plenty. He had passed away a year ago.

"I'm not the one to hold a man to a rash word. To think of a wedding at our age! Wouldn't that be the grand occasion—with none to hand me over but my own son and the neighbors lined up to laugh on either side. No, I had the one good man, and one is all I'll have. I'll lay it down flat. Even if I were an airy girl again I'd not be the one for you who wants a female mild as turnip water. Have sense," she told him.

He knocked the fresh tobacco from his pipe. "You misjudge me, Peg. A man alone is a great pity, but a wife is company. I'll pray you change your mind."

In a pig's rump I will, said the voice in her skull's vault. "Then pray to Saint Jude who loves a lost cause," she said aloud. A long straying on you, said the voice, as Jarvis Fitzgerald, a fine well-standing figure of a man got smaller in her sight.

She stood toiling with her hair before the little mirror in her room, sick to her soul of the body: the constant caring for it and its constant complaints. The shingles illness stung like a bodice of briars. Soon she'd get soft in the head, and they'd have to lead her on a leash to the State Home. A fine physique. Well, what did he know. In the long ago she'd stood tall as a guarding goat. She'd had hair the red of Indian corn. Now it is as the psalm says, she thought, "My moisture is turned into the drought of summer." She'd pulled down the shades to make a cool night season.

Her room was a welter of feathery doilies, china figurines, and patterned fabrics. She had three clocks, counting her lavalier watch, and each told a different hour. There was a small fireplace of marble, its hearth blocked by a piece of green tin. Scapulars hung from the lamp, and you had to walk a slim path around the iron bed to get somewhere. On the dresser she kept an altar to the Virgin, a jar of pennies for the Missions, and a heap of bone jewelry. She stood toiling with her hair, remembering the long ago when the sea bashed the cliffs by the cottage where they'd lived.

She was born in 1854, four years after the famine. She'd heard tales of that time—the people living on barnacles and nettles, the coffin ships sent out with sacred medals and holy water fastened to their prows. Her father swore he'd never trust Ireland to feed them again. She'd gone into service under an English gentlewoman when she was fourteen. Behind the diamond windows of the rich she'd learned there was nothing worse than being under the hand of other people.

And she'd learned about the secret yearnings of men. She

attributed the worse vices to the English. As a domestic, she'd
learned that the jerky walk and glandular madness of certain old
men stemmed from their wild ways as boys. Some of them
believed that if they sinned with a virgin they'd be cured. Her
employer's second cousin had come into her room one night,
and she'd poured the washbowl's water over his head. The next
morning she gave her notice.

By that time she was sixteen, and her father had saved enough
money for the trip to America. They piled their belongings
behind them in the wagon, and Peg turned to fix the West
Country in her head. She saw a woman walking with a load of
brushwood on her back like a pair of raveling wings. In the distance, the ashen water and a figure sitting on the seawall.

In her day girls were raised to be pure and not transgress.
Then, my sorrow! she thought, some learned all the mortifica-
tions of the saints at their husband's hands. Not that Jarvis would
expect wifely duties of that kind. He was as Godly as De Valera.
She knew he'd not tamper with her. Like herself, he'd believe
the act was for procreation—or sin. Still she didn't want his flannel breeches on her bedside chair, his skin next to her sleeping
skin, a crescent of hair oil on her pillows, a bedful of tobacco
sweat. Her own smell of camphor and wintergreen was a place
to dwell.

Not once had Michael told her to belt up or had a rod onto
her. He was a gent. On their wedding night he had dropped to
his knees and prayed before entering the high iron frame and
coarse sheets. That first time she was reminded of a visit from
the dentist: the screech along the nerves and the duty to open
against your deepest instinct. She had no good words but the
Irish for the body and what happened in the marriage bed.
Gaelic was more direct, less soiled than English. A month before
a niece gave birth, the young woman had asked Peg where the
baby would come out, and Peg hadn't the words to make her
much the wiser.

And the things she knew to tell wouldn't have comforted the girl. Many a strong tough woman I've seen laid low in the anguish, bellowing to Mary, and some never came to themselves again, she thought. Wasn't God far from the words of their roaring! In some houses, the men sat round the fire nice and chatty wondering why didn't the woman stir herself and pass the babe in a mad rush, getting the release from her task. Or a husband would run in and cry Oh, God be with us stop, his blood shaking from the sound. Her Michael had always gone to his brother's house when her time came, which suited Peg nicely. She'd put a tea towel between her teeth, so her courage might be firm as Queen Maeve's of long ago. It wasn't the pain down in the bowels but the fiery needle of no heed sewing through your spine that put the amazement on you. Each time was different except for her thinking this time I'm at the end of my soul! This time I'll be cliff grass when it's over!

Now some women were more nicely formed. But for her the family way meant the toothache, the leg cramps, the vomiting, the dropsy, and the jaundice. One infant was born yellow, and Peg's hands swelled fat as creamcrocks, so she could hardly haul water from the well to wash the baby's clothes. She'd had three girls and three boys. Once the doctor had used instruments to pull from her a dead child. Only the baby's fingers had their natural color. They said that once you touched a dead person you wouldn't have any loneliness in you. But stroking that sweet and goodly girl had put the solitude of the world in her. And then Thomas had died at two—of empyema, the doctor said.

Well, she had always feared God and done her duty. Now she had grandchildren, each more afraid of her than the other, all of them too shy to give sharp ear to her marvels. And that is a shame, she thought, for it is as the psalm says, "My tongue is the pen of a ready writer." A woman didn't tell hero stories, after all, only ghost stories. Hers were so potent the children ran when they saw her coming, though she gave them Mary Janes and more at Christmas.

"I hear you had a visitor this morning," her son Jim said from the doorway. He was in his suspenders and rolled-up shirt-sleeves. Peg stopped sorting her baubles into groups on the bed and began knitting to put the appearance of work upon her. "A gentleman caller."

"You wouldn't mean Jarvis Fitzgerald." Jim's Dolly must have been listening from the kitchen. Peg could imagine her picking with her ears by the window, her hair in rags around her Temperance Lady face, to hear what Jarvis had to say. Dolly has the spite in her nose for me; she'd give me the ropes side of the house if she had her way, thought the head inside Peg's head.

"Is that who it was?" Jim sat himself down on the spread. He was her pet son, a boy of fun and tricks. It was years since she had seen him clearly. She remembered him dressed finely on his days off, his hat at an angle. And there were spokes of blue and gray in his glance, which she had memorized. His eyes had rays in them like a dartboard's. Even as a child he wouldn't flinch when things hit him. No matter how hot the day, Jim Flynn would assure you the breeze would soon be in from the river, people said. People said he'd stake his last dollar against the sun's setting. And she couldn't deny his liking for a wager. But those people hadn't heard his fine wide laugh. She thought he looked always as if he should have an accordion strapped to his chest, so ready for happiness he was. It wasn't true either that he was bone-lazy. He worked as a train conductor five days a week, but she'd seen his Dolly place a quarter of a pound of butter out for tea, squandering his pay. And didn't she, his mother, eat out of his pocket, pushing him to the poorhouse with every bite?

"What did you and Mr. Fitzgerald discuss, might I ask?" Jim said. He toyed with a coral necklace, staring idly into nothing. Then he removed a small pad of paper from his pocket.

"Home rule." Her eyes fell on a garnet ring given her by Michael.

"Ah. And I heard he touched on matters of the heart. I heard he asked you to be his lady wife." Jim scribbled on the pad. Toting up his bill with the turf accountant, she thought.

"At his great age he'll be wanting a lady nurse. You'd have to buy a pair of wheelbarrows to roll us to the altar. That would be a sweet sight for the parish, indeed. But I'll not shame your father's memory with such talk."

He smiled. "What's wrong with old Fitz? The man has no vices that I know of. And he's here every morning, so don't say you don't like his company."

"Would you have your own mother marry a stranger? You get the award."

"He couldn't be more of a stranger than Dad was when you married. You'd only known him a month, remember?"

"God rest him." She kissed the crucifix she wore on a chain, thinking we were a made match. When I die, will the dust praise him? "And what are you composing as we speak?" she asked.

"Young Peter has a touch of the croup. I'm just reminding myself to buy mustard for a plaster. But to return to our subject, Mr. Fitzgerald is a decent, God-fearing citizen. Well-spoken, too." Jim grinned, and put the pad away. Jarvis was famous for his earnest sermons on political matters.

"His talk is like a peat fire. Lovely at first, but it chokes you after a while. Your father and I were as close as the Shannon and the Suck."

"Jarvis is a widower himself, isn't he?"

"So he's not of a queer nature," she conceded. "Oh, he's a good enough creature. But I'd sooner walk naked through the streets than take a husband at my age." Here she'd been thinking how ashamed they'd be to have her marry, yet it seemed the very thing Jim wanted. And why wouldn't he? Didn't he have the full of the house of croupy children, and she and Dolly in each other's haircombs all day?

"Wasn't he married to Mary Hurlehey?" Jim asked. His hands flew over the tobacco he was rolling. He didn't once look down.

"Now there was a ramblin' rose. He might as well have put a roof of stone on a house of thatch." If she left, they'd have room for the children, and she wouldn't be pushing in on them. But she'd be on the shift for shelter, living like a tink in the weather unless she married. And if she stayed, she'd have to hide in her room or have on her conscience the spoiling of a home.

"I just wanted to point out that a man has his pride." He picked up the garnet ring and studied it. "If you offend him he'll be without a wife forever before he'll have you. You're a stubborn woman, but don't be too hasty in saying no to a fair offer."

"Your father said, 'Peg, I might as well argue with the wind that strokes the water as with yourself.' A rare man he was!"

Jim sighed and rose to leave. Then he hesitated. "What's that noise? Hear it? In the chimney?"

"The chirping and scratching? I heard it but was afraid to say aught in case it was the imagination of the ears."

"It sounds as if some animal's caught there. I don't see how it got in with the flue sealed."

"The flue sealed, is it! This morning after Jarvis left I was down to the canal with a sack like a picaroon. Didn't I trap a seagull and put it up the chimney because yourself said it needed cleaning and so we couldn't use it. Last winter I wished for a good blaze." There hadn't been a fire in the hearth since she and Michael were young.

Jim's broad face furrowed in a scowl. "Oh Ma, you didn't! Jesus, Mary, and Joseph! Have you taken leave of your senses? How did you ever sneak the bird past Dolly?" He continued, greatly stirred, saying he would buy her a stove if she felt chilly.

And how could she remember winter on a ninety-degree day? At last he left to get the long-handled broom.

She would put her hair in a snood, take her shawl and go to Edward McWilliams's wake. Then Jim's family could have the house to themselves for a while. How wearisome it must be to live with an old woman who brought livestock in the building. She was shaking with humiliation. Hadn't she raised Jim from a tiny mite only to find the back of his hand given her now?

He had said Jarvis was proud. She knew the Fitzgeralds had been the most spoken-of family in Western Ireland. Even during the famine they'd had a budgetful of yellow gold and sauce with their potatoes. "Well, he's cold poor now," she said aloud. Though he thought he'd be a mouthful in this country, he'd never advanced beyond foreman at the mill. As for those who whispered of a fortune hidden in his house, let them try to live on whispers. His lady wife! As if she'd be rich and wear white stockings. She'd planned on having safe moorings here for the rest of her life. But when a person thinks it's nice 'tis how it's a mocking trick, she thought, overcome with self-pity.

Jim hurried in with his stern face on. "A seagull! You'd sell your shawl rather than do anything the normal way." He opened the flue and pushed the straw end of the broom up the chimney. The beating stopped, and his face cleared. "I think it's gone. Are you going to see the hydroairplane? I hear it's docked in the canal."

"I am not." She selected an earring from the trinkets on the spread and held it out to him. "Would you be giving this to your Dolly from myself? It's lost its mate, but it'll make a lovely brooch."

Edward McWilliams was stretched in the front parlor with eleven lit candles at his head and feet. The twelfth candle went unlit to stand for Judas. A lamp glowed red in the corner of the room, and the air hung thick as a blanket of flowers. People stood around chatting or sat in rows before the casket, waiting for the lovely young priest to say a prayer. None of the women could do enough for the young Father. They at least would stay until he spoke. Jarvis was there, looking ill at ease since the afternoon mourners were mostly female. Peg waited until he stood alone, then went over.

"Did you know Edward McWilliams well?" he asked.

"Not at all," she admitted.

"Then why are you here to pay respects?"

"They say death makes your praying more sincere," she said with a flick of her shawl. Putting her hand to her mouth she added, "I heard it was the cancer killed him. But whisper! I have a recipe for that." She had to get someone to write down her cancer cure before she cleared off.

"I heard his last words were 'Show me the mercy you'd show a beast and shoot me,'" Jarvis whispered back.

"He was a great dramatist then, was he?"

"The despair runs in that family," he told her. "They're from the West Country, you know. His father died after leaping in a holy well, may they be safe where it's told."

"They say a holy death is a happy death," she noted piously.

"But to die without penance or anointing rites, without the Host!" Jarvis sighed. "And didn't he change his mind after the leap and come up with the moss in his hair. And Pat O'Boyle, staggering home on a toot, shot him for the Antichrist."

"It is short until we join him on high," she said sweetly.

"There's nothing but a while in this life for anyone," Jarvis agreed. After a bit he added, "I've heard that heaven's a yard and a half above the height of a man."

"Wouldn't that be the way of it," she said. "To be just out of reach." The subqueen in her mind wondered why people feared death if death meant entering forever to bright welcomes from your darling dear ones. But she held her tongue.

"I was after coming to inquire for you tonight. I don't suppose you've considered the story I opened this morning?"

So he'd still want her, though she poured a hundred discouragements on his head! "I have," she said.

"Well, let it to me, Woman. Has your answer changed?"

"It has." She wouldn't dig her heels in any longer.

Jarvis brightened. "Then the matter is right. God never failed the patient heart."

"Patient, is it. It's been all of the eight hours since you honored me with your attentions, my good gentleman."

"You're right, Peg," he said. "It's well late for us to be patient."

She would have to do for him for the rest of his life. The thought made her want to flee the fuzzy, red-lit room. Talking with Jarvis was like trying to sit still on a prickly horsehair couch, she thought.

She went home and told them right before supper. Then, entering the little room off the kitchen where they ate, she saw that Jim's Dolly had set out enough cutlery for courses. And a fruitcake left from Christmas, jeweled with candied fruit like a dark crown, sat on the sideboard. They had to eat in shifts or suffer bruised elbows at the table. Usually she took a tray of tea to her room, but tonight Jim insisted she join them. The babies would eat in the parlor. But when Jim's Dolly placed a chop before her she found she had no edge on her teeth. "I thought you were partial to lamb," Dolly chided.

"I'll have a tomato with a whiff of sugar on it. I have the liking of the world for that," she said.

"Why didn't you invite Jarvis over to see his new home?" Jim asked.

"When a woman marries she goes to her husband," Peg said. She thought of Jarvis's rented room, the hunks of sun falling through its windows and herself perishing with the heat. What wouldn't she give for a hole of her own! A steady hut on a stump of land out of the water, an old boat turned upside down as hens would live in.

"Nonsense!" said Jim. "You have to stay here with your family, with all of your things."

"You really must live with us, Mother," Dolly added. "This was your house before we moved in."

Why is it my nose would bleed if I met her without warning in the dark, Peg thought. You can't hate a woman because she has no complexion on her. Isn't it that when I sit with her for thirty minutes I feel I've been dead and buried that full half hour? How it must distress Jim, the two women raking each other! But what if she'd been wrong, and her son had no grudge against her living here? There was still no going against the promise she'd made Jarvis. And she'd never bring a husband into their crowded lot, another someone to bump into on the backstairs.

Later, as her room grew dark, Jim came up with a bottle he'd stashed before Prohibition became law. "What if herself finds out you've been drinking?" Peg asked. "She'll Carry Nation you for a week."

"A man has a right to celebrate his mother's wedding."

They had a glass and laid into talk with each other. Peg said a psalm that went "The king's daughter is all glorious within: her clothing is of wrought gold," having learned it by heart from her mother. And Jim told her of the great events he'd read in the evening's paper. Does it not seem Jim would like me to stay, she thought.

"It's much I admire those people whose lives would make books you'd need two hands to lift," she told him. It would be grand to do one bold, soul-gambling deed before she died. But a wedding! The ancient bride and groom hobnobbing with the gossiping guests . . . that was never it. Who would dance on the table to "The Hard Summer"? Then to live with Jarvis

Fitzgerald's worryings until the end day of her life. And wouldn't he seem the wisp in place of the brush whenever she thought of Michael? "It's close in here. I'm thinking I need a breath of air. I won't be long," she said.

It was a dusky nine o'clock by then, and the evening was made dimmer by her fading eyes. She walked along the towpath near the canal until she saw a new shape near the opposite shore. Was this the flying thing? She moved closer to the water to get a better look. It was moored next to a grove of gas lamps and hallowed by their churchly yellow glow. The canal was tall and dark as a priest's gown; the Northern locks must be open wide.

It was a perfect night: calm and desolate. Since there was no one to see, she sat down on the bank, dangling her feet over the darkness like a girl. She let one foot, then the other, dip into the water, brogues and all. It was the first cool she'd felt in weeks. She set down her cane, and slid forward a bit so that the waves reached up her shins, wetting the dense black lisle of her stockings. She'd never understood why a person was urged to pray for the souls of the faithful departed. The subqueen inside said to pray for the unfaithful: tinker, hawker, gypsy, Protestant, and Jew. Oh my God, I am heartfully sorry, she said, easing herself into the state waterway, which at first felt coldly foreign, then as her skirts turned to fetters, warmer, more familiar.

A Shadow Table

Charlotte Garrahan

IN FOX'S SWEET SHOPPE, I once saw a woman take off her shoe, unscrew the heel, and drink from it like a shotglass. I could almost taste the vinegar of homebrew mixed with the grit from her lizard pump. Thirst, I said, the eighth deadly sin, right after gluttony. And my fiancé, Ray Northrup, smiled between spoonfuls of his ice-cream soup.

Frozen treats named for hot places—Hawaii Frappés, Pompei Phosphates—were all the rage, but Ray was the only one who liked his ice cream cooked. We were leaving that day for Connecticut where I would meet his family. As he ate, I packed the makings of a special birthday dessert in a cooler. As long as things stayed chilled, we'd be all right.

Stamford was in a different state than Watervliet, and it was a long, cold trip down. Ray said driving made him so hungry he wanted to rip the lid off and eat the dessert ingredients with his bare hands. I knew what he meant. I was a lot hungrier than he was, though I'd never admit it. Starvation is easier than moderation. That's why we had Prohibition instead of temperance and why I'd eaten nothing but tea and crackers for two weeks.

It was a time of boyish silhouettes—corsets that flattened the bosom, dropped waistlines that dissolved the waist. The minute I'd noticed my hips thickening, I'd disciplined myself to thinness. But the more I tried to reduce, the more attracted I became to food. Once I understood how much food meant to me, I began to fear it. Still, I wanted to be around it—to smell it, touch it. That's how I came to be a waitress. I wanted to serve food. And I wanted to serve Ray.

We both were starving. We had that in common. The difference was, I tamed my hunger by not eating and Ray tamed his by eating to his heart's content. We were well-suited as Jack Spratt and wife.

Working at the Sweet Shoppe, I'd learned you could cook with cold instead of heat. Once the stove was the heart of the home. Now it was the icebox. I counted on the draft seeping through the car windows to preserve the dessert ingredients on the way down to Connecticut. To amuse ourselves, we listed anything green we spotted outside. Ray said it would quench our thirst for spring. But on that snowy drive, there wasn't much green to be found—some pine trees, maybe, a child's hat.

Night had fallen by the time we got to Stamford. As we pulled in the driveway, I made out stone fences and a big white house. It was lovely at first sight, even in the dark.

"Someone's coming," I said.

Ray said, "Oh, that must be our maid."

I laughed.

Then I saw she was wearing a white paper tiara like the frill on a lamb chop, and I faltered on the path behind him, distracted.

"Hello, Bridget. Is Mother awake?" His father was abroad on business. "Are there any leftovers?" he said.

Waitressing appeals to people who like to leave a place neater and cleaner than they found it. I felt equal to the responsibilities of the Sweet Shoppe, which included wiping a lot of white marble, humoring customers who wanted their ice cream on top of their topping, and turning a blind eye to the owner's bootlegging business. I think Ray fell for me because I was so unlike any other girl he'd met. He could confide in me and not feel judged, and this meant a lot to him. It meant he could bring up the notion of sweet suppers, for one thing. Just us, he said. Just desserts. Would you? Why, sure I would, I said.

Our sweet suppers took place after hours at the Shoppe. I served sponges, dumplings, puffs, puddings, creams, jellies, delights, supremes, bettys, gems, jewels, rolls, tortes, tarts, meringues, kisses and floating islands. Ray feasted while I sipped tea. At first he wanted me to join in, but soon my fasting began to seem natural. He never nagged me to eat or noticed my weight loss, and this made me feel acceptable. Ray was a student of Rensselaer Polytechnic Institute, remember, not a student of human nature. His interests were mechanical, scientific. When it came to people, he was innocent. He wasn't a soul searcher, I knew he'd never delve, and being with him was peaceful for that reason.

Private. It was private.

The other day I came across an old photo album. The pictures show my sisters and me at home, standing in front of broken barbed-wire fences and splintery woodpiles with drainpipes and clotheslines and dead trees growing out of our heads. I could tell which photos were taken by Ray because he posed me between plum blossoms. My family had no sense of background. Some might say we were raised to aim low, but I'd say we chose our disappointments just as others choose their battles. After Catholic High, I'd received a scholarship to St. Rose and turned it down so I could make money and help out at home. My neighbor went to St. Rose and afterwards she got a big desk job with the State. A big desk with her name on it.

The Northrups' living room had tall windows and flowers in crystal. It had easy chairs, and bridge lamps that swiveled to throw the light just so, an upright piano and twirling banisters. Wallpaper with a small raised figure. Their dining room suite looked like swans trying to be furniture. Ray introduced me to the maid, who actually did a little curtsy. I did one back, and he laughed and squeezed my hand, but I could tell from her expression that it was the wrong thing to do. I made a mental note: do not curtsy to the servants.

She grabbed the cooler, and Ray asked what birthday dessert I'd planned. He asked in a dreamy way, but my answer was no-nonsense. I said it was one of those unforgiving delicacies that had to be made perfectly the first time; there'd be no second chance. Remember, Ray liked his ice cream cooked. It was hard for him to understand the danger of melting. Couldn't you refreeze it? he said. Tinkering with mechanical things, he'd come to believe anything broken could be fixed. Couldn't you buy more and start again? Nothing could be ruined for him, you see. He was a hopeless optimist. This meant he saw me through a mist and thought all he had to do was say *here's Charlotte* and everyone would gasp and say what a find he'd found. I had no such expectation.

When the maid left, he ran his finger down the piano keys and said he'd often thought of me being there. Then he shrugged his shoulders like a little thrill had passed through and said maybe we could have one of our sweet suppers some night after his mother had gone to bed. Now wait a minute, I thought. Making a birthday dessert for his sister was one thing, but sneaking around a strange kitchen, playing with sugar— "I don't know," I said. "What if your mother wakes up?" I was eager to meet her and get first impressions over with.

"She won't."

"Reach for a Lucky instead of a sweet." I smiled and offered
him a cigarette.

⁓

I fully expected our families to have differences. Mother had no
patience with la-di-da ladies. All her buddies were men. She felt
comfortable bossing them; she liked to hold the reins. Although
she couldn't swim, she once ran into Lake George, shoes and all,
and saved a child from drowning. She had such confidence. If I
married Ray, I'd have to leave her, my family, Watervliet, the
Catholic Church, and live in Connecticut the rest of my life.
Where was I most wanted? Who needed me most? That's how
I thought about it. Sometimes I considered what I'd be giving
up either way. I thought about giving up a lot.

I once asked Ray if Episcopals had Lent. Why yes, he said. So
I asked if he'd ever given up sweets for Lent. Why no, he said,
he'd never given up anything. How could anyone live without
abstinence? That was my question.

The Church had some odd answers. My aunt, who was a Sister
of Mercy, knew them all. She told me if I married a Protestant,
I'd be excommunicated and go to hell. If I married Ray, she said
she'd pray every night that he would die before me. That way, the
marriage would be over, and I could go to heaven. But how could
it be heaven without Ray? I asked. Charlotte, you can't change
paradise to please yourself, she said. What I wanted wasn't part of
the picture. It was easier to think of what I didn't want.

Like the time I didn't want to be a waitress. It happened right
after a father came in the Sweet Shoppe with his little girl. She
was a beautiful child in perfect health. It must have been a big
day because she was all dolled up in dotted swiss and patent
leather shoes she kept showing off. The father ordered our
Xanadu Special Nut Sundae for her, and I served it with a smile.
I can still see my hands on the dish, handing it over. The next
thing I knew, this beautiful child was choking. The father

jumped up and called to me for help, but I froze to the spot as everything went topsy-turvy. He turned her upside down and held her by her ankles and shook her till the bow fell from her hair and you could see her drawers and tears ran into her bangs. He yelled hit her, hit her! because he didn't have a free hand to do it himself. Another customer started hitting her, but it didn't do any good, so the father laid her on the floor, where she had a fit. The other customer yelled get a spoon, she'll swallow her tongue! I did, but she was still by then.

You can see how flawed I was. Yet people said I was good. Psychology was just getting started, and no one put any stock in it. Everybody came up with their own theories. Mine was: Some people are doomed to be good. They can't help it any more than Episcopals can help being Episcopal. Saints don't deserve special credit—they'd be worse if their nature allowed.

Anyway, I was no Goody Two-shoes. My boss, Harry Fox, saw to that. He had a still in the cellar of the Sweet Shoppe where he manufactured Father Harry's Medicine for Coughs That Hang On. I thought his slogan, *If Not, Why Not,* made people remember why not. Mother could have come up with something better. She had some catchy sayings: *Don't come home if you get killed. The past is always with us. A move is as bad as an accident. Time won't tell.*

Actually, it was a Sweet Shoppe accident that led to my romance with Ray. I was pouring coffee for him when the chief of police walked in. My boss, Harry Fox, bunked into me as he ran out, and the boiling coffee splashed onto my arm. Ray drove me to Troy Hospital, where they diagnosed a third-degree burn. Don't worry, Doll, Harry said, when he saw the scar. It's a long way from your heart.

⁓

As Ray showed me around his family's home that first night, I noticed everything was imported from afar. They had French scrap baskets, Venetian glassware, Japanese lacquer trays, Dutch silver boudoir lamps, a Chinese dinner gong, and Yorkshire singing canaries. "But nothing from Watervliet till you," Ray said, and I laughed.

"A gift from Mother," he said, handing me a book from an end table. I'd been wondering why his mother hadn't stayed up to greet us. This made me feel more welcome.

"*Honorable Daughter,*" I read.

"It's almost her Bible."

"I'll start it tonight."

"There's an inscription."

" '*To Grace, the sweetest child in the world.*' " Grace was Ray's sister, the birthday girl. There was a picture of a plum blossom on the opposite page.

"Mother used to read it to us before we went to sleep."

"I hope Grace likes her dessert." Why was Mrs. Northrup giving me her daughter's book?

"Sugar Girl," Ray said. "There's something you should know."

Some people would have demanded the secret there and then, others would have nagged it out gradually, but the author of *Honorable Daughter* would have done exactly what I did. Like me, she'd been taught that questions were unladylike. She had this tendency to bow and scrape and back respectfully out of a room, and a heart that could be killed with shame.

We had a late dinner. The maid had left, so I did her duties. As a waitress, you learn to be attentive to the needs of others. Ray was easy. All he needed was understanding and permission to live a little.

As we sipped our coffee, he asked me to forgive him for something that might seem sneaky but was more a sin of omission. He was worried I'd mistrust him, but I did not share this fear. Something inside me had decided to love him all my life, and I knew he couldn't talk me out of it. You loved someone or you didn't.

He took my hand. "Will you read the book? *Honorable Daughter?*"

Now I was no reader of books. I liked the newspaper. "Why, sure I will," I said, with a smile.

Ray nodded. He cleared his throat. "Mother and Father lived in Japan for years," he said. "My sister Grace died while they were there. I was so young I hardly remember."

"Your sister Grace?" My voice went loud with shock. "She passed away?"

"I'm sorry I never mentioned it. It's just, I didn't want to be glum." He blushed and fumbled for a cigarette. "Mother still celebrates Grace's birthday every year with a shadow table in her honor. It's a Japanese custom. Do you understand, old pal?" He fanned the smoke away from my face. "Do you?"

"I do," I said.

And we fell silent. We sat there, looking out the window at the snow coming down in tatters. The dining room was drafty; it was like being in the car except we weren't going anywhere. I was thinking of the day my brother James died. He was two, and I was nine. He'd had his oatmeal that morning, like always, and put the empty bowl on his head, like he always did, to make us laugh. *All gone!* he said. It always made us laugh. He had this little cough, nothing serious. Then about an hour after breakfast, his breathing got raspy, and Mother told me to fetch the Vicks VapoRub. She put some on, but in no time he was struggling. His lips turned blue, but he was too sick to cry the way a baby should. Mother held him in her lap, and that's where he died. It all happened so quickly. I hid in the back kitchen. I'd never seen Mother so upset, and it scared me.

The wake was in our tiny parlor. I recall it very mistily. There were flowers and a plate of divinity brought by a neighbor. Papa led me over and told me to kiss James goodbye. I was shocked by how cold he was, like a baby made of snow. The hearse was pulled by horses with big plumes on their heads and big dark oily eyes and smoke pouring from their noses. Men carried the casket out. It was small and white as a wedding cake. And every Sunday after this, Mother would pack a picnic, and we'd walk to the cemetery to eat and play around James's grave. Of course I understood a shadow table.

In my room that night, I started reading *Honorable Daughter*, as promised. The author, Kikuno Takamoto, wrote about her childhood in old Japan, in a world of propriety and restraint. As a samurai girl, Kikuno had been taught to discipline her mind and body even in sleep. Boys could sleep carelessly outstretched, but girls had to curl themselves into the character *kinoji*, meaning "spirit of control." Like the plum blossom, their bridal flower that bloomed in snow, girls had to bear hardship and injustice without complaint and move without abrupt unceremony. Kikuno said she'd once been scolded for shifting her position slightly during a lesson, and the shame still burned in her a lifetime later.

Reading this, I remembered my boss's daughter, who refused to raise her hand or speak in school. Harry Fox said he'd tried everything from coaxing to whipping. She had been whipped till he declared he would not whip her anymore, as it did not help. He'd threatened to wash her mouth out with soap if she did not speak. What more can I do? he'd asked.

The snow crackled like a fire against the window as I read, and I lost track of time. It must have been after midnight when I came to the true story of the handmaid. She'd committed an unforgivable breach of etiquette by talking alone with a beautiful youth. Suicide was the only honorable option. Accepting her fate, she washed off her rouge, tied her hair with the paper death bow, donned her white death robe, and went to the room where her lord was waiting. There was a ceremony for suicide, and she knew it. She kneeled and bowed deeply to her lord. Then, facing west, she tightly bound her folded knees with her long crepe sash and pressed her dagger to her throat. But instead of dying bravely, she clumsily flung out one arm, staining the wall with her open hand.

Her story reminded me that you could get hurt while serving others. Once my hand got crushed in a swinging door. Another time, while drying dishes, I'd forced my hand inside a glass and could not get it out. I panicked, the glass broke, and blood went flying.

But my most humiliated moment happened during a sweet supper with Ray. He was eating a burnt sugar cake and I was having tea and crackers. I took a sip of tea and started choking so badly that the tea came out my nose. It was over in a minute, and we tried to go on as if nothing had happened. Ray began talking about a sage who'd cut off his eyelids in mortification after falling asleep during meditation and how the first tea bushes had sprouted from his eyelids. That must have been a sweet sight, I said. And we laughed and never mentioned my disgrace again. Silence is the best medicine, they say.

That night in Connecticut, I dreamed of frozen flowers. I dreamed I was eating them. They were noisy things to eat. In the morning, I saw the picture on the bedroom wall was one Mother had at home, *The Helping Hand*. It shows a little girl and an old fisherman rowing a boat. The little girl looks so honored to be helping. If Harry Fox asked my advice again, I'd say honor thy daughter. That's a commandment.

Of course, I felt for Mrs. Northrup over the loss of Grace. And her passion for Japan filled me with awe. I supposed she'd have impeccable manners and want everything just so. Had I packed enough ladyfingers? My dessert seemed even more critical now that I knew about the shadow table.

The next morning, Ray had errands in town, so we ate quickly. His mother never had breakfast. After he left, I asked Bridget, the maid, about the food I'd brought, and she led me to an unheated sun porch where the less perishable ingredients had been stacked beside a linen-covered box. She went about her business then, and I began my inventory. Snow rustled against the house, and I thought a blizzard must be brewing.

As I counted the ladyfingers, I glimpsed something moving on the edge of the waxed paper. I focused then and saw a big greenish white caterpillar moseying along, all fat and creamy. I gasped, for I'd never seen a bug so out of this world. It was quaint as a toy. As I backed away, I was startled by a voice. *I see you've met one of my little friends.*

I turned to find a smartly dressed lady in the doorway. "How do you do," I said.

"I've made pets of them." She held out her finger and the bug toddled onto it. It looked like a dollop of whipped cream. "You're not frightened, are you? Because that would be foolish." She moved her finger closer to my face. "They don't have lungs, but they do have a heart. You can see it beating."

"They're like—animals," I said.

"They're domesticated insects. *Bombyx mori.* They'll eat out of your hand."

"That sound. I thought it was snow."

"It's their jaws. They nibble constantly. Yet they're dainty about food. One wilted leaf will send them foraging."

She let the caterpillar creep into the box next to my ingredients. Then she opened another container. "They spin these cocoons to protect themselves. But alas, it doesn't help."

Eager to change the subject, I said I'd like to be useful during my visit. "If there's any cooking I can do . . ."

"You could boil the cocoons," she said. "They have to be boiled alive, poor dears."

The blood drained from my head. They must be a delicacy like lobster. I'd rather drink a pint of gall, I thought. "Why surely," I said.

"I keep some for the next generation," she continued. "Their eggs can be stored in the refrigerator for years. I have some in there now."

"Do they go for"—I waved at my ingredients—"sweets?"

"Sweets? I should say not! They like mulberry leaves. Though mine are raised on lettuce."

With that, she hustled off, and I plopped into a chair, still gripping the ladyfingers.

When Ray got home, he showed me around the garden, which was planned especially for winter. He lit a candle in a stone lantern designed to hold snow on its roof, and we admired the shadow it cast.

"These trees," he said, taking my hand and leading me over, "were planted to frame that distant steeple. It's called captured scenery. Another Japanese idea." I shivered and he moved closer. Hunger made me feel the cold. "You met Mother's silk-worms."

"Silkworms."

"Bridget boils a few cocoons for the thread, but Mother isn't really interested in their silk." He rubbed my hands as if he could start a fire with them. "Mother said you were *wabi*."

"What's that?"

"A compliment."

"Tell me about the shadow supper."

"Shadow supper?" He frowned a little.

"The memorial dinner. On Grace's birthday."

"Oh, the shadow table. It's Mother's version of an old custom. It's also *wabi*."

"Translate, please."

"Genuine," he said, as we walked toward the house. "Good."

We were sitting in the living room, listening to a radio Ray had built himself, when Mrs. Northrup came in. She handed me a blue silk kimono, saying it was a gift and wasn't it a pity no one did such exquisite work anymore. Then she took up some lacework or tatting. Her thread was coiled around a wooden spike in the center of a bucket. Ray, meanwhile, was tuning in a distant station.

"Can you guess what this once was?" She nodded at the bucket.

"An ice-cream churn?"

"You must be an expert on those, given your line of work."

"Tell Charlotte about the shadow table," Ray said. He had one ear glued to the radio.

"This was a head bucket," his mother continued. "When a samurai committed suicide—"

"The shadow table," Ray interrupted, "is for an absent family member. Their place is set, and they're served their favorite foods." He turned to his mother. "Charlotte's planning a grand dessert for Grace's shadow table."

"Grace's dessert will be pure snow," his mother said. "Pure snow, fresh from the sky, gathered from a tree, and seasoned with maple syrup. That was her favorite."

"Charlotte went to a lot of trouble—"

"That's okay," I said quickly. "It should be pure snow."

"Snow nothing!" said Ray, in exasperation. "Where's my radio map?" And he went off looking for it.

Mrs. Northrup licked her thread. "Raymond is being honored, you know."

I nodded. I hadn't known.

"At the radio awards ceremony tomorrow." And she told me

the nominees' dates brought sweets to celebrate their escorts. That was the custom. Rubbing her thread to a point, she said my dressy dessert would be ideal.

"To honor Ray? Why, surely."

"Then it's settled," Mrs. Northrup said, her needle threaded.

I spent the next day splitting, crumbing, mixing, whipping, beating, boiling, standing, draining, pouring, setting, and chilling, in honor of Ray.

That evening, we took Mr. Northrup's Packard to the awards dinner. There was no sign saying Country Club. You just had to know about it, like a speakeasy. The grounds were largely snowy fields with green links underneath. A maid was taking the desserts at the door. Please, I said, handing mine over, keep this cold.

Inside, people clustered around set-ups of White Rock and ginger ale. A girl called out, Old flame! Old sweetheart! She hustled over, dragging her date, and Ray introduced us. They were Pearl and Oliver. Pearl's dress was the last word—black crepe with steel discs. Slashed arms. She had platinum hair and a chinchilla wrap. I could see it was a reversible affair and very costly.

"How is Honorable Mother?" Pearl said. Ray and Oliver were checking our coats. "Still raising her silkworms? Has she tried to bribe you with an old kimono?"

"Bribe?"

"No girl's good enough. Hold out for the jewelry. Did she give you material for an obi?"

"I beg your—"

"A cummerbund made from twelve yards of brocade. You fold it in and fold it in till it's this thick." She measured air with her fingers. "It's a shame to hide such magnificent stuff. I had mine made into a train. Oh, and I still have that queer little book about Japan."

"*Honorable Daughter?*"

She laughed. "My favorite was the soldier whose enemies didn't lock the prison because they knew he was too polite to leave."

"Too honorable," I said.

"Far too honorable. Ray was raised on that hogwash. It explains a lot."

"Like what?"

"Oh, you know." She wrinkled her nose.

I folded my arms and looked her in the eye. "Ray is good," I said. "He's a prince."

"If you like that kind of thing," Pearl said, as we followed the boys to our table.

Once we sat down, Ray produced a silver flask and poured some in our drinks. He was saying he'd been nominated for a silly prize given to the man whose homemade radio could pull in the most distant station. Pearl pointed her long cigarette holder at me. "You'll be the one to present the prize, as your initiation." Now wait a minute, I thought.

Meanwhile, my dessert had been placed on the table. Oliver said it should be called Mount Everest Surprise because if we ate all that, we'd suffer the fate of the last expedition. And he told how some climbers failed near the summit, and two made the top only to die there of exposure. Or possibly one slipped, and being roped together, the pair fell to their deaths in the eternal ice of the Himalayas. As he was talking, something white flew across the table and hit Ray's lapel.

"Charlotte, your dessert has met with an accident," Pearl said, flinging another spoonful. "It has been injured. Your dessert has suffered. It has been wronged."

Ray shook his head as if she were a spoiled child and dabbed at his tuxedo. Catching my eye, he smiled and licked some whipped cream from his finger with a blissful expression. Another spoonful sailed across then, landing in his hair. He held up his palms, signaling stop, but she scooped up more sugar ammunition. Oliver was laughing and the band was playing hard. Ray mouthed, I'll be back, as he got up and moved off through the smoke and saxophones. Old flame, Pearl called after him, it was entirely my fault, I could just weep with sorrow. Black olives, salted nuts, and peppermints littered the table, the ashtrays were overflowing, and the help had mostly left. I saw my dessert was in ruins, beyond repair.

"Ray looked like he'd been used to wrap a workman's lunch," Pearl said with satisfaction. She took a swig from Oliver's flask. "Let's speak Japanese," she commanded. "Charlotte first."

"I only know one word."

"Tell."

"*Wabi.*"

"What's it mean?" Oliver asked.

"Boring," Pearl said. "Amuse me."

Oliver stuck out one of his legs and tripped a waiter carrying an ice bucket.

"That man nearly fell," I said. Somebody could get hurt.

"I'll leave the fellow a large tip," Oliver said.

The band was taking a break, and someone was playing a ukulele and singing "Show Me the Way to Go Home" under the table next to ours. Pearl leaned over and whispered in my ear: *Why do you want to come here anyway? No one knows you, and you won't have any friends.*

I couldn't sit a minute longer looking at the crumbs and ashes. I began stacking the dirty dishes along my arm, so I could clear the table in one trip. That's quite a balancing act, Lottie, Pearl said, shoving her slave bracelets higher. That's quite a stunt. Oliver, look what a good little waitress she is.

I sidled between the drunks and dancers and set the dishes down near the kitchen. Then I saw Ray was back at our table. He kept swiveling in his chair, looking around, and I knew he was looking for me. I could see last summer's freckles on his skin and his lush, lush lips. That contrast always killed me. What else did my Sugar Boy look like? Like every young man in love, I guess, except that he was mine.

Though the band wasn't playing, some couples were dancing. One group had spread their tablecloth on the floor for a picnic. A girl was bent over double, laughing. Every time she straightened up, she was struck by another bout of hilarity, and so she jackknifed back and forth, like someone bowing or being sick. There was such a din I hardly heard my name being paged for the award presentation. People were throwing sweets at each other, and I was afraid I'd get hit with a pie before I made it to the stage. I knew in Japan silence was the greatest tribute given an accomplishment, yet I wanted applause for Ray; I wanted the lift of pride it would bring.

When I got to the podium, the bandleader handed me an envelope, but before I could open it, a gust of wind hurricaned up from the floor. Later I realized there was a fan hidden under the stage, positioned to perfectly shame. But when it happened I didn't know what was happening. I froze in place, too petrified to move, while my skirt went up like a flame, exposing everything, and the room erupted in wolf whistles and laughter. These mockeries blended with a roaring in my ears. I hadn't eaten all day, remember. I'd only had doctored drinks. I reached toward the mike to steady myself as a powerful weakness surged through me, and I knew I was going before I was gone.

Ray was bending over me when I came to. I heard people saying give her space, air, water, uncut Park Avenue gin. He kept telling me I was all right, and I tried to act that way as we hurried to the car. He said they were asses. He said Pearl was a vampire. I asked who won the award, and he said another fellow, and he was sorry because it would have given him such pleasure to throw it back in their faces.

We got in his father's car, and he took a drink from his flask. When he was upset, Ray liked to talk about things at a distance. Now he brought up bootleg silk—how once upon a time, Persian monks hid silkworm eggs in their walking sticks and smuggled them out of China. I marveled that something so delicate could make it through that long journey alive.

I had a bad headache and felt queasy. I tried to fight it, but my body was in charge. It was frightening to be so out of control. Everything's coming up, I said. Here? he said. Now? He stopped the car and rushed around and opened my door. We were blocking the clubhouse driveway; everyone was in back of us, in their cars, all eyes. No, I said. Not outside. I wanted to be sick in the car, in private. I thought I could use the cooler. I didn't want an audience.

Ray tugged on my arm and tried to help me out of the car. No, I said. Please. He said his parents would never understand, while the people here didn't matter. I knew he wanted to avoid a mess, but the urgency in his voice sounded like annoyance. I knew he was being practical, but I felt forced.

He didn't understand how deeply shaming this would be.

Until that instant, I would have trusted him with my life. Now I felt he'd let me suffer to keep things smooth. I felt sacrificed. But I had no choice. I was in his hands. And when a door is held open, you go through.

Snow filled my shoes, and the scar on the white of my arm from the old accident, the scalding, glowed like a plum blossom in the moonlight. People swerved around us, honking and yelling and hitting me with their headlights as I sank to my knees.

Afterwards, he asked if I was all right. My shoe had come off, and he picked it up and shook the snow out. Everyone else had left. He asked if I'd like to go back and get my dessert, so we could eat it at home—because from the little taste he'd had, it was really something, an accomplishment. Sugar Girl, why don't you answer? he said.

He said he knew he was flawed, a letdown, but I was the only unselfish person he'd ever met, he only felt at home with me, and wasn't that the true test of friendship. Then he said he was thirsty and gave his flask a little shake. All gone, he said.

At that moment, I wanted nothing more than to wash my mouth out with snow.

As we stood there shivering, he started talking about Japanese lovers, how they never kissed. "How do they express their devotion without kissing?" he asked. "Is it possible?"

It was only because of my education in Connecticut that I knew the answer.

"Why, sure it is," I said. "Don't you remember? In moments of passion, they gently turn their backs on each other." I held out a handful of snow, and he put his mouth to it, cold and pure and burning.

THE NIGHTINGALES OF TROY

Annie Garrahan

T HE VISITING NURSE had been waiting ten minutes for her last case of the day, a has-been priest. Her raccoon coat was folded inside out on a chair, and she'd placed a clean newspaper under her black bag. When she opened the venetian blinds, hygienic winter light glazed the oilcloth and dresser scarves of the Phoenix Hotel. How far could that Jesuit get with his halting gait and metabolic disease? She kept her eyes peeled. If he turned up, she'd ask him why God made the Depression. Annie Garrahan was vehement with things that had given her the slip.

I want to help you, but first I have to hurt you, she often warned her patients. When she'd said this to Bernard Jolley, he told her a good nurse was an alloy of compassion and brass. For once they agreed. A too-sympathetic nurse was a danger. She sniffed, taking a culture of the air, testing for evidence of liquor. Had he bothered with his insulin? No regular priest would live in the Phoenix. Jolley was a freelance, an outcast.

He had three illicit passions: the river, the theater, and strong drink. Years ago, he'd put on church pageants, Father Jolley's

Follies, and though the Jesuits sanctioned theater as a means of edification, they'd deemed him a vulgarian. And every spring, he'd go looking for the origin of the Hudson River in the heart of the Adirondacks. Still, these excesses might have been tolerated if drink had not dulled his spiritual vigilance. Drink was his great sin.

As she walked to the hotel office, young Nurse Garrahan repeated her class motto like a prayer: *Esse Quam Videri*. To be rather than to seem. Jolley was not what he seemed. He was an unpriestly priest. Worse, he was a dreamer. Give me reality or give me death, she thought, as she knocked on Sam Livingston's solid oak door.

Like daylight and science, Sam Livingston's purpose was to make the world so ordinary that people could bear to live in it. Nurse Garrahan told him she could fix the best menu for atonic constipation he ever tasted. It hits the spot, she said.

She was tired of chasing Bernard Jolley through the bitter streets of Troy, New York. She thought Jolley needed a dog— something adoring to follow him around and press its cold black nose into his knee as he held forth. He wasn't satisfied unless he was tearing the heart out of the obvious. Just thinking of his longwindedness made her woozy.

"Cocamilk's best for an upset stomach." Sam opened a miniature Frigidaire and produced two bottles. "My housekeeper, Mrs. Fredrickson, won a contest with this. First prize for most nourishing soft drink. Say when," and he poured milk into a half glass of cola. Annie took a sip.

"Tastes swell!"

"I'm thinking of adding it to The Ship's menu," Sam said somberly. In addition to the Phoenix Hotel, he owned a floating dance pavilion. "Something special, to outclass the competition."

"The weather and disease are my competition," Annie said. "And now this hobo priest. "

"What's Jolley's problem, anyhow?"

Annie appreciated Sam's direct and simple speech, the way he referred to the Phoenix Hotel as The Place and the Ship of Joy as The Ship. He was sensible, yet his blue eyes always looked mildly surprised. There was a sweet yet manly scent about him, a blend of cigarettes and menthol, Barbasol and talcum. "Sugar." She added reluctantly, "And the DTs."

Sam shook his head. He was thirty-nine, a man of the world. "C'mon." His heavy key ring jingled with industry. "I'll show you The Place and give you the best shoeshine you ever had. You're only as young as your feet, you know."

As they walked the hallways, Annie was soothed by their no-skid rubber tiles. She took comfort in the stark usefulness of the restaurant's napkin dispensers, the chrome toothpick holders and hefty china cups. When they entered Sam's hotel flat, a transfusion of well-being surged through her, and she almost cried for cheerfulness. The carpet roiled with ferny ferns, the wallpaper was big with orchids, the drapes with jungle gardenias. These were heavyweight flowers, flowers with muscles. They bulged and flexed and leapt from the walls, larger than life.

She planted herself on the chintz sofa in glad anticipation while Sam fetched his shoeshine kit. Kneeling at her feet, he began to swab and brush her pumps. First he polished, using an old toothbrush on the tight spots; then he waterproofed with an emollient he'd crafted himself from pine sap, mink oil, and beeswax. He roughed the soles with sandpaper, buffed the leather with his bare hands, and sat back on his heels. "You're in business," he declared.

"Yes sir!" Annie affirmed. She felt reborn.

As Sam was putting away his polishes, she glimpsed a collection of cure-alls in the cupboard. These remedies testified to a secret delicacy in him, and her nursely vocation flared like a flame. At first her family might not approve of a divorced former bootlegger, fourteen years her senior. They wouldn't like the rumors of fifty-gallon copper kettles in a frame barn on 113th Street, the aliases he was said to assume, the bullet scar on his left arm, the fact that he was a Protestant. But they'd come around. Sam was her chance. As a registered nurse, she had what he needed. Here was someone she could save, an opportunity to use her training. She clicked her heels and clenched her hands, inspired, in fact, thrilled to the bone.

But her immediate problem was Bernard Jolley. She told Sam she feared the priest had gone off on a spree. Delirium tremens usually followed a hard debauch, and she wanted to start treatment before hallucinations or wet brain developed. He'll be fit to be tied, Nurse Garrahan predicted.

"We might try a restraining sheet fastened to the headboard in a simple clove hitch," Sam said, "though a mattress on the floor is safest. What'd they say in nursing school?"

Annie rolled her eyes and waved her hand to push the thought away. She couldn't give a priest a prolonged warm tub bath, let alone perform high colonic irrigations of normal saline.

Sam lit a cigarette, and Annie noticed the signet ring, yellow gold with a diamond, on his little finger. Diamond was the hardest stone, and gold never tarnished. As she stared at the ring, she remembered an article in her nursing journal on radium treatment. Radium looked like salt, but it was rare and costly. It was kept inside a lead-lined safe, whose combination was guarded by the radium custodian, a graduated nurse, paid to keep track of every gram since all the radium in the world would fill only a pint bottle, and radium took nineteen thousand years to decompose to lead.

Nineteen thousand years! Why should radium last that long? Or diamonds, or gold? Why were they almost perpetual while people were fragile, gone in a flash? When Sam died, someone would twist the ring from his finger, and the ring would continue, but Sam would be gone forever. There was heaven, oh yes. But objects inherited the earth. It was so unfair, it made her mad. She glanced at her watch, seeking reassurance.

As she was resisting these unnormal thoughts, Annie became aware of a calming aroma, the fragrance of bakery blended with rose water. She sensed an approaching gentleness and was looking toward the open door when a motherly face peered in.

It was Sam's housekeeper, Mrs. Gertrude Fredrickson. Call me Freddy, she said. On her left breast, over her heart, Annie noticed an unusual brooch: a tiny snapshot of a boy encased in glass and framed in gold. Freddy was carrying a tray. "I made a pineapple pie, and it'll taste even better if I share it," she said. While the housekeeper was in the kitchen, Sam confided that Mrs. Fredrickson must have been a Girl Scout troop leader at one time because she was always inviting him to do beadwork or tool leather with her after hours.

Freddy's eyelashes fluttered helplessly as she handed Sam his plate. Why, she's lovesick, Annie thought, with a twinge of sympathy. The housekeeper told them Bernard Jolley's bed hadn't been disturbed all week. "Are you the hotel nurse?" she asked, and Annie smiled and denied it.

But that's exactly what she became. There was a great need for nursing at the Phoenix Hotel, and Annie was there every day on her lunch hour, looking for Father Jolley. She'd reported him missing, but she still thought he'd turn up. Meanwhile, the other ailing residents required Ovaltine for sleeplessness, Mazon soap for ringworm, Petrolagar for constipation. When Annie learned of Sam's stomach ulcer, she arrived with bowls of junket and sparkling gelatins known to aid the healing of inflamed mucosa.

Soon the tenants were lining up outside Sam's office, waiting for Nurse Garrahan to appear in her navy dress with detachable white collar and cuffs.

One day, a short bristling woman cut through the line, rushed pell-mell past Annie, seized an open bottle of pills and hurled the contents at the assembled tenants. Annie's protest faded when she recognized the hooligan as the supervisor of visiting nurses, Victorine Crawley.

She'd heard Nurse Crawley lived in a hotel, but she'd never dreamed it was the Phoenix. They'd been in training together, and after graduation, Victorine Crawley had advanced quickly in the profession. Annie glimpsed the silver whistle, used to summon staff, around her neck. *She's always there when she needs you.* That caption, said to be a printer's error, had appeared under her yearbook photo. Her ears were cunningly made and adorned with earrings shaped like Florence Nightingale lamps. These earrings were rumored to be lockets filled with an unidentified white substance. Annie admired them.

"Do you think you're being a good nurse?" Victorine Crawley demanded. This"—she brandished the empty bottle— "is how you're treating your employers. You're throwing medicine at these people! Can I be more expressive?" With that, she hustled off to rap knuckles and reprimand inferiors elsewhere in her district. She won't be happy till everyone's as miserable as she is, a tenant quipped. But Annie was too disturbed by the charges to laugh. A good nurse was all she wanted to be.

To be rather than to seem. A good nurse defended the real and true against the half-baked or mysterious. She raised resistance against disorders that made the normal seem awful. Raising resistance was Annie's vocation. She did it mostly by talking. When she was in training, the other probationers would gather outside her door, suppressing giggles as they listened to her solitary murmurs: *Clara Barton, glamour, coffee enemas.* Though they'd teased, the others had to admit her monologues could rouse the dead. They'd witnessed as she leaned over the comatose, urging them to rise and shine, talking until their lips quivered and their pinpoint pupils dilated, until their color improved and they demanded steamed clams with butter sauce and crackers.

When Victorine Crawley got wind of this gift, she'd nabbed Annie in the hall. I am dismayed, she said, by your yen for self-glory. The same meaning lurked beneath today's accusation: You think you're special, don't you, starting a clinic in the hotel where I live, on my stomping ground. Annie could imagine the report she'd file: Nurse Garrahan must curb her tendency to freelance and assume a doctor's role. . . .

The pills tossed by Victorine Crawley struck Mrs. Fredrickson's seven-year-old son, Eugene, and his whippet, Moonshine. Annie recognized the boy from Freddy's brooch and Sam's descriptions. He'd been waiting to get cough medicine for his mother. Eugene's father had died, but the housekeeper saw that her boy had nicer clothes than most: the toes of his shoes had not been cut out to make room for growth; the moth holes in his sweater were small. His wren-brown hair appeared gray as his mother's, and his horn-rimmed glasses were so similar he might have inherited them, too. His whippet, a racing dog abandoned by a former tenant, was windbroken and highstrung.

Eugene had built a model of Sam's floating dance pavilion, the Ship of Joy, and he often stopped there on his way home from school. The two of them would lean over the railing to dip their hands in the frigid Hudson, Sam's superstitious ritual. He took the boy to prizefights to make him more rugged, and when they passed in the hall, he'd softly punch him and say how's the boss.

For two weeks, Annie tried to imagine where Bernard Jolley might have gone. Thinking like a Jesuit was a terrible effort. At last, Sam suggested they set out in his Cadillac to look for Jolley at his usual haunts. Soon they were drifting past brick storefronts and two-families, heading for the smudge of trees along the Hudson River.

"Everything's melting." Sam let out the clutch.

"The river's awful high."

They squinted at the Hudson, a tidal estuary composed of power laundry and textile runoff, bleaching and dyeing agents, milk products, paper, and unclassified wastes. Annie frowned. Jolley had infected her with this knowledge. Thanks to him, she'd never spend a night on the river without thinking of American eels ruffling the moonlit surface, gulping oxygen through the nares in their snouts. She gave her nurse's bag a little kick. Eels fed on carrion and breathed through their skins. Their sense of smell was good as a dog's, and they could travel overland when conditions were wet. She pressed the lock on her door and peered through the mist. Silver lampreys covered with mucus lived in the toxic depths. Boneless, jawless parasites with rasp-like teeth that burrowed through a host's skin to feed on blood and tissue. But lampreys were rare. That was the nice thing about them. That set your mind at rest. Now northern water snakes . . .

"I don't know how a lame priest can dance," Sam said. "Did you ever see Jolley dance?"

"I told him, if you want to be The Dancing Priest, you have to be more social." She scanned the shirt workers and schoolkids at the bus stop. "I hope he hasn't gone on one of his pilgrimages in this miserable weather."

Given a chance, Jolley said he would climb Mount Marcy, the highest peak in the Empire State. He would follow Calamity Brook, then trail the Opalescent River till it became Lake Tear of the Clouds, the splash of blue that was the Hudson's rumored source. She checked her nurse's bag for the small bottle of insulin. If acidosis had set in, she could revive him hypodermically.

As they turned onto 109th Street, the fog parted and they had a clear view of the Ship of Joy. On the hurricane deck, near the smokestack, a figure lorded it over the river. As they got closer, Annie saw its outstretched arms were formed from an oar, its backbone from a mop pole. Its swab of hair was haloed by a dented hubcap and fishing nets strung with bottle openers jangled from its extremities. It was swathed in a long black frock.

"To scare the gulls," Sam said. "You lose business if people slip on bird do or a rat runs up somebody's leg. The Ship is the only dance garden with a scarecrow. You have to consider the competition. The Blue Heaven gets big names—Sammy Kaye's Orchestra, Cab Calloway. I get Horton Spur, the Boy Who Bounces, and Margie Barrett, the Fiddling Tap Dancer. "

"You could put out some traps."

"The scarecrow's unique. It's a mascot, a good-luck charm."

"It's dressed better than some of your clientele."

"There's no cover, that's why. Like the ads say, *Exclusive—not expensive.*"

Annie smiled. If Sam wanted the Ship of Joy to be exclusive, he shouldn't have started the soup kitchen on Mondays, when the dance pavilion was closed for business. He shouldn't let the destitute lounge on the deck chairs in nice weather. He was chronically kindhearted, that was the problem. It posed a danger for her. How could she advance in her profession if she spent her spare time helping him buy storm windows for his old people at the Phoenix or new shoes for his sister with the expensive foot? How could she save him when he was busy saving other people?

"One thing," Sam continued. "The Blue Heaven is too dark. What are they trying to hide with that candlelight? A dirty kitchen. Could be bugs. I like to see what I'm eating. That's what I like about you, Annie. You put your cards on the table."

"I thought you liked the way I smell like Ivory soap."

"That's right. And I like nurses. I like the way they kiss with their eyes open." Sam's smile was both debonair and shy. "Let's try the Oakwood," he suggested. "Jolley goes there to visit with God."

Five minutes later, the Cadillac swooped through the iron gates, past the ornate crematorium of the Oakwood Cemetery. Once they were inside, Sam pulled over. He fished out his pocket compass and studied the red-tipped needle floating under glass. Annie, meanwhile, had come upon her new lipstick in her bag. She swabbed at her mouth and felt the oxygen promise of vermilion—the color of transfusions, high blood counts, nourishing hemoglobin—restore her smile. She approved of things in mint condition. Her taste ran to sanitary, progressive angles that did not gather dust.

That was the problem with the Oakwood; it wasn't modernistic. It was a vast puzzle of unnamed gravel roads winding through evergreens and bony birches and hills that rose to hide whatever tipsy cross you'd chosen as a landmark. They drove past sooty slabs and headstones, ghostweights that kept the passed-away from spinning in their graves till time had time to soothe their rest. Annie saw the lamb sweet as glucose at the good shepherd's feet, and twin angels kneeling in the muck, their wings fibrillating through the mist. It was the mud she disliked most. That mud could ruin a new pair of pumps. She peered at marble houses with barred windows, padlocked doors, and tiny yards tucked into iron fences. The Oakwood was a good place to catch your death of dampness, when all was said and done. An ashen-skinned angel flew by in its granite nightgown, its eyes downcast, its arm pointing upwards through the fog.

Sam stopped the car alongside an ancient family vault, and they got out to have a smoke. "Don't fall in any open graves," he called. But Annie was already standing beside him in the headlights, puffing without inhaling from her Old Gold.

Sam Livingston bought graves the way other men bought

neckties, and he liked to advise young Nurse Garrahan on the pros and cons of available lots. It seemed the sections with the best views had no breathing room. They were crowded, hard to mow, or close to traffic, while the spacious sites were located under messy shade trees or afflicted with poor drainage. In fact, no grave had won his perfect confidence. Yet Annie did not understand his wish to be buried aboveground, in a mausoleum full of fungus and powdery mildew. Sam could imagine tree-of-heaven plants, unkillable weeds that hatched in crevices, uprooted stones, and grew eight feet overnight. He could imagine being buried alive, the satin suffocation of a casket. What he could not imagine was the end of all imagining. She dropped her cigarette and ground it underfoot.

"Friends, some things are best disposed of by burning."

They spun around to see Bernard Jolley materialize from a cloud of exhaust. His black vestments were absorbed by darkness, but his face flared forth—a sallow, phosphorescent structure with too many bones. The sweaty smell of sanctity hung around him, and his eyes were gray as griddles.

"Holy smoke," Annie said.

Father Jolley was middle-aged, but he seemed timeless. His glass eye made his sunken glance more steadfast—he looked as if he were always ready to cry "behold!" When he talked, his lips squirmed and seemed unconnected to the rest of his face, which stayed inexpressive as a fish. Really, the intensity of his calm irritated Annie. She felt if she stuck her tongue out at him, he'd place a communion wafer on it.

She searched her bag and handed him the baked sweet potato she'd packed that morning. The cheerful yam was well-tolerated by diabetics, if properly masticated.

Jolley said, "Nurse Garrahan, you are a brick. I hope I may prevail upon you to star in my next production."

Some vain and spangled part of Annie liked the sound of this. She was secretly amazed that she was not already in the limelight, making curtsies so deep her permanent wave brushed the crowns of the crowned heads who were her public.

"*The Nightingales of Troy*. A water ballet, combining medical and aesthetic values, to be performed in the Hudson River."

"I never saw a nightingale in Troy," Annie said. "But then, I'm from Watervliet."

"I never saw one in Lansingburgh," Sam added.

Jolley limped into the white specter of a headlight and waved his sweet potato at the heavens. Blessed are they who do not see but believe, he said, and Annie was afraid he would start chattering in Latin or launch into a litany of dictionary words and foreign phrases, an utterance with every hair in place that wound on and on in longwinded loops of booklearned pronouncements until she lost her bearings and wanted to strike a hear-no-evil stance with her hands over her ears.

Not the songbird, Jolley said, clasping the sweet potato to his breast. Florence Nightingales. A show that dramatizes the importance of home nursing care to the housebound invalids of Troy. And he stroked and punched the dark to make them see the synchronized Rockette kicks of swimmers in Red Cross bathing caps and the flailing limbs of those going down for the third time while the bell tolled on Sam's ship, the Ship of Joy. He was all gray matter and hot air, he was dirty but luminous, holding the tuber aloft like a torch. Why, he's burning up, Nurse Garrahan thought. And when he finished, his silence was momentous, as if he expected them to say, Father, you have told us things we've wanted to know for a hundred years, and now our lives will never be the same.

"Bernard, I've been meaning to ask you," Sam said. "How did you come by the nickname of The Dancing Priest?"

Jolley sniffed the sweet potato absentmindedly. Then he put it in his pocket. "How can we know the dancer from the dance?"

"And another thing," Sam said. "Can the river get sore and hold a grudge?"

"Ancient customs of propitiation arose from such convictions."

Annie cleared her throat.

"Burning was the preferred method of sacrifice. The Druids placed their victims in willow cages, I believe."

She started humming "Moonlight Bay."

"Do you think the river minds the speedboat rides I sell in good weather?" Sam asked.

"It was not always thus. There was a time when a person who longed for absolute peace and quiet could find it by going on a river trip."

Sam said, "I don't mind the upkeep. Shoveling snow off the roof or flushing toilets all night to keep the pipes from freezing. It's the ice floes, the floods."

"The river has been injured. It was not always thus."

Those swimming ballerinas should be greased up with a good coat of lard, Annie thought, before they took the plunge.

"My housekeeper was born with the caul and has second sight. She told me there's a jinx on The Ship. Do you know how to remove a jinx, Bernard? Can you tone it down some way?"

"There are rites. The *Ritual Romanus*. I could drop salt into water so as to form a cross . . ."

"Then I got a business proposition. I'd like to hire you to take the spell off The Ship."

"I could," Jolley raised his right hand, "utter the words 'Get thee gone, vanquished and cowed, when thou art bidden in the name of the Lord—' "

"That's the ticket," said Sam.

"And when the malignant spirit has fled, I could pour holy water in the river."

"I need a specimen, Father," Annie said. "Are you experiencing unusual thirst or intense itching? Any tingling of the toes and fingers?"

"Nurse Garrahan, you are an object lesson."

"How's the potato, Father?" she continued. "When's the ballet?" The Nightingales of Troy would develop new and terrible diseases after their dip. There would be no toxoid available. It sounded educational.

"The potato is a first-class feast, which I will save for a time of need. I am on retreat. The saints will provide spiritual essence to drink and consecrated energy to eat. Then, if God allows, I may sanctify the river's depths with reserves of spiritual power that can be invoked for the benefit of mankind."

Sam nodded and Annie shook her head. She thought the depths should be left alone. The surface was as it should be, that's why it had become the surface. She approved of dissections when the scalpel stuck to reality. But the hocus-pocus of hidden meanings earned her scorn—the purpose of science was to stamp out that mumbo jumbo. Instead of saying the rosary before she went to sleep, Annie would list the structures through which fat passed on its route from the intestine to the cardiac chamber, beginning with the tiniest villi, wending through the lacteal and larger lymphatic vessel, rising toward the thoracic duct and left innominate vein to permeate the superior vena cava and enter the red springs of the heart.

The Hudson was a famously fickle river. In January 1935, after days of subzero temperatures, it thawed and rose fifteen feet above sea level. Rafts of ice tumbled down on the current. Then the rain started, and half of Sam Livingston's roomers came down with the grip. The ones who couldn't work and pay their bills gave him their wedding rings as security. No one was evicted. Sam stayed in business by being his own janitor, handyman, desk clerk, plumber, and electrician. He'd tend bar till three in the morning, sleep for four hours, and start again, mopping floors and unloading beer kegs. He said he felt a lump of blue coal smoldering in his chest, but his ticker was strong, so it must be his stomach. Annie agreed. It must be an ulcer, and lifting a single heavy object could destroy the cobweb delicacy of fibrosis that constituted healing.

Mrs. Fredrickson stretched the meat budget with jellied beef, liver loaf, and broiled tongue. But on Saturdays, Annie pan-fried a tenderloin for Sam, served it with canned Niblets, creamed onions, and rice pudding, and Sam deemed this the finest meal he'd ever eaten. To ease his lumbago, she covered his back with flannel and passed a heated iron over it. On Thursdays, her half day off, the ailing residents lined up at Sam's office, and Nurse Garrahan treated them with Foley's Honey and Tar or Vicks VapoRub. She dressed infections, removed foreign bodies, painted throats, lanced boils, and irrigated ears. She even treated little Eugene's asthmatic whippet. In return, Eugene kept an eye out for her supervisor, Victorine Crawley.

One day Bernard Jolley appeared, back from his retreat. He was carrying a painting Mrs. Fredrickson had given him of Lake Tear of the Clouds, the Hudson's elusive source. Freddy had painted it herself, entirely from imagination, in a style simple as a child's. In fact, Lake Tear looked much like the painting of Lake Louise she'd given Sam. Still, Annie was impressed. She wished she could do some frivolous thing that would add an extra note of beauty to the intimate circle in which she was placed. But she didn't have a nickel's worth of creativity. Her talents were entirely practical.

Her snappy brown eyes took in a bit of river through the office window, and icicles thawing to the size of hypos. The drapes smelled musty. *Fungus,* she muttered, *flood.* Now when Annie made her rounds of North Troy, the brakes of her Chevy coupe got soaked, and she thought longingly of blizzards. Blizzards were invigorating, while infections—pneumonia, typhoid, even poliomyelitis—followed warm spells. She had to be ready.

As an added incentive, *Visiting Nurse Magazine* was offering

an undisclosed award for the best piece of equipment improvised from materials found in the average home. That night in
Sam's office, Annie punched tiny holes in an empty can and fitted it over an old oil lamp. She took a sheet of Phoenix sta-
tionery from the desk. "What nurse can resist a new 'practical
device!" she wrote, and described her invention, which had less
than six parts, did not require salt to boil, and would not burn
the patient. "Gives plenty of steam for vapor medications!"
Annie enthused in brash, backslanting script. She'd try it first on
Eugene's dog, to help his wheezing. She lit the wick and waited
for steam to rise above the flame.

The next day rain flattened the feather on Annie's Robin
Hood hat as she mailed her contest letter. By the time she got
to Sam's office, her shoes were soaked. Instead of a shine, he gave
her a new pair of oxfords.

"With a flexible steel arch. To absorb the jolts." Sam lit an Old
Gold and took a drag. He'd spent the morning on the flat back
roof of the Phoenix, looking for broken seams. "My bucket's got
a hole in it," he confided.

"What bucket?"

"My cocobola." He tapped his index finger against his head.
"It's these dreams. Something dark, pulling a wave over my
face." The rain drummed fretfully against the walls. "See, The
Ship bankrolls The Place. It keeps me afloat. Now Mrs.
Fredrickson says . . ." He stopped and studied the ashtray ashes
as if reading tea leaves. "What do these dreams mean, anyhow?"

"They mean you've lost your pep."

"Could be. You're young. . . ." Sam rubbed his temples and
forced energy into his voice. "The old goat's feeling sorry for
himself. You deserve better, Annie." He paused. "But it would
bust my heart wide open if you left."

Annie smiled. "I can be your official brow wiper." And she
explained how a nurse used to be stationed by a surgeon to perform that task.

Sam smiled back. But when Annie tried to thank him for the new shoes, he took her hand, held her with his lake-blue eyes, and spoke so gravely that a premonition ruffled her nerves.

"Get Jolley to bless The Ship."

Then he leaned back in his chair, tilted his fedora over his face, and fell fast asleep.

Mrs. Fredrickson said Bernard Jolley was probably holding forth in the breadline or giving sacred lectures to show people at the Blue Heaven. After an hour's search, Annie found him in the Oakwood Crematorium Chapel. First she tried flattery, calling him Father. Then she tried guilt, mentioning freeloaders. At last Jolley said, Tell Sam Livingston I'll perform the *Ritual Romanus* on the Ship of Joy and sanctify the river's depths at noon tomorrow.

When Annie and Sam arrived at the river the next day, Eugene and Moonshine came racing toward them. The boy ran smack into Sam, wrapped his arms around Sam's leg, and hollered, The river's coming in The Ship! Sam dashed away, and Annie kept the child from following. Sam will go down with The Ship! Eugene wailed.

"Don't be crying," Annie commanded. Fear was a communicable disease. She squatted down to level with him. "Little man! How can you help me if you're bawling? I want you to go tell your mother about The Ship. Can you do that?" Eugene nodded and ran off.

It was with some misgiving that Annie followed Sam on board. She gripped the rope railings and tottered up the gangplank while the wind tried to shove her in the river and the scarecrow spun. A murky, sulfurous smell drifted from the vessel's innards. She could hear Sam shouting down in the hold. The Ship's bell began tolling then with a hollow bronze finality, and the employees gathered in the dance hall. Where was

Bernard Jolley? Probably dead drunk, passed out in the cozy darkness of some church. He'd stood her up again, the stinker.

Sam leaped onto the bandstand and sounded the orders to abandon ship. She's been hit by something big, probably an ice floe, he told them. As the staff left, he hurried over to Annie. He had mud in his trouser cuffs and folded squares of tissue paper in his hands. "Loose diamonds from the cooler," he said, giving her the safe's contents. He delved in his pockets for other treasures: deeds and registrations and leather nuggets of jewelry boxes. "Put these in your satchel, and don't drown on your way out," he cautioned, before disappearing into the hold.

From the safety of the Cadillac, Annie watched Sam toss furniture on shore. *Iceberg, Titanic, poor fella*, she murmured. The signs by the entrance—*The Floating Palace of Northern New York, Never a Dull Moment*—were ragged and stained. What did people have against dull moments, anyway? The best things in life were dull. Clean sheets, paid bills, mashed turnips, Freddy's paintings. The picture over Sam's desk must be Freddy's work. The simple shapes were unmistakable as was the handpainted title: NORTH RIVER STEAMBOAT. Jolley had explained how travelers used to try to take steamboats to places that couldn't be reached by water. The Hudson was mistaken for a shortcut to the Orient at first. Near its source, the river was free of cyanosis, and you wouldn't feel the urge to throw a box of chlorinated lime into the current.

Now the water was turbulent and armed with flotsam. Annie watched as The Ship listed to one side. The gangplank broke, the scarecrow flailed, and Sam fell to his knees. She squinted through fog at the spot where he had been, and at last caught a glimpse of him, dipping his finger in the river for luck. Then he jumped to shore.

"At least nobody got hurt," Sam said. His stormcoat dripped onto the upholstery. When he took off his gloves, his hands were lavender. "At least the Ship of Joy never lost a life." He coughed and reached toward the glove box. "But I took a shellacking on account of there was no insurance." He offered her a swig of cough syrup.

The smokestacks and scarecrow were still visible as the craft settled, and automobile trucks arrived. "I called hours ago. Maybe they can pull her out," Sam said. "It's funny how you worry. That safe is guaranteed waterproof, and I'm wondering did I close it. I'd like to get my money's worth." Annie understood. Anything that traveled through disaster and came out high and dry seemed miraculous. "Jolley's an odd bird," Sam went on. "He's a good conversationalist, an educated man, but he broke his promise."

"He's flighty that way." She frowned. Jolley was forever dissecting some offbeat subject. He'd explain how fish feel sound by means of a sixth sense located in Jell-O-coated hairs that reached out of the cells of their skins. He could not take a fish at face value. He would not let things be. Was that what it meant to be educated?

It was dark when the trucks hauled The Ship out of the river. She was glistening with mud and the clever little life-forms that called mud home. Leeches with suckers at both ends of their bodies. Worms that thrived in unoxygenated water. Midge larvae that fed on detritus. Annie thought Sam should change into dry clothes so they could go out for hot turkey sandwiches. But as soon as The Ship was on the bank, he left the car and climbed aboard. He worked the door and vanished inside.

Hear, hear! she scolded. Eels were generally more active at night. And she didn't like the sound of his cough.

A minute later, he came running back. "I spoke too soon. We had a stowaway."

Sam helped Annie from the car and propelled her toward The Ship. How did she come to this, a regular person who loved buttermilk and Kate Smith? She was not one to brave the depths. She was no crusader. Sam boosted her onto the deck,

gave her galoshes and an old ship's lantern. He carried a flashlight and her nurse's bag. Annie's teeth chattered as she followed
him to the hold, where the water reached her second-highest
boot buckle. She shuddered and balked as his light struck what
looked like a granite Frigidaire. The safe's door was open and
inside, curled and welded, snail-in-shell, was Bernard Jolley. He
blended so perfectly into this home away from home that she
couldn't see him at first. Then she made out his pearl-gray lips
and nails. As she touched his clammy skin in search of vital signs,
Nurse Garrahan, for the first time in her life, felt faint. She
waved smelling salts under his nostrils.

"These excesses of his embarrass the heart. I'm afraid there's
some morbid pathology in progress." And she leaned over his
face, uncertain whether to administer the kiss of life or the
sacrament of the dead. "He's prone to carousels, poor soul. He
rushes the growler, goes on a bender, and next thing you
know—" She couldn't find a pulse.

"He's gone," said Sam.

"You have to be more optimistic."

"He locked himself in that waterproof safe and went down
with The Ship."

"Well, you know the old saying—what goes down must
come up." She was still hoping for a coma.

Sam took off his hat.

"C'mon Father, that's enough shut-eye. Wake up now, sleepy-
head." She almost sang it. And because she was anxious, she
started humming a tune, *There was a man who had a dog* . . .

"He's passed, Annie."

It was true. The priest was cold and pale as the backside of a
leaf. She released his wrist.

"He was unusual, poor man," she said. "Did he ever tell you
how he was criticized by his order for theatrical tendencies?
Self-glorifying, they called it."

"He's met his maker," Sam said. "He's asleep in the deep."

"He used to put on shows in our parish, with everyone in bathrobes and him pounding out anthems on the piano while the scenery nearly fainted." She sang a few words—"There was a man who had a dog and Bingo was his name-o—"

Jolley wheezed, his right hand jerked. He opened one eye and spoke: *Ad majorem Dei gloriam.*

"Son of a bitch," said Sam, and smoothed his hand over his hair.

As she left The Ship, Annie kept her eyes down, looking out for eels. She thought of the larvae, transparent, shaped like willow leaves, that began in the Sargasso Sea and drifted a thousand miles to the Hudson, changing to glass eels on the way, gaining pigment as they moved, turning into snakey things that twitched and jigged when yanked out of the river and were despised by fishermen for just that reason.

After The Ship sank, Sam came down with lobar pneumonia. The symptoms were unmistakable: ferocious coughing, chills, high fever, a bounding, rapid pulse. He got so upset at the thought of paying for a doctor that Annie didn't dare call one.

Before dragging himself to bed, he pointed to a half-smoked Old Gold in his office. "My lucky charm," he said. "That means I'll be back. Don't throw that out."

Annie took a leave from her job, claiming family illness. If Sam could be sustained for seven to nine days he would, in the absence of complications, get well. In the early, congestive stage, her homemade inhalation burner provided medicated vapor. She gave alcohol rubs, applied turpentine stupes and kerosene fomentations. She forced fluids. As the disease progressed, Sam's fever climbed to 104; his breathing grew labored with an expiratory grunt; his lips turned blue. When he coughed, Annie splinted his chest with her hands. Her nurse's bag held medicine left from other cases: codeine and sodium luminal to ease the coughing and allow sleep; adrenaline, should circulation fail.

"Watch out," Sam yelled. "The jack of straw, the tattybogle shoyhoy, the hodmadod is here!" Delirium had begun. He couldn't be alone for fear he'd jump out the window, always left open with pneumonia patients. Mrs. Fredrickson offered to stand guard so Annie could sleep. Should she call a doctor? Reminding Sam of money worries might kill him. Rest was everything. Yet a too-sympathetic nurse was a danger. These conflicting wisdoms were all she had. What would she tell Victorine Crawley if the supervisor accused her of nursing a gravely ill patient not under a doctor's care?

On day four, as Annie passed Sam's office, she saw his half-smoked Old Gold was gone. Maybe Freddy had cleaned. She found the housekeeper making Victorine Crawley's bed, while Eugene sailed his miniature Ship of Joy on the rug. "*She* took it," the boy said. "Victorine. I seen her." He and Freddy rushed off to search, leaving Annie alone in enemy territory. The supervisor's Nightingale lamp earrings were on the dresser. Impulsively, she picked one up. It sprang open at her touch, revealing white crystals. Annie sniffed. Smelling salts. Its mate wasn't so yielding. She had to use her teeth. Folded inside, to her amazement, was a half-smoked Old Gold. She seized it.

She found Freddy searching Sam's office. "Is it true?" the housekeeper asked.

"What?" Victorine Crawley had a crush on Sam. Imagine.

"You brought Bernard Jolley back from the dead?"

"Who told you that?" With Sam's illness, she'd all but forgotten the priest.

"He called from the hospital. Is it true, Dearie?"

To be rather than to seem. "Nah. That's just a rumor."

She'd be barred from nursing if Victorine heard this gossip. It was just a matter of time. Her radium-faced watch glowed precisely, a reminder, as she hurried back to Sam.

Some priests thought they could walk on water, but Bernard Jolley had been humbled. He told everyone that Nurse Garrahan had rescued him from the depths of the Hudson River. He spoke of Lazarus, miracles, and Nurse Garrahan, all in the same breath. The rumors spread, and Annie continued to fear her conduct would be questioned. The problem was, while some despised Jolley's airs and graces, others found him hypnotizing. He treated everyone courteously, and it lowered people's resistance. "Permit me to tell you of my experience with . . ." And off he'd go, dramatizing why Adirondack deer needed their own Bread Line, why Lloyd's of London refused to insure the Dionne quintuplets. "This minute," he'd say, gazing solemnly at the ceiling, "Amelia Earhart is flying her red and gold monoplane into adverse winds." He had a standing offer of free soup at Troy Sandwich because he attracted business.

Now, during Sam's delirium, the ex-Jesuit returned, haggard but sober. When Sam imagined fiery vessels sailing down the river, Jolley made the monsters homely, explaining how old steamboats had become stone barges that in turn became dance gardens, like the Ship of Joy. And when Sam saw a lady with a lamp, Jolley identified her as Florence Nightingale, whom his grandmother had trained under in England. The real Florence Nightingale? Annie asked. *To be rather than to seem.* "A small, severe woman who taught the nurses to use white powder for bedsores and stopped patients from keeping food under their pillows," Jolley said. "Who cared more for the body than the soul, put scrubbing before praying, cleanliness before godliness."

"You haven't changed a bit," Annie remarked.

"All education which does not soften the heart is wasted. A nurse is tried as silver is tried, and dross is burned away. And if an ass goes traveling, he does not come back a horse," Jolley replied.

A long convalescence followed pneumonia. One mild day in March, Annie and Sam sat on the flat back roof of the hotel drinking river-brown Cocamilk highballs. Freddy had hung her Monday wash, but a crow had already soiled the sheets. It had befouled the Phoenix Hotel logo, embroidered in red near the hems, and Sam took this personally. He was sporting glossy black wingtips and his favorite fedora. Annie wore alligator pumps, earrings, and her Robin Hood hat. Her raccoon coat was draped over a chair from The Ship.

But the crow was the nattiest. Stunning and plump, it strutted over to peck at an invitation, decorated with tinsel, near Sam's feet. Jolley and Freddy had invited them to a rag party, a gathering of scarecrows. *Please dress as shabby as possible*, Freddy had written in a flowing hand.

"Like the boogieman." Sam blew smoke rings toward the crow. "You know what they say. 'A bird in the house means a death in the house.'"

His cigarette was the Old Gold she had saved from Victorine Crawley. Annie had kept it in a jewel box rescued from The Ship and now he was finishing it, as promised. The crow inspected some glittering ashes.

"What about parakeets?" Annie asked. Pneumonia means a death in the house, she thought. But she wouldn't say this. She wanted to be his nightingale, not his raven croaking nevermore.

As Annie saw it, Sam's superstitions hindered his practical strengths even as they gave his eyes their poetical glow. He had faith in the prophetic powers of fortune cookies and birthmarks; he trusted his luck to rabbit's feet and four-leaf clovers and understood why gamblers blew on dice and dogs circled three times before they lay down.

His recovery had encouraged the gossip about her gifts. She'd nursed him devotedly, sure, but she knew her talent boiled down to common sense. There was nothing spooky about it. Even her legendary ability to rouse the dead sprang from scientific observation.

Annie had simply noticed that no one spoke to comatose patients. No one encouraged them. And so she squeezed their hands and called their names. She leaned over them, begging them to awaken, and the tiny muscles around their eyes trembled as they strained to lift their lids. That's all there was to it. It wasn't wonderful. It was normal as crows.

Sam picked up his binoculars and focused on the riverbank where tramps were roasting a dark lump on a spit. "Four and twenty blackbirds," he said, "baked in a pie." The crow flew up to the clothesline, crying gawd, gawd! and Annie said it must be Jolley's bird, the one who could talk, sneeze, cough, and laugh.

"But he only laughs at his enemies and only talks to good-looking women with nice physiques wearing jewelry, fur, and feathers," Sam said. He smiled nonchalantly, and they watched the river, glinting like pig iron in the sun.

"The Rainbow," Annie reminded. Sam had promised to tell her his latest business idea, for without The Ship, he had no income. Now he described a derelict building he could buy and convert into a nightclub to be called the Rainbow Gardens.

"Like the rainbow after the flood," he said. "A sign of hope."

While Sam talked, Annie spied a clump of pink and white spring flowers by the river. But when she looked through the binoculars, the blossoms became dentures, an upper plate half sunk in mud, like pastel fungi. She was thinking that rainbows, like nightingales, weren't native to Troy. She'd never seen one, and she suspected they existed only in picture books. Rainbows weren't real. How could she respect them?

Sam read her mind.

"Rainbows are real. Those dreams where a buzzard covers my face, the Old Gold, Jolley's bird—they're mysteries, the unknown. But rainbows are real."

Annie admired Sam's worldliness. He could smell a sharper or charlatan a mile away, and the fortune-tellers he consulted were always sincere people. He was a licensed pilot with his own biplane and fur-lined leather flying suit. He played the saxophone. He was sophisticated, smooth. But now she thought his sentimental side was threatening his good sense.

"If rainbows are real, then the pot of gold at the end must be real, too," she joked. "Just think—you'll be on Easy Street."

"No, there's no riches." Sam smiled and shook his head. "Only the sun through rain and some ragged colors."

"Hey," Annie said. "That rag party they're throwing. I haven't a thing to wear."

And because they'd gotten too serious, they started laughing. The crow laughed, too. Then it swooped down and grabbed the last morsel of Sam's Old Gold.

"The little fella's over to his friend's," Annie said. "Freddy's outside toasting marshmallows and singing campfire songs."

The rag party had fallen on a chilly, drizzly Sunday. The whole hotel turned out, dressed in the spirit of poverty. People gathered in the alley, around Freddy's campfire, for tomato soup, potatoes baked in ashes, and bacon broiled on sticks.

In Presto's, the hotel restaurant, Jolley was holding tryouts for his water ballet, *The Nightingales of Troy*. Horton Spur, the Boy Who Bounces, and Margie Barrett, the Fiddling Tap Dancer, out of work since The Ship sank, were there to audition. Guests sprawled belly-down on the restaurant tables to demonstrate their swimming strokes while the Victrola played dance tunes. Freddy came in to recruit people for games of Drop the Handkerchief or Duck on the Rock. The restaurant door kept opening and closing, and Jolley's crow almost got crushed as it flew through. *A Trojan nightingale!* Tony the Tailor yelled.

Jolley had promised a big surprise before the day was out.

"He'll dance," Sam predicted. He and Annie were sitting in a booth to one side. "The Dancing Priest will dance. You wait and see." He moistened the reed on his saxophone, which had dried from neglect, and played the first notes of "Stormy Weather."

Annie checked her nurse's bag for bran, laundry starch, baking soda, salt, and boric acid. For her audition, she planned to dramatize how these common household items could yield soothing medicated baths for skin irritations. Sam would provide musical accompaniment. They were about to make jackasses of themselves, she felt sure. She wanted to end her demonstration with the Nightingale Pledge, but she couldn't remember the words. There was something about elevating the standard of the profession, and how could she promise that, dressed as a tramp, with a sooty face, in a black shroud swiped from a scarecrow?

Sam coughed, and Annie offered him a BiSoDol mint to aid his alkali resistance. Smoking and playing saxophone were hard on his lungs, still susceptible to adhesions, spontaneous collapse, empyema, abscess, bronchiectasis, and spreading involvement. She'd saved him; there'd been no late complications. But his delirious visions had gotten under his skin. He still talked about the boat he'd seen, slow as a haywagon, with sails and sidewheels, boiling up the Hudson. "It makes you think," he said. "Where does the past go?"

The crow flew by, inches from Annie's ear. Shoo! she cried, swinging at it. Birds were carriers of disease. She was secretly terrified of them.

Jolley was standing on a chair, holding forth. "Scarecrows began as human sacrifices," he declaimed, and the entire room leaned forward, transfixed. Only his bird, pecking at the lunch counter, seemed bored. Eat crow! it heckled. "Crows taste like duck," Jolley noted. Then he told how the heavens had darkened for hours as great flocks of passenger pigeons flew over. "Alas, they were delicious. That's why they're gone forever, eaten up."

Sam placed a parcel addressed to Annie on the restaurant table. "That could be fairy dust," he suggested. "There's no return address, and it's light as a feather."

Annie shook the package. "My undisclosed prize!" She'd just remembered her contest entry. "Whatever it is, I can use it."

"Whatever it is, you deserve it," Sam affirmed. "Did you enter your tip for removing castor oil stains from genuine silk?"

"I wish I could remove weird visions from your brain," she teased.

Underneath the brown paper lay a little box, wrapped in rags. Annie unbandaged it and opened the lid. A pale yellow stone gleamed from the black velvet depths, and a tag, in Sam's wind-blown script, read *The way you look tonight* . . .

"Gawd almighty!" she exclaimed. Then Nurse Garrahan did what she always did when surprised or moved: she pinched her nostrils as if stopping a sneeze or nosebleed.

Sam said it was a canary diamond from the cooler that could be an engagement ring or a friendship band. That was up to her.

"Can't it be both?" Annie said with a smile wide as wings.

Heartened, Sam confessed he'd fallen for her the first time he tasted her rice pudding, and Annie, suddenly exuberant, said she liked to be useful as well as ornamental. In this distracted glow, she heard Jolley introducing Mrs. Gertrude Fredrickson, who would perform a pantomime of things falling asleep to Margie Barrett's violin accompaniment.

They watched as Freddy, with a series of interpretive jerks, sways, flutters, and vibrations, suggested a clock winding down, a tree in autumn, a tired goldfish, a dying campfire, and a vacuum cleaner's gradual malfunction. Her final piece, "The Phoenix," she dedicated to Sam Livingston.

As Miss Barrett played "There's a Small Hotel," Freddy embodied the soul of a great bird sinking into ash. When the music stopped, she lay quite still. Just as Annie was about to rush up and resuscitate her, the stout housekeeper stirred, opened one eye, and peered coquettishly at Sam. He waved and nodded his approval. That was all it took. Freddy heaved to her feet, flapping triumphantly. Poor soul, Annie thought, she's trying to encourage him. Sam and Eugene are all she's got.

As Freddy curtsied bashfully, Jolley stepped forward. "Florence Nightingale was named for the city in which she was born," he said.

"I'm glad they didn't name me Watervliet," Annie whispered.

"After the war, she spent ten years in bed and never spoke in public again." Florence Nightingale lost confidence, Annie thought, imagine. "However!" Jolley continued. "She made one recording, in 1890." He paused, significantly. "We will hear that recording now."

He disappeared behind the lunch counter, and a terrible squawking burst forth: a raucous, rusty sound punctuated by high-pitched blasts of screech that pained the ear. If time could talk, it would sound like this, Annie thought. If the ages, if forever could. Some people put their hands over their ears.

After the last crackle faded, Jolley fixed Annie with his gaze and translated: *When I am no longer even a memory, just a name, I hope my voice may perpetuate the great work of my life. God bless my dear old comrades of Balaclava and bring them safe to shore.* Jolley liked to speak in parables. This time, Annie realized, the hidden meaning was for her. He'd played the old recording as a gift, a grace, to cheer her on. She waved and nodded, stately as a queen.

Once Jolley had taken his modest bow, Annie went back to Sam's office to find the Nightingale Pledge, for they were on next. As she was paging through a nursing textbook, three little boys came shrieking in. They yanked her toward the door, screaming, Eugene fell in the river! Where is he now? she said stupidly. In the river, we was sailing The Ship, he reached for it and fell in, they babbled. Before they finished, Annie was rushing back to Presto's.

Wait outside, she told the boys, and she dodged through the

party crowd to Sam, who sat alone, adjusting his saxophone mouthpiece.

"Eugene's in the river," she gasped.

Sam had cast off his constant vigilance for the afternoon; it took an instant for his party mood to shift. "What?"

"He fell in," she said. "Oh, hurry!"

Sam dropped his instrument and jumped up. He ran over to get Jolley while Annie grabbed her raccoon coat and nurse's bag.

In minutes, they were at the riverbank. The youngsters pointed to the spot where their friend had disappeared. Then Jolley saw Eugene's shoulder protruding from the water about twenty feet from shore. "He's caught in that tree branch," Sam said, kicking off his shoes. "I'll get him." But Jolley was already in the water, striding, then fiercely swimming.

"Wait. . . ." Annie grabbed Sam. "He's got him."

Water covered Jolley's face as he gripped the boy and started back. He had him. Jolley was rescuing Eugene from the cold currents of the Hudson. But it could take another half hour for the firemen to arrive with the inhalator, and the boy needed help right now. Annie threw her raccoon coat on the ground and knelt beside it. As she rummaged frantically through her bag, her glance fell on a pair of impeccable black shoes standing on her fur, using it for protection from the muck. Victorine Crawley. The supervisor hadn't attended the rag party. In her smart black dress and navy cape with crimson satin lining, she was the only one who looked respectable.

Sam waded in to take Eugene from Jolley. He stumbled up the bank with the boy in his arms and laid him down on Annie's coat. She found no pulse or respiration.

"What are you doing?" Victorine Crawley demanded.

Annie had placed the boy on his stomach, clasped his waist, and lifted him so the water could drain. She set him down, turned his head, and pressed his back while counting to three. Release, then repeat.

"Fix a hypo of adrenaline," she directed Victorine.

The supervisor had the rules of nursing conduct by heart, and she loved to display her learning. "It is only by a doctor's direct orders that a nurse can carry out that procedure," she said, crossing her arms. One patent leather shoe tapped irritably.

"There's no time!" Nurse Garrahan cried. Then her glance fell on Victorine's Nightingale earrings.

"Try your smelling salts!" she ordered. "Your earring." Infuriated by this impertinence, the supervisor seized Annie's wrist as she was attaching the needle to the syringe. "What you're doing is illegal. I will be forced to report it. You'll be prosecuted, I warn you."

Annie jerked free. "For God's sake, get out of the way! You don't scare me, you old crow."

In fact, she'd never been more frightened, but you had to stand up to a bully. You had to resist. She tore Eugene's shirt and wiped his arm with alcohol. Placing the needle-point in the adrenaline solution, she drew up the plunger and pressed to expel any air. Then she pinched the child's icy flesh and gave one sharp, quick stab. Breathe, Eugene, it's Annie, she said.

There was no response.

"You see?" Victorine was smirky with triumph. "You've given him an overdose. You'll pay for this."

"Eugene, can you hear me? Wake up!"

The supervisor drew her cape against the damp. "Do you believe in black magic? Or is this vanity? Your disregard for aseptic technique is a disgrace to the profession. More cannot be said."

Annie wondered where Sam, the one person who might call off Victorine, had gone to. Now she saw him restraining Freddy, her face ghastly with terror. Their eyes met and Annie felt a compassion that translated to calm.

"The soul of nursing must never be sacrificed for the technique," she said. It was something Jolley had told her. *The soul.*

Freddy called out then—save him! "Breathe," Annie commanded, massaging the boy's icy hands and legs. "Wake up, little fella." Then, leaning over, she whispered directly into his ear: "Come back."

"Nurse Garrahan." Victorine flicked her cape impatiently. "You're wasting your time with this gruesome display. Quackery can't bring back the dead, and he is dead, that's certain. He has no vital signs, no pulse or respiration."

"Shhh," Annie hissed. "He'll hear you. His mother will hear you. For shame!" Then she added, "I never waste time; it injures eternity." Another of Jolly's sayings. To her surprise, Victorine's eyes filled.

"Don't give me eternity. Any nurse worth her salt could see the child's dead."

She said it loudly, and Freddy, overhearing, moaned. The rain had ended, and as Annie turned toward her stricken friend, her eyes were pierced by a single hysterical beam of light. It was the setting sun reflecting off the tiny golden lamp in Victorine Crawley's earlobe. Nurse Garrahan's pleural cavity hurt; she felt wild, irate. Jumping up, she seized Victorine and yanked the charm from one of her ears. It sprang open, spilling its salts on Eugene's chest.

"You're a phony, a fake!" Annie cried. And with that, she hurled the Nightingale earring into the Hudson River.

She threw it so forcefully she would have fallen in herself had Sam not grabbed her. "We wasted time, precious time, arguing," Annie moaned. But she might have been talking to herself. For the supervisor, with fastidious sympathy, was informing Freddy of her son's death.

After entrusting Eugene to Sam, Jolley had gone back to save Moonshine. When Sam returned and asked for the priest, Eugene's frightened playmates pointed north, where the priest and dog had been swept away.

The *Troy Record* called Jolley's rescue efforts heroic. "For more than an hour," the paper noted, "Nurses Victorine Crawley and Annie Garrahan labored, trying to resuscitate the victim." Sam later expressed the belief that Eugene was dead when he took him from Jolley. But Annie was deeply shaken. Bad nurses stayed on duty even when unfit. She'd seen it happen. When Eugene died, a power rushed from her like blood from a wound. She felt it go, felt diminishment set in. Her gift, a gift she'd denied, had dissolved like salt in solution.

"I failed," she told Sam, "I failed the little fella." Now her hand trembled when she took a pulse, she sometimes confused the invalid's heartbeat with her own, and she suspected if the patient cried, she'd join right in. She tried to describe her shaken confidence to Sam, but all she could say was, "I practiced medicine instead of nursing. It's like—" And she stopped, at a loss.

"Like selling liquor on a beer permit?" Sam suggested.

"It's like Jolley said. 'If a horse goes traveling, it sometimes comes back an ass.'" That was the best she could do.

How could she shoulder the burdens of others in this state? How could she march into a sickroom and say Nurse Garrahan has spoken? She knew how to give anesthetic with a tea strainer, how to make a knee bandage from an inner tube, an ice pack from a rubber glove, a cradle from two coat hangers. But this knowledge no longer gave her confidence. She no longer believed a single flower in a test tube anchored to the bedpost would help a patient find new interest.

As Sam struggled to withstand his setbacks, Annie saw the limitations of science. She worried she'd become the picture of poor mental hygiene—the type who believed that wearing asafetida prevented diphtheria or that the best treatment for TB was to drink whiskey and go west. She might begin to think most deaths occurred when the Hudson was at ebb tide, or that a dish of salt placed on the chest ensured a better corpse.

In May, she resigned her position as Troy District Nurse, bought a White Swan uniform of Irish poplin, and went on private duty. She would accept only cases whose crisis had passed because she did not trust herself to make death seem a natural rather than a scary thing, as a good nurse should. *A good nurse makes death behave itself.*

During these weeks, Annie gradually began keeping the same odd hours as Sam. He'd close the bar at three a.m., and they'd share a bite to eat. At first, she prepared nutritious snacks, but these tidbits became more slapdash till at last the two of them were eating crackers from the box washed down with jelly jars of beer. Annie started to allow herself a jigger of gin at midnight; before long she was taking therapeutic nips as the need arose. Sam's parlor, which used to seem so cheerful, now reminded her of a dim aquarium stocked with carnivorous plants. If she stared at it long enough, the aquamarine rug, etched with snaky stems, would liquefy in peristaltic waves, queasy as infinity.

As they sat on the davenport sipping Manhattans, Sam described his fevered hallucinations. They'd begun with a vessel that resembled a sawmill mounted on a barge and set on fire. Above her flue, a constellation of ignited vapor soared like a splendid, frightening fountain in the dark. The next time he'd seen her, she'd grown large and lavish, silent and graceful as a mute swan. She had gardenia-white awnings and an upper deck where ladies paraded by lantern light in frocks as fresh as flowers. She looked like a perennial bed floating up the Hudson.

Annie's gaze fell on the painting above Sam's easy chair. Sunny water walled by leafy slopes, labeled *Lake Tear of the Clouds, Mount Marcy, New York.* It was the picture Freddy had given Jolley. After a few drinks, Annie could imagine the priest washing up on that Adirondack shore, alive. Would he remember to rotate the site of his injections? She liked to think so. She liked to think he'd joined the Troy Encampment of Odd Fellows or gone to live with booksy folk who could appreciate him.

Sam picked up a brown paper parcel from the end table. He'd brought it home days ago, and they'd forgotten all about it. "This could be gold bullion. There's no return address, and it's heavy as lead."

"Oh, that's probably my undisclosed prize," Annie said dismissively. "It's probably five pounds of fudge or a new iron. Whatever it is, I can't use it." She folded her arms defensively.

"Sure you can," said Sam. "Think how you used a cut lemon to remove match-striking marks from plaster walls."

He lit a cigarette as she tore at the wrapping. There was something red and harsh underneath.

"It's a—isn't it?" Annie said. "The tag says—I can't believe—" She read it to herself. "Let us pray!" And she yawned in disgust.

Sam read, "A brick from No. 10 South St., London, home of Florence Nightingale from 1865 to 1910."

"What am I supposed to do with it?"

"Think of the honor. This means you've arrived," Sam said.

"I'm thinking what use is it. I'm thinking I'd like to pitch it through a window. If you ask me, this prize gets the booby prize."

"I'll put it in the cooler," Sam said. Then liquor and the late hour made him philosophical. If you're close to someone, maybe you absorb part of their spirit when they die, he said. Their habits, good and bad. And maybe things like this brick do the same. Hold some trace.

At dawn, Annie went home to Watervliet and tossed in her slender iron bed, drawn to Sam's notion in spite of herself. But she did not believe the brick was her undisclosed award. It became an irritant, another deterrent to sound sleep.

Freddy had resumed her housekeeping duties, but mournful sounds crept from her flat, which shared a wall with Sam's. Once Annie would have rushed to comfort the sufferer. Now she wanted to pound her shoe on the wall. Freddy's torment reminded her of Eugene, and the guilt was unbearable.

She put her hands over her ears and sank into Sam's chair. Memories spun through her head. She remembered Sam saying he wanted the Ship of Joy to be a place where regular people could have a night on the Hudson. He said he'd tried to keep her free of extra tophamper so she'd sit high in the water, but he'd gotten in Dutch with the river and gone under. Since Eugene's death, Sam said he felt too stoop-shouldered and old to remodel the Rainbow Gardens. He felt like giving up the ghost.

"To Sam Livingston," Annie said, and raised her glass. "A hard life and a happy ending."

She poured herself another shot and stared out over Second Avenue toward the Hudson. It was a humid July night, and she'd opened the windows. A breeze drifted in, a zephyr warm as sugared breath. "*Spiritus frumenti* is indicated in any form of sepsis," she said, pouring herself another. "To Father Jolley, down the hatch." She must have dozed off then, for the next thing she felt was a voice in her nerves—felt rather than heard it, as if the words sounded in her ganglia and cells.

Good nurse. Good nurse.

Annie started humming "Shine On Harvest Moon" to drown this whisper out. Then, as she looked toward the river, she saw a figure jerking itself along on top of the water. It was limping and spinning, genuflecting and elevating its clasped hands on high as it hoofed and tripped and flung itself north. "Walking on water," Nurse Garrahan said disapprovingly. She grabbed Sam's binoculars and experienced a blast of recognition: she knew this curio inside out. She saw the bristled texture of his hobnail liver, saw his steerhorn stomach's telltale curve. She saw right through him to the shredded starlight on the water. He was not worried about breaking every scientific law. Annie jumped up and rapped her knuckles hard against the upper pane. "Hear, hear!" she barked. "Hear, hear!"

The Dancing Priest.

She leaned out and watched him to the vanishing point. *No man hath seen such scarecrows.* The sentence echoed through her marrow's marrow. Some psychological fibrosis must be setting in. Jolley had looked unmade, as if his stuffing were coming out. And he seemed to be raising a beard. If he were her patient, she would not allow it. Except for bards and hermits, bearded men were covering weak chins.

Had she been asleep when she saw him? Was Jolley living and she'd only dreamed him dead? Or was he dead and she'd dreamed him back alive? She was so tired! So tired she lay down on Sam's blue carpet as if it were a bed. Tiny anchors of gravity fastened her there.

"You had too much to drink, sweetheart," Sam said when he got home. Then he sighed and lay right down beside her.

It was as if Annie had stepped on a beached plank that suddenly sailed off with the tide. The unusual had gotten the upper hand somehow. Each night she waited by the window, hoping the crippled vision would not appear, and each night her faded chorus boy came faltering along, stomping on the river like a stage.

On the sixth night, she resolved to avoid the view. If Jolley could operate on a go-as-you-please basis, so could she. She once had enough pep to grow the materia medica herself, to raise a hillside of mandrake, if need be. Now she worried about losing touch with her profession. *Icebag, steamed flannel,* she murmured, *digitalis, morphine.* And then she drifted off.

It must have been around midnight when she felt a sentence taking shape. *They flee from me that sometime did me seke.* She crept to the window, and sensed him there beneath her, on dry land, lying in wait. "Hair of the dog," Annie said, and her hand flew to the brick she'd gotten in the mail. But as she drew her arm back for the pitch, she was distracted by an utterance:

I will not let you go unless I bless you.

She saw him then: a black and folding form, pliable as light. Or the absence of light.

Her skin formed tiny peaks and hairs stood up from every bump.

The loiterer pressed his hands together. *God save your child from the foolish sins of nurses. Keep her from the passively unspiritual, the hirelings at heart, the wagetakers and doers of the least, the backbiters, tarnishers of hope, mockers and hate-fomenters, the posturing, harebrained, narrow and obstinate, the deciduous of will. Protect her from all manner of misemployed and undevoted virgins, throughout the wide jurisdiction this whole delinquency presents.*

He swept the air from from east to west and again from earth to heaven.

He liked to do it, so she let him.

Then he sizzled into the distance like ghost butter.

As dawn approached, the sounds from Freddy's flat grew more desperate. Nurse Garrahan imagined the housekeeper striking her head against the wall, rolling on the floor, tearing her clothes, maybe biting her own flesh. She was about to go looking for Sam when suddenly the noises stopped.

Scald milk, boil water, Annie muttered. *Nourishment.* She started measuring ingredients, breaking eggs. Humming tunelessly, she placed her watch on the windowsill to serve as timer. A crow was scavenging the pavement. *Bad luck,* she whispered, *omen.* Impulsively, she grabbed the pan of boiling water. She'd show that bird the meaning of baptism! She'd douse it like a fire and be rid of the unknown, which was so much greater than the known. Leaning out, she calculated.

But as she was about to act, Annie heard Sam's voice. "Don't punish us like this," he said, and something in his tone alarmed her. Setting down the pot, she ran to the hall. A trail of wispy pinfeathers led from Freddy's flat, up the stairs, to the roof.

There she found Sam trying to reason with the housekeeper, who stood outside the black railing that marked the roof's edge. Victorine Crawley hovered nearby, in curlers and peignoir, threatening to call the fire department. Freddy clutched her feather duster, and in the ashen light of dawn, she reminded Annie of a rare bird on its perch. As she thought this, she saw the crow circling, a slink of gold in its beak. It flew closer, showing off its prize, and she recognized the trinket as her watch.

"Hear, hear!" she clapped. "Come back, you little stinker!" Sam, Victorine, and Freddy turned as one, astonished. Annie ran over and grabbed the housekeeper's feather duster. She waved it threateningly and squawked, hoping to scare the crow into dropping her watch. Instead it flapped fiercely toward her, hissing as it came, a big black spitball of a bird, bent, she felt sure, on pecking her eyes out. She yelped and scrambled backwards.

At that moment, Freddy moved. They all gasped, time held its breath. A rusty croak ending in a wheeze issued from the housekeeper. Then her chest spasmed with an emotion Annie gradually diagnosed as mirth. "Well, you can't die laughing," she noted. And Freddy let Sam help her back onto solid ground.

Victorine scuttled over. "Have you forgotten the Nightingale Pledge? 'I will abstain from whatever is deleterious and mischievous.'"

"Go fry ice," Annie replied. Someday she'd be eloquent, like Jolley. But now a creamy smell came wafting by. "I'm making rice pudding," she announced. "And it'll taste even better if I share it." Sam brightened. "Mrs. Fredrickson might appreciate a shoeshine," she added.

A scrim of light passed over Freddy's features. "You two are going to be hubby and wife," she predicted. "Your daughter will be a nurse—"

Annie beamed.

"Or a saint—"

Annie looked solemn.

"Or a poet."

Annie rolled her eyes. "I can hardly wait."

When she got back to Sam's flat, the eastern sky was the color of brickdust, and Freihofer's delivery wagon stood by the service entrance on 116th Street. The cart horse lifted a mighty foreleg and pawed impatiently. She saw his massive iron shoe, the green straw and manure packed in his hoof. "Hi Sandman," she said. The horse snorted, and cornucopias of steam rolled forth.

Once she'd asked Bernard Jolley whether his crow came when called. He comes whether he's called or not, Jolley said. As she remembered this, a crow swooped by. No bluebird of happiness, its eye was sharp as flinders, its coat the color of scorch, glossy as an oily puddle. If she had Jolley's eloquence, she'd say death was not what it seemed. "It wants to help you, but first it has to hurt you," she murmured. Black rainbows flickered in its feathers. A worm jigged in its beak.

DOROTHY LOVES MALEMAN

Edna Garrahan Kelly, Dorothy Garrahan

AFTER DOROTHY LOCKED her out on the roof, Edna regretted telling her the facts of life. Her sister was the kind of girl who got dressed and undressed inside her nightgown even when she was alone. The truth was too much for her. Edna blamed herself and worried. While tar stuck to her bare feet and wind toyed with her towel, while Dorothy lit match after match, and neighbors peeked through blackout curtains left over from the war, Edna worried her sister would burn herself. Even the shame of rescue—their former air warden helping her down the ladder, the intimate grip of his grease-monkey hands—could not stop Edna's fretting over what came next. Her mind was ablaze with dangerous maybes.

Sickness used to be the only thing that bothered her. Sickness and hospitals. The stuffy Automat and ether smell of those places made her queasy. Which was why, after the trauma on the roof, a week passed before Edna got the strength to visit her sister in Albany General. She waited in the Occupational Therapy room, next to a small display case labeled Patient Productions. It contained two figurines: a blurry little beast with sagging ears and a perky one with a tiny flag. A handwritten card said "The small white animal is made of absorbent cotton, soap, and talcum powder. It is mounted on a used blotter. The small dark animal holding the stars and stripes is made of toilet paper and ink— molded while wet."

When the attendant brought Dorothy, Edna was shocked at her sister's expression. Dorothy's face was sealed. Like she's behind the iron curtain, Edna thought. Every so often her eye-brows yanked together in a crease, as if revolutions were being crushed inside her skull.

"They punish you terrible here," her sister said. "It's murder." She tore at the box of chocolate peppermints Edna had brought. "I know I done wrong. But I paid my debt. I'm ready to go home now."

"When you're better," Edna said cautiously. "When you're better, you can go home."

"I can go home," Dorothy agreed. "I'm letting a smile be my umbrella now." Her brow seized up again.

Edna had to take three buses to get to the hospital. So when a friend who worked in Albany offered to drop her off early one morning, she accepted. She was about to press the buzzer of the locked ward when an attendant, her cart piled high with laun-dry, came edging out. Before the door slammed behind her, Edna walked in unnoticed. Dorothy said being an attendant ran in some people's families. She claimed some of them used to be farmhands and slaughterers before they got hired here. The doc-tor called these ideas confabulations.

When Edna got to her sister's room, she found a nurse hold-ing a hypodermic needle. It must be treatment time. Edna had the ability to shrink into herself and become so still she was almost invisible, ignorable as a wall. Now she disappeared into a massive wooden chair outside the door, out of the way, yet close enough to hear the whoosh and snap of shades. Insulin sleep treatment. It sounded peaceful. She didn't smoke, drink, or take aspirin. Even the "friendly stimulation" of Tetley tea made her uneasy. But insulin sounded natural. As the eldest sibling, she had given written permission. Her sister would receive two hours of coma six days a week for two months. "Receive," her doctor had said, like a coma was communion, the eucharist. It made Edna hope for miracles. For what they called transsomething in religion class.

The doctor called it stupor. You mean she'll have a good rest? Edna asked. And he said, It is a return to the oblivion which all of us have sought to recapture more or less successfully throughout our entire lives. Now she tried to imagine this special slumber. It would be deep. Profound, even. So profound the cracks would snooze in the plaster. The hissing radiators would hush. The light glistening on the needles and iron beds would doze off in the dark. Even the clock would dream between its ticks.

Edna gave in to a great yawn, her mouth stretched to a wide and silent note.

The nurse stepped out into the hall. "You're an early bird today," she said with a scolding smile. "No visiting till after lunch."

Her sister's doctor came striding toward them, a pin-striped, three-piece man. Smallfield. He had stared at a space over her shoulder when he explained the sleep treatments. It must be tough being a blind doctor, she'd thought, and it wasn't till he wrote a prescription that Edna realized he could see. He was the chief here, and you had to expect some standoffishness from prominent medical men. It consoled her to know they'd gotten the best. Smallfield had a young nurse with him. She wore no cap, which meant she was still a probationer.

"I'm here to observe your eight o'clock," the girl said to the RN.

"My insulin shock," said the RN.

"The schizophrenic with paranoid and catatonic tendencies," said Smallfield.

"My sister," Edna murmured from the sidelines. "She's not herself."

These people had only seen the broken-down, nervous Dorothy. She wanted to tell them what her sister had been like before. She'd been cheerful and thrifty. A girl from work would teach her a new dish, shrimp cocktail or cabbage rolls, and she'd become an advocate for it. She'd brush her sweaters to make them look angora. She's domesticated, Edna wanted to say. I knew her when.

When she could have stepped out of an MGM musical, she was so beautiful and flirtatious. When she could shake a leg and cut a rug. When she could have picked and chosen instead of worshiping a drunk like Frank Furioso. He'd broken their engagement after the war, and right before Thanksgiving he'd married another girl, which crushed her sister's heart. Then, to make a sad story tragic, Frank Furioso became their mailman. Dorothy thought he was visiting her whenever he delivered, and when he got fired, she thought he'd given her the boot all over again. It made her mad as all get-out.

Oh, Edna could have filled these people in! But they were so busy and official, she didn't dare to interrupt.

Smallfield commanded the young nurse to ask him questions. How does insulin shock treatment work, Doctor? she said in a shrinking violet voice.

"At present we are uncertain." He consulted his pocketwatch. "However, cerebral anoxemia with resultant cell destruction has been postulated as an explanation of the effects of physical treatment in mental disorders."

So the cells that made her sister sick would be destroyed.

"Her Wechsler-Bellevue test gave evidence of a feeble mind," he continued, studying his clipboard. "For example, she thought Paris was a thousand miles from New York and that the heart pumped air into the lungs. She did not know the height of the average American woman."

"Is this psychology?" Edna spoke up. "I never took that."

Smallfield looked at her for the first time.

"That's a relative," the RN said.

"Her sister," Edna said. "She's not herself."

"I suggest you wait in the solarium, little lady." And Smallfield turned away abruptly to continue his rounds.

The two nurses went into Dorothy's room. We begin by checking the tray, the older one said. Needles ampules tablets insulin adrenaline chloride cormine caffeine glucose. She rattled off this list, and the young one repeated after. Edna had supposed a sleep tray might contain lullabies, a cup of cocoa, bedtime stories. Maybe earplugs or a black dream mask. Instead she heard some kind of basin, alcohol, sponges, some kind of meter. The nurses had it down to a science. They had a routine. It went: Tourniquet, *tourniquet*! Blue litmus aspirating syringe, *blue litmus aspirating syringe*! Bowl of ice with nasal tube, *bowl of ice with nasal tube*! Karo syrup KY jelly, *Karo syrup KY jelly*! Tongue blades tongue forceps, *tongue blades tongue forceps*! Mouth gag, *mouth gag*!

"I'm passing away," Dorothy called out. "You're passing me away."

She sounded drunker than drunk. Slowed-down, retarded.

"Nonsense!" said the RN. "Write 'ten o'clock, excited,' " she told the student, and they continued with their medical badminton. How do we recognize coma? *Pinpoint pupils, which do not react to light! The absence of corneal reflex!* Why do we place a wick in the patient's mouth? *Salvation may cause drowning!* How do we determine that the nasal feeding tube is in the stomach rather than the trachea? *Aspirate a small amount of stomach contents and test!* Respiratory difficulty, convulsions, cyanosis? *Report it, report it, report it!*

Jeepers, Dorothy shouted, *Creepers!*

Edna felt dizzy. She hadn't eaten breakfast. Drugged dimness poured from the room like knocked-out light. Or locked-out light. She couldn't think straight. The whole ward was groaning. There were whinnies and barks. She wanted to run out and board the first bus that came along. *So darn dark,* her sister mumbled. *So cold.* Take care of Dorothy, Mother had said before she died, because I think Dorothy is going to be sick. Edna got up and peered into the room.

"Do you have any blankets?" she asked.

No, the Hotsy Totsy wasn't born in Germany! her sister crowed. *He wanted me, not her!*

The nurses looked up from their paperwork. "I beg your pardon?" the older one said.

Me not her! Dorothy hollered. *Let her be light!*

"She'll be up and about after lunch," the RN said. "Till then, would you kindly wait in the cafeteria?"

The moon passed away! Red horse with wings!

"Would you like something to read?" The student gestured to some books on the bureau.

Edna accepted her offer, just to be polite. When she got back outside, she saw she'd chosen *Emotional Hygiene, the Art of Understanding.* Opening it, she read, "In Cuba, the natives in the interior still go about on moonlight nights protected by umbrellas, for it is difficult to say what strange malady the moon has the power of imparting." There was a drawing of a pinstriped, three-piece man on a donkey. He was holding an umbrella under a crescent moon. Once upon a time, last night or yesterday, this picture might have amused her. But now even funny things seemed frightening. *You passed me away!* her sister cried.

Over the next hour, she heard Dorothy say she was hungry. She said she was cold. She said she was dying. Two attendants stood chatting by the nurses' station. Edna went over and asked them when the doctor would be back.

"What doctor?"

"Smallfield. My sister says she's dying."

"Oh, that's mental talk," the attendant said. She had black hair and eyes blue as gas flames.

"Smallfield," Edna repeated. "The one who acts like he's blind."

"Oh, Smallfield. That guy was our sister's doc. 'Take her home and treat her like a houseplant,' he said. And that's exactly what we did. Didn't we?"

The other attendant nodded. Her eyes were the same gas blue. "She'd sit and watch the snails whiz by."

Just then, the RN hurried out of Dorothy's room and took off in the direction of the nurses' lounge. Edna gathered her nerve and walked in on the student who'd been left in charge. Why the syrup, why the rubber sheets, why was she so riled up before? she asked. *Give sugar by mouth to revive, profuse perspiration, you're not supposed to be in here*, the girl said, in her daisies-won't-tell voice. Edna didn't want any trouble. Her sister was quiet now, and it seemed like a good time to grab a bite to eat.

When she returned from the cafeteria twenty minutes later, the RN was poking at her sister's eye with a Q-tip swab. Poor Fella, that old doll. Edna shook her head, remembering. Little Dorothy had gouged his eyes out in a jealous fit after their sister Annie was born. And ten-year-old Edna had laughed. There was something funny about a creature so tiny and so mad. Afterwards, Dorothy had crooned *Poor Fella Poor Fella* while big crocodile tears crawled down her face.

The tap of cuban heels on linoleum jarred Edna out of her nostalgia. Both the nurses were leaving. They waltzed by without a word. A moment later a new and alarming sound came from her sister's room. Like gasping at straws, Edna thought. Her nerves flared, and she jumped to her feet. She glanced wildly from side to side, but there was no one around to look after her sister. She would have to look.

When she did, she thought of horses, their foaming mouths and rolled-back eyes, their bucking and kicking. Phrases came to mind and branded themselves in. *Six days a week for two months, you passed me away.* Help, she called, help! Two hefty attendants moseyed in. That stockyard scent of meat and manure rising from their skin—was she dreaming it? One roly-poly held her sister down while the other fastened her wrists and ankles to the bed. The nurses rushed in next. The RN gave Dorothy an injection, then the two left in search of Dr. Smallfield. A few long minutes later, Dorothy started to wake up.

"How are you feeling?" Edna said. Her sister was blurred in the face.

"I don't ask how I feel," Dorothy mumbled. "That's the doctor's secret business."

As soon as she could sit up, the attendant brought her a sandwich. When Dorothy finished, her voice picked up strength. "I done everything you want. When will I get paroled?"

Edna was keeping an eye on the hall in case Smallfield appeared. He strolled by just then with the two nurses in tow. She rushed out. "About that permission," she said. The three kept walking. "I had no idea. I was shocked."

Smallfield deposited his cigarette in a sand-filled cuspidor by the nurses' station. "My dear, the shocks of peace are trivial," he said.

"Peace?"

Didn't anyone notice anything here? Sleepers, awaken! she wanted to shout. Rise and shine! Make the shades roll up, the sun behave!

"Tomorrow your relative could wake up a new man," the doctor said.

"From what I seen, she could wake up dead."

"I assure you, your loved one is quite alive. We've treated 400 patients with only four fatalities due to prolonged or irreversible stupor."

"And only five due to severe pulmonary complications," the student nurse added.

"Physician heal thyself!" Edna said. "What about your hypocritic oath? 'First do no harm!'"

"Is she always this hysterical?" the doctor asked the RN.

Hysterical. Like this was funny.

It was then she noticed her sister loitering way down at the other end of the ward, near the locked door. Dorothy was wearing Edna's hat and coat, and she had Edna's pocketbook over her arm. A visitor was coming in. Dorothy nodded at him like she owned the place, and he graciously held the door open for her as she sailed out.

Once I got out, I vowed to be normal. Calm as a star, steadfast and bristling. Watervliet girls do not know how to throw things, but I'd learn. First, I'd stop believing my sister Edna's wicked stories. Next, I'd kill the Hotsy Totsy. I'd train my hair to wave, get my lashes to curl up, separate, and say howdy like nature intended. My sister Edna had but one advantage. She was a good liar while I was bad at telling the truth. Yet I had an advantage, too. I could stand the cold longer than any of them. I swore someday I'd get my picture in the paper as the normalest of them all. Someday my prince would come. Then my Gleem teeth would be admired, and I'd be myself again, Dorothy Outgoing, Dorothy Bombshell. Dorothy Furioso, the blunt instrument of their suffering!

Oh, I was windbroken. I was an old maid. That's why they put me to sleep. The needle pricked me and I slept a hundred years. While hedges grew high around the windows, and the doctors tried to stir the sunnyside into me. When they woke me up, they wanted to know if the war was over. This was 1947. Of course, it was. Where had they been?

But their next question, how-are-you-Dorothy, was tricky. The right answer was I'm fine Doctor how are you? How are you was the important part. The doctors like you to take an interest in them. As soon as you do that, they will say that you are well.

There must have been some lamb-to-slaughter look about me. Mother always said I'd better find good friends as I was easily led. In high school, I'd been popular as meatloaf. Afterwards, I got a job at the plant, opened a little bank account and began saving for a Magic Chef range and Eureka vacuum cleaner, a husband and kids. I made a weekly novena to pray for these things. I was dying to settle down and be just like my sisters. We all was after the same life, beginning with a nice fellow and ending with a baby or at least a baby leopard coat. We had luxurious dreams, yet we was raised respectable. Everything came second to that.

The nuns had drummed decency into us to the point where we'd rather knock down an old lady and nab her hose than be caught downtown with bare legs. You think you have to be wealthy to be snooty? Think again. Poor people need someone to look down on too. My sisters would rather hold their noses and jump off the Green Island Bridge than endanger their good names in Watervliet. We was closeknit. The kind who keep their scandals under slipcovers, their troubles bottled up. We grew stiff upper lips or became cockeyed optimists to take our minds off the deep worries furrowing our souls. Loose lips sink ships! While tried and true expressions keep things normal, on an even keel.

But normal comes more natural to some than others. For me it was a struggle. I had bouts of wanderlust. Call it footlooseness. The fact is, I went AWOL.

It started last Thanksgiving, when the gang was gathered here in our childhood home. Mother left this house to me and Papa when she died. Dinky rooms with an oily filling station across the way and a live bait business in full swing next door. I'd saved green stamps to buy a sunburst clock, and at the foot of my bed, I kept the cedar chest that Frank Furioso, my maleman, gave me before the war. There was a thermometer with two little girls whose umbrellas turned pink when the sun shone, blue when it rained. That Thanksgiving, I remember, they was blue. The house was stuffed with my sisters and their husbands. With their furs and Jell-O jewels. The air was rich with the roasting bird, lambasted with happiness for one and all, the haves and have-nots.

They told me later I went out to get some clothes from the line that day and never looked back. Forty-eight hours passed before the police found me in Prospect Park. My toes was black from the cold, and I lost part of the little one. My nails fell out as I thawed.

Then the minute I got better, my sister Edna wanted to move in. Maybe the others put her up to it. Knowing her watchful ways, they might have thought she'd keep me under lock and key. Or maybe she'd already decided to latch on to what was mine. Edna was the only one of us who didn't have her own home. She probably thought the coast looked clear, with Papa convalescing at my sister Annie's.

Those eyes in the back of her head made me nervous. Yet I was so desperate to be like her, I put out the welcome mat. Some copycat part of me wanted to follow her hook, line, and sinker, down the beaten path of normalness. Besides, how could I turn away a refugee who was a close relation? Who was calm as milk and made mountains into molehills, the way I never could.

I kept wishing my heart was like one of those little Daisy canned hams. Stuck with cloves and sliced invitingly on the label but peaceful and whole inside. Fully cooked, skinless, boneless! My sister Edna had a heart like that. Practical as dirt. If anybody knew how to get Frank Furioso back, it would be her. She had her ear to the ground. My other sisters might get his name, rank, and serial number, but Edna could find out where he had his car winterproofed, what kind of girl he married right before Thanksgiving, and whether he called that girl his Angel Face or Velvet-Footed Vixen.

In her youth, Edna had used a swagger stick to turn the fellows' heads and drive away her rivals. She'd put rats in her hair to dazzle and tweezed her brows till they was needlethin. Many's the time I'd seen her toast her eyelash curler in the coal stove and spit on it for luck before using it on her lashes. To raise them up. The better to watch you with! Make no mistake, her curly eyes drove men like Frank Furioso mad.

As far as I could see, my sister Edna's life had only one liability. You know how cats will crawl into the lap of whoever hates and fears them most. *Drunks and nutcases was drawn to Edna that same way. It was her cross to bear. Dipsomaniacs were her least favorite people, yet she could not take a bus without one of them settling down to bend her ear. I told her she lured them by watching them. Her frilly lashes made her look fetching instead of menacing. Oh, I don't let those goofballs get to me, she said. As a girl, she'd crossed her heart and vowed to never let anything bother her, and even after her husband died in the war, she kept her pledge.*

I envied Edna her happy-go-lucky mind. Just like I envied the pluckers and curlers in her bag of beauty tricks. Those little pinchers had raised her up in glory. But one fine day they clawed her down in shame and torment, too.

We was in Frears, the grandest department store in Troy, when it happened. The two of us was riding the gate-front elevator when I noticed Edna standing at attention, peering through the airy metal slats. She'd spotted something on the main floor, far below. I sensed her tracking it. When I saw what it was, I took the name of the Lord. Maleman! It was Frank Furioso. Then the elevator landed, and he got in with us. And before we could say boo, he wrapped his muscleman arms around Edna from behind. He held her in this crushing bearhug without a buy or leave while I looked on.

Even in mufti, Frank Furioso was a dashing hulk of manhood. Six feet tall and rugged as the old cross. While my sister was short and blunt as a stump. Let go, she said, you're bothering me. Still he stuck to her like a cocklebur as the elevator lurched up. Edna kept twisting this way and that, struggling to pretend she was not enjoying herself. Let go, she said, you're crimping my style. Her skirt hiked up, and I pictured the bones in her girdle poking his stomach, her metal garters branding his thighs. When he leaned down to blow sweet nothings up her nose, I smelled the juniper berries, malted grains, rum, hops, and sugar ferment of his breath. It was intoxicating. I had nowhere to run, so I closed my eyes. Still I heard the slurping sloshy smack of his suction cups all over her. Then a new and smoochier sound disgusted the air. A muzzling and slathering and huffing and puffing. I peeked. And what I saw made the veins in my mind blush. It was dark pink. Jupiter! It was his stuckout tongue lapping at her nape, his tastebuds rub-a-dub against her skin.

I had an emotion then. Fury sadness. I felt jilted. Out in the cold.

Yet I turned the other cheek. Pride kicked in. I paid no attention to Edna's two-faced squawking. Next time the elevator opened, I strode right past her raised voice. From the ground floor, I watched them go up in the iron cage car. I watched Frank Furioso lift my sister and her pocketbook swing open, and I roared laughing. But when her hand started digging in her purse, I felt something drastic coming. "Lookit." I pointed. "That woman is bothering that man." I said it loud. Heads turned. Quiet condensed. Felix Frear, the owner, strolled over with his face tilted back like a person taking nosedrops.

Then the elevator landed, and my sister and beloved staggered forth as one. Edna looked out of order; the feather in her cap was crushed. Get him off me, she kept saying. Help. Felix Frear told them to leave his store immediately or he'd call the police. This got me picturing my sister's mug shot in the paper, and jealousy, the green monster, seized my heart. It distracted me from the silvery something glinting in her fingers, and before I could say Frank Furioso! she'd clamped the soft marble under his forearm with her eyelash curler. I saw she was using this pliers to hold him while pretending to ward him off.

"Shame!" I cried. "That woman's got her tweezers in that man!" All of a sudden, his face came to its senses, and Edna's attempt to bind him backfired. He gave her the heave-ho and rambled past me, taking his sweet time.

I'd been numb since my frostbite in the park. Now hot tears ached unwept against my eyeballs. I have met the enemy and she is us, I thought. My own flesh and blood. Not his war bride from Albany. I was living with the competition, sharing her bread and water.

A lady marched by.

She looked good and mad. Her bouncy pompadour pounded her brow at each step. Yet I didn't recognize her as myself, the Hotsy Totsy part of me, till Edna pulled up panting at my side and grabbed my arm.

"Where the heck was you? You had me worried," she said. "I only hope and pray he don't turn up again."

Hope! He'd given me the hope chest, not her. She had no claim. And hers was a wicked prayer. She was asking God to make me lonely all my life. Edna often said she didn't want no man around to confuse her cooking. And I believed this. My sister didn't want Frank Furioso. But she didn't want me to have him neither.

I was trusting, that was the trouble. I'd trusted Edna, and she took advantage. She moved in and stole my boyfriend, and next she'd steal the roof over my head. I'd been on sick leave since Thanksgiving, going stir-crazy in the house with her. As the next few weeks dragged by, I got so worried about having her underfoot I sometimes forgot my maleman. Frank Furioso faded to sweetness and light. Then I'd remember: I had to make him crave me again. Make him annul his marriage, move in here, and throw my sister out. For this to happen, I'd have to be normal as salt. I had to learn Edna's bewitching ways. Imitate what made her tick. So I could beat her up at her own game.

And I had to kill the Hotsy Totsy. I'd need a rock of ages calm to tiptoe down the aisle as Frank Furioso's bride.

"You could do better," Edna said. "If you married him, you'd have to cook Eyetalian food the rest of your life. You're young yet. You could go places. Be like me. Independent."

"Okey-dokey," I told her, nice as ice. "I'll be like you."

Once upon a time, my smile was the life of the party. I'd gone dancing with Frank Furioso, and he squeezed when he wanted to dip. We tried a pizza pie and drank one cider through two straws. He gave me a ring and a prayer. I wished I could have him eating out of my hand and sipping champagne from my shoes like in the old days. Yet I was realistic. I would settle for less. People said a little Frank Furioso went a long way. I'd take that little and make the most of it. I'd take him in name only. I'd take him as a snapshot in the corner of my vanity where I could dote upon him always. I'd take him dead or alive.

After the elevator upset, I started locking the door when Edna went out on errands. So when she got home, she had to knock. To be honest, I always thought twice about letting her in. And I always acted surprised to see her.

"Sis!" I said. "You been doing some shoplifting." Then I laughed like it was a joke.

I made a habit of shaking her hand hello to show who was in charge. But this one time she had so many bundles I couldn't find a free finger. She walked past me, and I trailed behind like something on a leash, curious. My sister was not petite so much as condensed. All I could see through the hedge of boxes was her teeth, which stuck out something fierce. I was hoping the dentist could make me some false buck teeth like hers. I could hear the snowy crackle of tissue paper and the bony bang of hangers coming from her bedroom. The unworn, costly smell of a new garment hung in the air.

"It'll be hot as Hades, but it won't show the dirt," she said.

She was holding up a stunning sheer yoked dress. Other purchases lay scattered about: sharp new pumps, a tricornered Empress Eugénie hat, crochet gloves, and nylon hose. All this booty was in one matching color: black.

"Looks like a funeral outfit."

"Mourning," she said. "For the service." I remembered then. Her dead hero husband would be honored.

"Can I try it on?"

People treated me different since my breakdown. They acted careful, like I was a problem child. I hated this kid glove treatment. I preferred the kind of pampering accorded war widows. Maybe one of those black widow costumes could win me that respect and martyr standing.

"No sir." She shut the dress in the wardrobe so hard it rocked. "Remember we promised not to borrow each other's stuff."

But she had borrowed something of mine. In fact, she had stole him, which made our promise null and void.

"That Frenchy perfume of yours," I said. "I tried it out."

At this, her face got still as a storm's eye. She picked the little glass bottle off the dresser and held it up to the light, measuring and mumbling. *Tusk-tusk*, she said, *tisk-tisk*. Then she put the perfume inside her top drawer, way to the back.

This drawer was full of Edna's nest eggs. It was where she kept her junk jewelry and ironed corsages. It was full of her powerful mudpacks and pure cold creams. Her yeast tablets and bubble baths. Tiny tubes of unguentine and jars of fancy elbow grease. I knew because I liked to experiment with these belongings while she was out. There was legal documents, too, like the written guarantee for her last permanent wave, and her expired marriage license. That was wrapped around a cunning valentine locket.

Of all her treasures, this tiny locket lured me most. I could hardly keep my hands off it. I loved the way the heart door opened on pictures of Edna and her husband. And I loved the way their faces pressed together, cheek to cheek in secret, when it closed.

"When it comes to perfume," she was saying, "the only kind some men appreciate is ninety-proof." She shot me a look.

"Ninety-proof!" I echoed. I was thinking locket, locket, so loud I was scared she'd hear my mind. I lit a cigarette to calm my nerves, and opened the window to let out the smoke. Two insects, hinged together at the rear, was walking across the top half of the glass. It was a buggy thing to do, nothing more. But I needed a conversation piece, so I called her attention to them.

"Must be mating," she said. "Birds do it, bees do it."

"Good thing people don't," I said.

"What are you talking about?" She put her wedding ring in a little dish on the dresser like she always did before a bath. That was the only time she took it off.

"You know. With people, constant nearness causes kids. It's like catching the grip. Germ warfare." I was surprised a married woman hadn't heard. I ignored her sparkly laughter and kept on. "If men and women are exposed to each other enough, it causes kids. Everybody knows this. One rubs off on the other."

I could hear her cackling over the bath she was running. Her mockery always made my words sound dumb. When she reappeared, I said "Okay, smarty-pants. You tell me."

"You got a point." She grabbed a few items from her dresser. "Like the doctor says, even a stopped clock's right twice a day." Then she broke out in laughs again.

I sat on the bed, taking fast drags from my cigarette. My legs was crossed, and the top one was swinging like a struck reflex. I wouldn't look at her, but I could feel her looking at me.

"All right," she said, "I'll tell you." And her voice was starched serious. "You're almost forty. It's time you knew the facts of life." I was eleven when we had our last heart-to-heart. That was when she told me I was going to grow hair under my arms and bleed. I'd waited years for that underarm bleeding to begin. Now I braced myself for more dirty lies.

"The man goes in the woman," she said. She said it fast, on her way back to the bathroom, like she wanted to get it over with. "It's called intercourse."

"Phooey!" She wouldn't outfox me this time. "If that was true, people would have died out by now." I reached up and flicked those bugs away. "Besides," I said, "this is a democracy. You can believe whatever facts of life you want. It's called freedom of the press."

I could hear her chuckling from the bathroom. I walked in and glared at her in her bubbles. "Anyhow, you'd never catch me doing that!"

"Long as I don't catch you doing it with Frank Furioso." She draped a washcloth over her chest, which was mostly covered anyway. "Listen to your big sister. That one took alcohol with his mother's milk. He was here last night at three a.m., prowling around, tooting his own horn. He must be off his wagon again. Those pills let you sleep right through it, but I was worried he'd bother the neighbors. I had to get after him."

Well, I was mad. I was mad that he'd come back and she had not woke me. And I realized her sorry lie was meant to drive me away from him. That was why she said people did that dirty, bedbug thing together. I felt the Hotsy Totsy rearing up. She could ooze through any crack, that girl!

The locket, Dorothy, the Hotsy Totsy said. Get the locket from the drawer.

I went over to the open drawer and took it out. My hand shook, but I was at her command. She had me tear off the marriage license it was wrapped in.

Put the locket in your mouth, she said. The man goes inside the woman! Then stick out your tongue and show her the heartbug on it.

The Hotsy Totsy always got her way. That was what scared me. I went into the bathroom and stuck my tongue out at Edna. As soon as she saw the locket sitting there, she jumped from the tub, grabbed a towel, and went for me. I backed away, but the bathroom door was half closed, cutting off my escape. Her feet made a webbed, rubbery splat on the linoleum. I could feel the steam heat rising from her pores, hear the air passing through her tubes with a tiny bagpipe wheeze, as she got near. I tried for the door, but her pixie fingers grabbed my wrist and twisted it behind my back. Her other arm got me in a stranglehold. I was fighting to breathe, growling and chok-ing, when one of my gasps caught the locket and sucked it down my throat. It went down easy.

"Give," she said. "Spit."

"Gone," I said. "It'll all. Come." I couldn't hardly talk. "Out in." I tried to bite her, and she grabbed hold of my ear. "The wash." I stomped on her bare foot with my shod one. She eased up then, so I ran into the bedroom and swiped her wedding ring from the dish.

"I'm going to tell the doctor on you." She came limping in. "This time they'll take out part of your brain."

"Stay," I said, holding up the ring. "You're the bait. See if you can't get my maleman here now. Fetch!" And I threw her diamond out the window onto the roof.

Boing. The roof was flat, the day warmy. That ring wasn't going nowhere, unless maybe the wind . . . Snap went Edna's joints as she climbed out. Crash bang went the window when the Hotsy Totsy slammed and locked it. She was a rip, that girl! Next the Hotsy Totsy *raced down the stairs and came back with a dusty bottle of crème de mint. Ninety-proof! She had me grab the black dress from the wardrobe, take it to the window, and drench it with that emerald sticky stuff. I felt sorry. Yet I was at her beck and call. I listened to the drip-drip of Edna on the shingles, listened to her saying what she'd do if I did not let her in. I noticed everything she mentioned could not be accomplished from the roof. Then it hit me. She was not pulling her weight. She was not dancing to my tune or sending out her siren song as ordered. I struck a match.*

"Do the Big Apple," I yelled. "Follow the bouncing ball, or I'll burn down the house."

On the day her sister escaped from Albany General, Edna had to hitchhike home to Watervliet. Dorothy had taken her pocket-book, leaving her without bus fare, and she was too proud to panhandle. At least it was a fine day, and she was sensibly dressed. She had her worries to keep her warm.

When she finally reached their yard, the evening paper was unraveling on the front path. A familiar face caught her eye. "Happy Housewife Likes Freihofer's!" the headline cheered. The article said her sister Dorothy had purchased more Freihofer's baked goods than any other customer last month. A photo showed her posing by a breadwagon, her smile a flashy crescent between the shadow of her hat and the tower of boxes in her arms. Dorothy had won a two-dollar gift certificate. She had attained celebrity.

Edna glanced up, and a second shock spiked through her nerves. The doorknob at the front entrance was missing, and a perfect little circle of night had broken out in its place. The hardware around the hole looked pried at, charmed to curlicues. One metal corner twirled up like the tip of an elf's shoe. She tried the door. It would not budge. She started around the side of the house, then stopped abruptly, teetering in place. A mousy shriek popped from her throat. She'd almost stepped on a snake in the grass. Then she noticed a clump of twitchy wires at one end of the viper and a white dial at the other. It was only their telephone. Yet the bad novelty of it out here on the lawn fed her fears.

The knob on the side door was missing, too, and as Edna continued around the back, she met with another distraction. For a second, she thought some rare mammal from Australia had migrated to their yard. The creature's mauve-beige hide glowed gently in the dying light. It had one large exterior lung, and its antlers rustled as she approached. As she got closer, she gradually identified her sister's Eureka vacuum cleaner. Beribboned dance cards swung from its handles; their stubby pencils clacked woodenly in the breeze. The flag they'd given Edna at her husband's service, still fused in triangular folds, was placed like a wreath on the cleaner's base and the cross from Mother's coffin shoved in front of it. A chalice of green liquid—antifreeze? crème de mint?—had been set on one side of the appliance and a casserole on the other. A framed photograph was propped against its shaft. Frank Furioso's wolfish grin shone from the picture's swagged depths. *Dorothy Loves Maleman* was scrawled on its glass in loopy red lipstick.

Edna knew a shrine when she saw one. Darkness was falling. Her feet ached, and her spine felt heavy, as though she had a dowager's hump or a monkey on her back. What now, she thought, what next?

The MOBILGAS sign came on across the way, a white circle with a red Pegasus ascending. The beast flew daintily upwards, as though wings were normal for a horse as hooves. He threw more light into the yard than the full moon. Maybe that was where her sister's wits had fled—to the moon. Maybe they were buried in the dark dimples of its placid face, benignly smiling, full of *nice* forever. Edna stared at the moon accusingly. It made her mad.

Once she got inside, she'd call the ambulance and they'd take her sister back to the hospital. She'd send Dorothy on her merry way and look for a little place of her own. A little peace of her own. Because since her sister's breakdown, Edna hadn't been herself. You've been at her service, kid, she thought. Wise up!

"Dorothy?" Edna fed her voice, strained as baby food, through the knob hole. "I'll dance if you'll let me in. Put My Time Is Your Time on the victrola. Put Don't Fence Me In, You'd Be So Nice to Come Home To. Put on the one that goes—" And she broke down in song like tears.

Only a crazy bird chirped back.

"Listen, I got something for you." She waved the newspaper. "There'll be no hard feelings, honest."

"Liar."

Her sister had spoken. Edna shivered with relief. The temperature was dropping. There was an old Indian blanket in the toolshed. The place was full of mildew and spiders and so dark she had to stroke the air like a swimmer to find the walls. While she was searching, she remembered. This was where Dorothy hid an extra key. Edna ran her hand down wooden beams, picking up splinters, till she came upon it. Then she went to the back entrance. She used the pin of her brooch to rip the screen, and the key opened the heavy inner door.

Yoo-hoo! she called. Anybody home? Freihofer's boxes gleamed waxily on the kitchen table. Three steps led up to the front parlor, where Mother's old-fashioned furniture loomed large as oxen, and Dorothy's trinkets were overcome by mahogany and doilies. Her sister's room was on the right. Edna saw mussed linen erupting from the hope chest at the foot of the bed, Poor Fella smiling blindly from a chair, the statue of Our Lady crushing the serpent under her bare foot. At last her eyes found Dorothy on the bed, half hidden by sheets from her trousseau. Her initials and Frank Furioso's writhed and twined in monogrammed ecstasy across her breast. She was wearing Edna's black dress over her hospital gown. Its institutional fabric filled the sweetheart neckline. She stared at the ceiling, her arms straight by her sides, rigid as a petrified woman. But she was breathing. Edna relaxed a little. Breathing was a sign of life.

"Why did you lock me out?"

Dorothy ignored her. She's in her own little world, Edna thought, like always. Her sister would never get to know her. And that was fine and dandy. Living with Dorothy was like living alone.

"Tell you what." Edna sat on the bed. "I'll take you to the Sunset Inn for dinner. You can wear my dress."

Dorothy looked at her then. Her eyes were full of solitary confinement. "Who do you think you are?" she said.

Edna's stomach seized with anxiety. If she wasn't careful, she'd turn into her sister Charlotte, a worrier who'd slept propped up on her elbow for months when she'd minded Dorothy. People should be made of stronger stuff. They should be unbreakable as light, at least. When God made you, he threw away the pattern, she'd told Dorothy once. Why? her sister had said, wasn't it any good?

Dorothy's little room was dense with belongings. Scatterpins. A pair of china poodles on one golden chain. Objects her sister had strived toward, saved for. Dustcatchers! Yet Edna felt protective toward them. She wanted to safeguard the thoughtless things of the world. Her watchfulness began with the walls and ceiling and extended to the dumb dirt of the planet, whirling through the doorless dark. She'd heard how the Shakers, who'd lived in Watervliet ages ago, had spun and danced as part of their religion. They'd placed a gold band around a woman's head, a band that said "Touch not mine anointed." Edna liked that idea.

She struggled to stay awake. She had to rouse, to rally. She had to call the ambulance. Dance, she told herself. That'll liven you up. Put on Someone to Watch Over Me, Full Moon and Empty Arms, Now Is the Hour. . . . She swayed in place. Her eyelids felt leaden, weighed down by coins. Sleep was seductive as a drug. It had an undertow. Salvation May Cause Drowning, Edna thought, as she sank into the linen drifts next to her sister. Give Sugar By Mouth, My Funny Valentine!

The Glorious Mysteries

Charlotte Garrahan Willoughby

A s the second eldest daughter, it was my job to tell Papa his sister Lou was having trouble breathing. "Oh, she'll get over that," he said.

This morning I called to tell him Lou was gone. "You know, I've been thinking about her," he said. I could hear him drawing on his pipe. "She was always an oddball."

Those words kept repeating on me as I stood in the parlor of the house on Seventh Avenue, trying to decide whether I could sneak outside for a smoke. If I'd opened my pocketbook once, I'd opened it a dozen times, checking for matches. The house belonged to my maiden aunts, Min, Bess, and—I nearly said Lou. We always spoke of the Garrahan aunts in just that order: Min, Bess, and Lou. There was a naturalness to the habit by now.

You have to understand. My aunts were not modern people. Their house made you feel the previous century was still at large. It was brown as a horehound drop, inside and out, with mossy green shades on every windowpane. The parlor had some tintypey furniture under hand-tatted linen doilies and a wide-open Bible on a library table. There was a picture of the Sacred

Heart of Jesus on the wall with a sick call set and the crucifix from somebody's coffin laid out underneath. The mahogany radio was the most with-it thing in sight.

As I reached for my pocketbook again, I disturbed Lou's sewing basket. Something white and sharp jumped out at me. I LIKE IKE! it said. I gave a yelp. Only a campaign button from the last election. But in this room it seemed offbeat as something come from outer space. I was struck by it. It gave me butterflies. A can of Fluffo, a box of Tide—anything recent looked strange in the house on Seventh Avenue. I straightened the seam in my stocking and realized I was still wearing my Puritan uniform and white seamless mesh from yesterday. I hadn't had time to change after being up all night with Aunt Lou at St. Mary's Hospital.

"Charlotte, get in here and rest," Min called.

I joined them in the dining room, which was nearly cheerful. The table was pine with a sunny sheen, stenciled with green and yellow Dutch tulips. A corner cabinet showed off some Fiestaware and a set of china with a handpainted underglaze.

"Sit down before I knock you down," Aunt Min said, setting a cup of Postum on the table in front of me and wiping her hands on her pinafore. "Sit, Scottie," she told the dog. She was bossy as a floorwalker.

She and Bess were discussing the details of Lou's wake. I was there to help, and I couldn't leave till everything was set. Right now they were deciding the easy stuff, like what to put on the holy card.

"First come the Joyful Mysteries, then the Sorrowful Mysteries, and last are the Glorious Mysteries," Aunt Bess said. Her hands were folded on a stack of altar linens with lace that deep, waiting to be laundered. She always seemed to be wearing gloves whether she was or not.

"No, the right order is Joyful, Glorious, and Sorrowful. Isn't it, Char?" Min said, to draw me out. She usually looked a little puzzled, like somebody trying to do arithmetic in dim light.

I knew they were talking about the rosary, though I am not a religious person. I was still working as a waitress despite my husband, Itch, wanting me to quit, and when I heard the Glorious Mysteries I thought of a Chinese blue plate special. I wouldn't let on, though. I wouldn't give them any lip. Maybe it's that I'm their second-eldest niece, or that I do their taxes, or that my godmother was a Sister of Mercy. For some reason, the Garrahans seemed to think a lot of me. I wanted to stay in their good graces.

"We'll tell the paper she worked for Cluett's, the Model Shirt Company, and the George P. Ide Collar Shop," Bess said.

Min, Bess, and Lou had a nice little arrangement in their day. Bess and Lou went out to earn a living as seamstresses, while Min stayed home to cook and clean. The whole setup worked like a charm. You had to admire it.

"And they'll want her full name. Louise Theresa Garrahan. After Saint Theresa, the Little Flower," Min added. She was watering her patient lucy on the sill. "Just like my middle name, Zita, is after the Saint of Pots and Pans." Min considered housekeeping her vocation. In the spring and fall, she'd rip everything apart and wash the walls from ceiling to floor. "Remember how Lou got her first name?" she asked.

"You wouldn't remember because you weren't born yet," Bess told her.

"Bess and them got Mother to name Louise after a cow," Min went on. "Some old Holstein. On account of the cow was the first thing Mother saw after she saw Lou."

"She was our best milk cow. A Guernsey," Bess corrected. Even in old age, Aunt Bess had stunning skin. The sort that never shines but always boasts a dusting of down like cornstarch. She also had a beauty mark. Min had nothing of the kind. Louise had been sweet-tempered but homely as a hedge fence. Her complexion was sallow, almost jaundiced, and pools of wrinkles widened out over her face like somebody had thrown a pebble in it. The aunts all had middle parts and hair yanked back into buns. Only Lou's hair was rusty pink, and her nose was a shame, being like a beak, pushed to one side, and bumped. You noticed it. None of the Garrahans were the kind of ladies who'd wear their stockings rolled to the ankle, but Lou's fashion sense was truly lacking. It must have been because she felt the cold that she favored big, shabby, shapeless brown sweaters year-round. She was the shyest of the sisters to boot.

"Remember how Lou wanted to go on the stage?" Min's laugh was short and jolly.

I wasn't surprised to see the aunts were treating Lou's death like something they had gotten over even as they were going through it. That was the Garrahan way. St. Thomas Aquinas said to purge all passion; despair was a sin against the Holy Ghost.

"Remember how she used to talk about opening her own dress shop called the Up to Date?" Min said. "And how she answered the phone 'Ahoy! Ahoy!' instead of 'Hello'?"

"I think she should wear her dark blue suit, relieved by lace at the neck," Bess said. She reached down to straighten Scottie's collar.

"And when we went to visit Sister Immaculata, remember how Lou stayed home to go to the movies?" Min asked. Every summer Min and Bess took the train all the way from Troy to Asbury Park, New Jersey, to vacation with the nuns who were our relatives. They thought that was living, vacationing with the nuns.

"She'd go twice a day if the picture changed," I offered.

"What should we do about her tooth?" asked Min. She sashayed around to pour me more grain beverage from a teapot shaped like a cottage.

"I think we should let Roy Fleming decide," said Bess. That was the undertaker. We all knew about Lou's tooth. Every morning before work, she'd mold a front tooth out of wax and wedge it into place. How couldn't anybody know?

"Roy Fleming looks down his nose at us. And Fleming's is too far. We won't get a good turnout. MacChesney's needs our business." Min sat down in a definite way.

Bess adjusted her reading glasses and unfolded an issue of *The Evangelist*. "Send her good dark blue over to Fleming's," she said.

"I don't know, Bess." Min took a swipe at the table with her apron. Maybe it's because of my arthritis, but I admired the nimbleness of her hands. They were always up to something. "Before she went, Lou said something to me that's got me thinking." Min stopped and stared at a bannister of sun falling through the bay window. "It's got me thinking she should wear that dress she made herself."

"Not *that* dress!" Bess's famous good skin turned radish red. If she'd gotten the breaks—if their mother hadn't died after Min's birth, say—I think Bess might have gone to the Convent of the Sacred Heart and wound up the high muckety-muck of some women's club. I see her as the ringleader of her own salon. And I don't mean hairdressing. "We dasn't. What would the priest say? And the board of health!" She asked the saints to preserve us.

"I only want to honor my sister's wishes," Min threw in.

"Anyway, it won't fit," Bess added.

"Now you're fibbing. Lou never got stocky," Min said, shaking a finger.

Bess raised her chin and pursed her lips. "I mean to say, it won't fit in the coffin."

"That's as may be," said Min. But you could tell she wasn't giving an inch. If they'd had a mother, any of these girls might have made something of themselves. Min was practical. She might have become a rockhound or taken up animal husbandry. I see her with pick in hand. I see her as a beekeeper, sticking her whole arm into the hive. Any of these girls might have had more drive than their brothers. Look at Papa. He hadn't been right since his prostate operation. They might as well have taken his brain out, Mother used to say. As for me, I was sitting there dead on my feet, sipping little pretend sips from my cup of dust.

"Charlotte, you look all in. Why don't you go lie down while I fix us a bite to eat?" Min said with a kindly smile. I'd been eating Min's cooking since I was a kid, so I knew what was coming. She was a believer in all-day boiling. "We're having the specialty of the house," she said. Her specialties included mutton with flour gravy gray as a rat and chicken stewed in its pinfeathers. She kept the heavy syrup from canned fruit and fed it to her guests as juice. "And for dessert, my pieplant pie," Min said. This was cake crumbs she'd saved in a jar, scraped together with suet, condensed milk, and rhubarb conserve, slow-baked.

"Once, when you were little," Bess said, "Min made you a cup of cocoa and left out the sugar."

"It must have been terrible bitter. But you drank it politely, like a good child," Min noted.

"Another time, Char said she couldn't eat your creamed corn because of the hairs in it." Bess touched the net that kept her bun in place.

"'Hairs! That's silk,' I told her." Min shook her head.

And I'd eaten her creamed corn, too, though I was particular about hair in my food. As a girl, I'd fasted on tea and crackers, which ruined my looks and health and digestion forever. That is why every time I ate Min's cooking I got sick as a dog.

"Nothing too heavy," Min continued. She poured the kettle dregs of cereal coffee onto a gardenia in a galvanized tub. "In honor of your dyspepsia. It must be hard to be a waitress with your nervous stomach."

"I'd rather serve people than be catered to myself." I got up to bring my cup out to the sink. I wasn't one to lounge around like the Queen of Sheba letting people wait on me. But I knew better than to interfere with Min's kitchen. She had a real bad cook's temper. I've worked with a flock of chefs, and she could hold her own with any of them in the giving-some-poor-soul-what-for department. She'd get mad as heck if anybody questioned her seasonings. Thinking of Min's cooking made me remember how Louise claimed to have tastebuds not just on her tongue but all over the inside of her mouth—on the sides and roof and lips and halfway down her throat. She was funny that way. You had to wonder whether Min's cooking wasn't another cross for her to bear.

I decided to lay low for a while on the chaise lounge in the parlor. I must have been suffering from tired blood. Somehow, I couldn't get comfortable. Everything looked cockeyed. I had the loop-de-loop feeling you get when terra firma says so long. A little table that was also a bookshelf held poetry called *Heart Throbs* and other doodads. *The Silver Chalice, The Life of Christ.* I tried to focus on that with no luck. I tested myself by trying to remember what month it was. May came to mind.

It seemed like only yesterday I was a kid, sitting here with Min, Bess, and Lou, watching the style—including the choir prima donnas and lead tenors—going to high mass at St. Patrick's. Louise could do fine stitching. If one of her nieces appeared in a new blouse, she'd eye it and pinch it and report on the weave and quality. She'd say, "I think that outfit should be a little shorter," and kneel down and hem it where you stood. We'd exchange opinions on the Freihofer breadman who tried to slip treats in with their regular order. We'd talk about the all-girl band they'd seen at Proctor's Theater or how people became saints. I'd ask what they thought of eating pitted cherries at the movies or describe a pair of spectator shoes I was saving to buy. When we mentioned items we wanted, we could see their faces taking notes. Before we left, Min, Bess, and Lou would vanish into their bedrooms. We'd hear the pocketbook clasps snapping. Each one would call us into her room so her sisters wouldn't know how much she gave. Min gave five cents, Bess ten, Louise twenty-five. "Here you are, Old-Timer," Lou would say.

Remembering that made me think oddball was a tough thing for Papa to call his sister. And this morning was not the first time I'd heard him say it. In the car on the way home from Mother's funeral, Louise told us she'd have to go right back to the shop. They needed her to do something special with the machines, some smocking or dart-and-gusset work just she could do. They'd only given her the morning off. That was the first time I heard Papa call her an oddball.

It was but a week ago she'd come down with a cold. When she got so she couldn't breathe right, Min rubbed camphorated oil on her chest and made a mustard plaster for her. Their medical man gave her something, but her temperature was 104, her pulse was racing, and she was delirious when my sister Annie, the family nurse, arrived. Annie phoned for an ambulance right away.

At St. Mary's last night, I didn't like the sound of Louise at all. She kept breathing fast and then stopping. This was around dawn, when the night shift changes, and they bring in the trays. I hailed a nurse who was coming on duty. She must have thought I was a cafeteria worker and not a relative because of my uniform. "She's having trouble breathing," I said, pointing to Louise. Oh, honey, the nurse says. That's the death rattle. It won't be long now. When she saw me smoothing Lou's mussed blankets, she said that's Cheyne-Stokes respiration. Her lungs have consolidated.

I guess there's a name for everything these days, I thought. After that I waited, listening to Louise struggle, puffing and puffing and then quitting cold. Every time she stopped, I held my own breath, wondering if she'd breathe again.

You have to understand. The Garrahans were saintlier than any nuns I'd known. Lou's life had been nothing but innocence and kindliness. And there she was, tucked in that ward with hospital corners where no one knew her, like some castaway, with nothing to make her feel at home, no rings or handkerchiefs of Irish linen, without a friend in the world. When she opened her eyes, I saw despair and abandonment and terror in them, and I had to think where was the happy death they said true Catholics died? I couldn't get over the way God had turned his back on this poor good little thing in her last moments.

"Time to keep body and soul together," Min called from the dining room.

"Doesn't that smell grand!" I said. I thought it smelled like she'd cooked Scottie. At least she served measly portions. I took a slice of toast she'd sulfurated on the coal-burning part of the stove.

"—And he was a man whose second helpings were as ample as his first," Min was saying. "It did your heart good to see him. Charlotte, don't be stinting yourself on the gravy."

"Have you made up your mind about everything?" I asked. They'd put me at the head of the table.

"All but the dress." Aunt Bess swiped daintily at her mouth. "Louise said something to *me* before she went. What she said meant she musn't wear any such dress."

"What did she say, Bess?" Min asked. She was nosy as a terrier.

Bess shook her head.

"What did Lou say to *you*, Min?" I wondered.

"I wish I could tell you, Charlotte." And I could see she wanted to in the worst way. "Then you'd know she has to wear that dress she made herself."

"Say." I took a stab at my boiled cutlet. "If neither of you will tell what she said, how will we decide?"

Min passed me the gravy. "I don't mind telling *you*, Char. It's Bess I worry about. It's Bess who would be shocked."

Aunt Bess made wit's-end, tongue-ticking sounds.

"I know!" Min said. And her ears seemed to perk with eagerness. "Let's you and me go into my room, Char, and I'll whisper it."

I could see Bess thinking the jig would be up if this happened. "All right," she said with a sigh. "And I'll tell Charlotte in private, too."

With that, Min and I adjourned to her room, which hadn't changed in forty years. There was a three-quarter size bed, a throw rug on the oilcloth floor, and some pinch-pleated drapes. Aunt Bess's room was just as plain. It didn't take long for me to hear their little secrets. I returned to the table feeling almost victorious.

"Well, Old-Timers, I have a surprise for you," I said, taking a swig of peach syrup like it was a Tom Collins. "Louise said the same thing to both of you. She said, 'Bury me in my Rose of Sharon Mermaid Dress.'"

Bess twisted her Catholic Daughters of America ring. "God help us," she said.

Min sneaked a scrap of mystery meat to Scottie under the table. "What could be clearer?" she said.

"I won't have it." Bess tapped her black oxford like a gavel on the floor. "People would say we were putting on airs. The Rose of Sharon, my foot. And Mermaid! A dress like that is impious. We could all be excommunicated."

"It's what Lou wanted. The Rose of Sharon," Min reflected. "Wasn't she the one whose teeth were like a flock of sheep that are even-shorn?"

"Louise wasn't herself when she asked for this. She was raving. It's our duty to save her from sin, not lead her into it. Any fool can see that, Mary Zita. She's our sister. We have to take care of her!" Bess always spoke sparingly. I'd never seen her so riled up.

"It's not that I approve of that—that taxi dance dress." Min's face looked discombobulated. "But I'm not worried about Louise's soul, either. Remember she made the Nine First Fridays. And she was wearing the Scapular of the Sacred Heart when she died."

"Louise loved God. I won't have her wearing that—thing—for all eternity—for all to see," Bess said. Her milkwhite nose was trembling.

"Louise loved God the way chorus girls love furs," Min said, snatching Bess's plate away while Bess's fork was in the air.

"Dear Hearts," I said. Min and Bess had been best chums, ticking together like the hands on a clock till this minute. I was worried about them. I honestly was. "Don't be arguing over a dress. Louise wouldn't want that." I could hardly believe they were squabbling over something so picayune. "I have an idea. The solution has just come to me." I must have been getting punch-drunk or I'd have kept mum. Talking to the aunts right then was like playing pickup sticks. You had to be delicate and move one part without rattling the other.

"Let's let Scottie decide," I said.

There was a queasy silence. The aunts looked baffled.

"There's that trick Scottie does." The dog only had one trick, and believe me, it wasn't much.

"You don't mean the one where we wag a bone over his head and he spins around and around till he gets all balled up and falls over playing dead?" Min said.

"That's it. The solution is, you stand on one side of the room, Min, and Bess gets on the other. I wave the bone over Scottie's head, and whichever one of you he falls toward decides about the dress."

Either they were weary or their supernatural respect for me made them go along. Louise always did like Scottie, Min said finally, and we were in business. I feel like a jackass now for not getting them to toss a coin. But that is the wisdom of hindsight.

Min handed me a greasy gray bone fresh from the pot, and

we took up our positions. Those Scottie dogs get awful excited.
I twirled the bone above his head, and he spun himself faster
and faster, yipping and yapping. Then didn't he fall over with his
head on my foot and commence to slobbering on my good
white work shoe like I was his only friend. There was no if, and,
or but.

"Looks like it's up to you, Char," Min said.

"Now hold your horses." I hemmed and hawed. It was not
my place to act as judge and jury, taking sides.

"If Charlotte's going to decide, she has to see the dress," Min
said.

"Charlotte doesn't want to see that dress," Bess said.

I had to admit to being a little curious about what manner of
garment we had in our possession.

"We'll show you, Char. And you can give us your opinion,"
said Min.

She led the way into Louise's bedroom. Like the other two, it
was small and dim, with a window right on top of the neighbors,
a little iron bed, and a dresser with some silvery lady things—a
brush, mirror, and comb set—on it. Min opened the closet and
rummaged around till she found a garment bag that looked
handmade of maybe muslin. She ripped open the metal snaps,
and I was nearly asphyxiated by a sudden gust of camphor with
a mild undertow of vanilla. The Garrahans put camphor into
every blessed drawer to protect their wardrobe from moths. Once
at Christmas, Bess gave me a box of candy she'd stored all year in
camphor. It smelled to high heaven. Camphor was also a cure-all
used to ward off germs and maintain health. The well-known
remedy Save the Baby had a camphor base. Mother used to warm
the tonic up and feed it to us on a spoon. Min, Bess, and Lou
wore little crocheted bags filled with camphor around their
necks. So I guess I should have been ready for it. But I wasn't, no
more than I was ready for the dress itself.

I jumped back onto Bess's toe when I saw it. I put my hand

over my heart like someone at a parade when the flag passes. Even in the gloom, the material was stunning, with a finish unlike any I'd known. It changed colors depending on which way you turned. It was as if the manufacturer had taken embers, spun them into thread, and woven that molten stuff into dry goods. The fabric was burnished coral in the folds yet bright rouge in the higher places where it grabbed the light. There was nothing indecent about the cut, I could see that. I could see it would cover every mortal inch of her.

Buttons began at the right neckline, zagged to the left, and plunged on the bias to the thigh. Around the hips a swanky swathing of rose sateen gathered in a vee that gradually blurted out into a fishtail someplace near the ground. But what knocked the wind out of me was the tailoring. Every single solitary seam was showing. The seams were even and pinked at the edges with delicate sawteeth.

You heard stories of exotic furs in the family. You heard of marmot maybe in the aunts' far-distant past. You heard of caracal coats cut to look like Persian lamb. But I'd never seen the aunts wear anything beyond crispy clean housedresses in dimity prints or solid suits. This was something different. I had to admit it.

"Mercy," I said. "My word!" Lou must have sweat blood over this was my thought exactly.

"Decent people will see it and start to weep—" Bess began.

"It's," I paused. "Inside out."

"—to think she had such sisters as would let her be laid out in this," Bess finished.

"That's the way Lou planned it," Min said, brushing some imaginary dust from the bodice. "She thought her best stitching went to waste on the inside. This shows all her fancywork to the hilt. Wait! I almost forgot. It has a tail." And from the bottom of the bag she hauled out a seething massiveness of mauve charmeuse.

"A train," I said. I reached out, almost against my will, and petted the dress's tiny gray collar. It felt warm and numb as frost-bite. "Marmot?" I whispered, full of wonder.

"That's mouse, child," said Min. "When we lived in the country, your Uncle Bill trapped rodents in the pantry. He'd tan their hides and give them to Lou. He was a good egg."

"The board of health!" said Bess, clinging to the white metal bedpost like a mast.

"But can you tell me," Min said, twisting herself away from the dress to look me dead in the eye, "why anybody would want to be buried in a dress like this? I call it a mystery."

I was feeling kind of woozy, like I'd had one highball too many. You got the jitters, kid, I told myself and sat down, thunk, on the bed. "Folks, I think I might take a little nap after all."

"Min, Charlotte here is all in," said Bess.

"And no wonder! Off you go—to the Land of Nod," said Min.

"Have a good rest now. Sleep tight." And they backed out of the room, taking great care to be quiet, like I was already under, leaving the dress on display in the open closet.

Having been awake for twenty-four hours, you'd have thought I'd fall into a deep snooze posthaste. But I lay there awhile with the aunts' voices dozing through my head like the Latin at Mass. Gradually I drifted off, and it must have been an hour or two later that I woke to find myself petrified from head to toe. I couldn't shut my eyes or lift so much as a pinkie. As I lay there paralyzed, I noticed a flickering Something taking shape at the foot of the bed. This shimmering Whatnot appeared to be loosening a watery garment. Then, making it look easy, this Whajamacallit opened its chest like the skin was a jacket to show me everything within. I saw the satin lining and I saw the heart, which was on fire. Flames careened from it with every beat. Before I had time to be completely surprised, the Mystery reached inside, pulled the heart right out of its body, and held it in midair—suspended, red, and wrapped in twine. It gave off a perishing light!

My own heart was racing, and a liniment warmth was creeping through my side and spreading out. This feeling was new and not like aches and pains. It was then I mustered all the oomph I had left and sat up in the iced air of after-trance, out of breath, on Louise's bed.

"Well, Rip Van Winkle, did you get your forty winks?" Min asked as I staggered into the parlor.

I sat down on the prickly edge of the horsehair love seat. What I wouldn't have given for an old-fashioned just then. Under ordinary circumstances, wild beasts could not have dragged what happened from me. But I was so befuddled that the experience began to tell itself without a by-your-leave.

"That's a humdinger," Min said when I finished. "I never hope to have a dream like that."

"At least I got my second wind," I said. It was true. My get-up-and-go had returned. And I couldn't believe I'd gotten through the day without a smoke. Maybe I'd quit after all.

"A dream like that will put hair on your chest. Something you ate must have disagreed with you." Min laughed her jolly laugh.

"No," said Bess. "Have you forgotten? This is a household consecrated to the Sacred Heart. Father Carey performed the Enthronement of the Sacred Heart in the Home ceremony in this room last year." She went over to their little bookshelf and grabbed a thin gray pamphlet. "I can't see without my glasses. But here's the record of payment in somebody's hand. Look, Charlotte."

"Five dollars to Father Carey for performing The Enthronement of the Scared Heart in the Home," I read. "Pardon me. *Sacred* Heart. But somebody wrote 'scared.' "

"It's a sign," said Bess.

"We've been given a sign," Min said. "I can't get over it."

"Did the heart appear in a clutch of flames, banded by a crown of thorns and surmounted by a cross at the top?" Bess asked.

"I don't know about the cross," I said.

"I believe you've had an apparition of the Sacred Heart," Bess said. Her eyes were big as banjos.

"For heaven's sake," I said. I was beginning to lose patience with the religious jiggery-pokery. I honestly was. "I don't think it was anything of the kind. I honestly don't."

"What does it mean, Bess?" Min asked. "Read more, Charlotte."

"'Enthronement implies that hereafter this image will have its place in the home and be honored by its inmates,'" I read. "'By such means, Christ asks us to make reparation for the indignities inflicted upon him by others and for the ingratitude directed against his heart. Our reparation would soften in some sort the bitter sorrow he felt in being abandoned by his Apostles.'"

"But the dress," Min said. "What's it telling us to do about the dress?"

A hush came over the room. It was so thick you could hear the dust burp, as my husband, Itch, would say.

Finally Bess spoke. "Didn't Lou knit a sweater with heart-shaped buttons once?"

Min said she wasn't sure, but she'd go check. We all trooped after her into Lou's room. She pushed the Rose of Sharon Mermaid Dress aside and began rooting through the other few items in the closet. "Here!" She flung on the bed what looked like some old rag Scottie had dug up. It was plate-scraping-leftover brown, and so dilapidated. But the buttons were hearts. I'll give them that.

"We'll put this over the dress. And no one will be the wiser," Bess said.

Min looked at her with real admiration. You'd have thought

she'd solved a problem hard as King Solomon's about the baby with the two mothers. "And we'll tear off that darn tail," Min added.

Why didn't some one of them switch on a lamp? It was getting dismaler by the minute. When I'd arrived at the house on Seventh Avenue, it was a beautiful spring morning, with sun all over the place. Now night was moving in. I'd have to hurry if I was to catch the last bus home. "Is there anything else I can do?" I asked. I'd been hoping since morning to get home before dark. And now I'd have to steer by the stars.

Min had the sweater on a hanger and was trying to work the heart buttons through the holes. They were giving her grief. "You try, Char," she said.

For once I was happy to say my arthritis was acting up.

"I can't imagine Louise making something that wasn't just so. I can't imagine her picking buttons too big for the holes," Min said.

"I can't get over it," Bess said.

I told them again I was going, but they were wrangling in a genteel manner, and I don't think they heard. Bess wanted to redo the buttonholes, Min wanted to put the thing on Louise backwards so the gap wouldn't show. As I walked by the bay window, I waved to them, but I couldn't catch their eyes. All I could see was their center parts bowed over the sweater, and their hands crossing as they tried to force the wayward hearts through the holes and button it up, nice and tight.

THE REAL ELEANOR RIGBY

Ruth Livingston

RUTH LIVINGSTON WAS the loneliest girl in North America. She was the only Catholic High student who subscribed to *Zen Teen, the Journal of Juvenile Macrobiotics* published by the Youth in Asia Foundation (Euthanasia! Someone should point out the unhappy homonym), the only member of the Sodality of the Blessed Virgin who'd read *Tropic of Cancer*. Once when she mentioned Henry Miller, the entire group thought she was referring to the amiable, goateed host of the popular TV show *Sing Along with Mitch.*

Arthur Miller maybe, but Mitch!

In a weak moment, Ruth had joined her school's chapter of *Up with People*, the moral rearmament choral group. She'd performed with them once or twice, but she was asked to leave after taking liberties with the windshield wiper waves. Now she spent her weekends immured in her room, cataloguing items in *BeatleLuv Unlimited* magazine and *IshMail*, the Melville Society newsletter.

"John, Paul, George, and Herman!" her mother said. "If you ask me, *Moby-Dick* is one dull book. Where's the romance, the love interest? If you ask me, Herman was a fink."

Ruth felt deeply misunderstood. Like Melville, she wanted to ship out to Liverpool.

No one shared her obsessions except Sunny Metzger, a Lutheran who attended Troy High. The two girls were desperate virgins, isolated by their attraction to the non-Troy and exotic. Ruth had heard all about Sunny's brief fling with an Estonian boy who wanted her to eat borscht while he snapped Polaroids. She heard how one famished night Sunny agreed, and afterwards, during the sad, postculinary intimacy, the boy drove her to Albany Airport to watch the planes take off. They had sat in the car outside the runway's chainlink till Sunny's hair smelled like jet fuel, a musky residue of adventure that Ruth envied, though the Estonian boy never called again.

Every night Ruth fell asleep with her transistor radio under her head like a renunciate's stone pillow. The local station was always holding contests. Their call letters, WTRY, stood for Troy, but in their elastic ID jingles, she heard the command *to strive*. Third caller, try again, fifth caller, try again, the DJ would say. One lucky midnight she became the ninth caller and won a pen touched by the Beatles. It arrived by mail a week later.

"It's a second-class relic," Ruth said, placing the sealed envelope in the middle of the kitchen table. Her mother was ironing nearby. Sunny was sipping a Diet Rite.

"Well, I call it pretty chintzy. At least they could give you a first-class prize," Mrs. Livingston said.

"C'mon, Ma. First-class relics are rare." First-class relics were taken from the body or any of its integrant parts, such as limbs, ashes, and bones. How many times had she explained? But her mother was an Easter-duty Catholic. What could you expect.

"Well, I still say it's pretty darn cheap."

"A third-class welic, now, that would be cheap," Sunny

offered. "A third-class welic is anything that's touched a first- or second-class welic. You can't take a welic like that theriously." Sunny lisped when she got excited. Sometimes she stuttered. "Hey, Ru! Now we can make our own third-clath welicths," she said. "We could thell them."

They had learned about relics during a special weekend retreat taught by a foreign priest full of discouraged Catholic lore. Sunny had sat in the back, and the visiting cleric did not recognize her as an interloper. His presentation was part show and tell, part autopsy. He explained how a particle extracted from a saint had been placed in a locket, covered by crystal, bound by red thread, and sealed with the insignia of office. Then he opened the back cover of the locket and showed them a swatch of red wax that looked like a hundred-year-old heart, wizened and dripping with antiquity.

Sunny raised her hand. "Father, I know a second-class welic is an object that has come in contact with a living saint, like the instruments wherewith a martyr has been tortured, the chains by which he was bound, the clothes he wore, or objects he used. But what about Saint Peter's shadow, or a saint's bray-bray-braces? I mean, it's just a high-high-"—a couple of boys snickered, and Brew Thudlinsky, the school bully, belched derisively—"hypothesis, Father, but what class would a saint's con-con-contact lenses be?"

And though the priest spoke perfect English, he had sighed in Spanish. "For the sake of simplicity, let's stick with the bones," he said.

The pen the Beatles touched was enrobed in a red plastic pencil case. Ruth eased the zipper back. As the tiny metal fangs gave way, a faint gas, a perfume of petroleum products, essence of black vinyl and steel strings, escaped, and there it was: an instrument of monastic plainness nestled in the scarlet darkness. A cheap black ballpoint. A new warmth possessed her. Hope, the thing with feathers, was perching in her soul.

"Are you sure it's not the albatross like in that other poem?" Sunny asked.

A relic might be *coronse spinse D.N.J.C.*, taken from the crown of thorns, or *de velo*, from the veil. It might be *ex parecordi*, from the stomach or intestines; *ex pelle*, from the skin; *ex capillus*, from the hair; *ex carne*, from the flesh. It could be *ex stipite affixionis*, from the whipping post, or *ex tela serica quae tetigit cor*, from the silk cloth which touched the heart.

"Or maybe it's the liver. That extinct bird Liverpool was named for."

"This is Hope," Ruth said. "You'll know it when you feel it." Hope felt like a summer clearance when the worn merchandise was offered up and whisked away.

Her mother hung up a blouse with a vehemence that made the hangers shriek. "It doesn't take much to make you girls happy, does it?" she said.

"Knock, knock!" Mrs. Livingston had yelled on the day Herman Melville entered Ruth's life. She was sequestered in her bedroom, which resembled a clipping service run by a poltergeist. The floor was a brittle strudel of back issues and loose paper. Narrow paths had been cleared between the door, bed, and stereo.

"What a booby trap," her mother said, walking the plank of carpet. "It kind of makes you glad paper has only two sides." She placed a book on the bed next to Ruth. "Old junk from the Phoenix." The Phoenix, a historic residential hotel, had belonged to Ruth's father. He had died a year ago.

Typee: a Peep at Polynesian Life by Herman Melville, Ruth read. New York, Wiley and Putnam 1846. When she opened it, a dank, riverish smell rose from the pages.

"*Typee* is a cookbook and a sex manual," she told Sunny during their nightly phone call. "It's a hunger novel."

Melville's book told the story of two starving pals, Tommo and Toby, on their perilous journey into the heart of the Marquesas. The infinite care with which these deserters parceled out their sea biscuits, the division of a little sustenance into less, worked upon Ruth's imagination. Every night she gave Sunny a synopsis. Tommo and Toby have been captured by natives! Toby has escaped, but Tommo is being treated well! Today the island girls gathered a thimbleful of salt. They spread a big leaf on the ground, dropped a few grains on it, and invited Tommo to taste them as a sign of their esteem. "From the extravagant value placed upon the article," Ruth read, "I verily believed, that with a bushel of common Liverpool salt, all the real estate in Typee might have been purchased."

"I verily believe it, too," Sunny said.

The girls passed *Typee* back and forth, reading and rereading. They went to the Troy Public Library and checked out everything on Herman Melville. One night Ruth called with a major discovery. "Herman wrote *Typee* in Lansingburgh. He was living on 114th Street, near the Phoenix Hotel." The next day, she called the Lansingburgh Historical Society, and they gave her the phone number of a ninety-five-year-old man named Tim Brunswick, whose father was rumored to have actually known Herman Melville.

"I'd like to meet him," she told her mother.

"I wish you could find someone your own age," Mrs. Livingston sighed.

When Ruth's mother realized the girls were determined to visit the ancient Melville expert, she offered them a ride. Tim Brunswick lived in a trailer on the banks of the Hudson River. He met them at the door with a quivery little dog in his arms. A toy poodle? Sunny asked.

"A Maltese," said Tim Brunswick. "Name of Blimey." He led

them into a tiny parlor lined with gray file cabinets. A picture window showed a dismal river view, and a saxophone gleamed dully in one corner like the esophagus of a golden beast. The room shivered when the wind blew, as if it might lunge into the Hudson at any minute. Ruth felt a little seasick.

"Did your father really know Herman Melville, Mr. Brunswick?" Sunny asked.

"Everybody in the Burgh knew him. Dad went to school with his kid brother, Tom. Those boys worshiped Melville." Blimey buried his tiny nose in his master's shirt, and Tim Brunswick peered at Mrs. Livingston over his bifocals. His eyes were a vibrant baby-blue. "I also knew your husband, Sam Livingston. He was a serious person. Quiet, but accommodating."

"That's why he needed me." Mrs. Livingston crossed her legs and started swinging the top one with aggressive abandon. "I was fun-loving as all get-out."

"Lansingburgh was quite a place in his day. It has quite a history." And Tim Brunswick told them how the first Dutch settlers had named the village Steen Arabia, and how in Melville's time, the 1840s, peach trees and willows had grown along the Hudson, which was then a busy shipyard. "Melville and a local girl, Mary Parmalee, used to stroll on the riverbank, reading Tennyson to each other. 'Far on the ringing plains of windy Troy. I am a part of all that I have met—' "

"Mary Parmalee!" Ruth's mother interrupted. "What a pretty name! How did I wind up being plain old Annie Livingston?"

"What was Herman like?" Sunny asked eagerly.

"Like a real sailor, Dad said. Suntanned. And he walked with this racy kind of swagger, what they called the sailor's roll. It was considered very suggestive in his day."

"Yeah?" Sunny smiled encouragingly.

"Yeah. Melville walked like he was on a rocking boat, kind of bowlegged-like—" And Tim Brunswick set the dog down on his chair and lurched around the table, demonstrating. Then he came to a halt and swayed tipsily above the little Maltese.

"Blimey!" exclaimed Sunny.

"You betcha!" said Tim Brunswick. "The ladies love a sailor. All the belles of Lansingburgh were after Herman Melville. Ladies led sheltered lives in those days, and he was a man of the world, swashbuckling, like Errol Flynn. He was what we'd call a sex symbol today."

"I don't understand symbolism, do you?" Mrs. Livingston appealed. "That's why I don't understand *Moby-Dick*." She shifted restlessly on the narrow love seat. "It's full of symbolism."

"Some books you have to read twice to understand," Ruth said.

"And some you'd never understand if you read till time immortal. *Gone With the Wind*! Now there was a book."

Ruth handed Tim Brunswick her copy of *Typee*. "This was in my father's safe at the Phoenix Hotel."

He opened the book and examined it. "You'd better take good care of this, young lady. This is a first edition. It might even be an association copy."

"Wow!" Sunny said. "What's that?"

"A book Melville owned himself. He might have given it to the innkeeper in payment for his drinking tab."

"You mean Herman touched *Typee*? That makes it a thecond-clath welic."

"Say again?"

"An object rich with spiritual electricity," Ruth translated. "An object made luminous by contact with a radiant being."

As they walked to the car, she looked for evidence of peach trees by the Hudson. She felt the past must exist behind, beside, inside, or under the present. The problem was time. Time came between things, shutting them off in loneliness and ignorance. And time had dimension. It wasn't flat like paper. Time had substance, yet it was invisible, like all important things.

"All the lonely sailors," Ruth said. Where did they all come from?

Ruth had long believed she had the power to pull things toward her with her mind. Now she sensed something desirable approaching, and she urged it on, envisioning a limo with dark windows, a single-masted schooner. A yellow submarine.

A week later, Mrs. Livingston came running upstairs in a state of high emergency. "The Beatle Buggy's outside!" she said. "It looks like a Ford Fairlane. Hurry!"

WTRY was giving away tickets to see the group at Shea Stadium. The winners also would attend the junior press conference in New York. Ruth and Sunny had sent in a hundred entries with "Jay Blue is sexy!" scrawled all over them. They'd found the DJ's name in the phone book under BLUE, JAY and called to say they admired his jingles. Now he sat in her mother's living room, a palpable absence of sound taking shape around him. His quietude felt lifeless, as if uttering inanities at the speed of light for a living drained him of élan vital. Maybe he's a mild-mannered mortician by day and a swinging DJ by night, Ruth thought. It'll be a gas, Jay Blue said in the forced baritone that was his air voice. He scratched his head and his mod-style toupee, said to be made of genuine mink, slipped down and touched the top of his sunglasses. Then he stood up and handed Ruth the tickets, and Mrs. Livingston burst into applause. "Since her father died, she's hardly left her room. Maybe this will get her out of the house."

"Say, that's a good idea," said Jay Blue.

Ruth held the receiver at arm's length after telling Sunny. "We have to stop screaming and think," she yelled into the mouthpiece.

"Thop threaming and think!"

"We need a way to get close to them. We need the perfect gift."

The usual offerings—gum wrappers woven into an eighteen-foot strip, a life-sized portrait of Ringo made entirely of uncooked elbow macaroni—would not do. All that chewing and plaiting and dyeing and gluing did not reflect well upon the giver. They'd have to come up with something unique. Something the Beatles might actually want. The perfect gift could open doors. It must be something that would not melt or die on the bus to New York, something that could be carried while sprinting in a miniskirt.

"For the man who has everything," Ruth continued, "a relic would make a very special present."

"Why would the Beatles want a pen they touched?"

"Not that, Hairspray Brains! *Typee*."

Sunny squealed in shock. "If we give them *Typee*, what are we going to re-re-read?"

"There are other books in the world, you know." Ruth affected a supercilious tone. "We could read *Billy Budd*. Or *Moby-Dick*." In fact, she was tired of second-class relics. If she could get close to the Beatles, she might achieve the hands-on, naked knowledge that came from touching a primary source.

"Why not give them uth," Sunny suggested.

"Give them us?"

"Remember Regina." This cousin of Sunny's had lost her virginity at Jose's Deli, and her description—the really amazing pain, the counterboy's commands to open wider—made sex sound like a terrible trip to the dentist. Now Sunny said she thought they could do better. Since Herman was unavailable, she thought the Beatles might be equal to the task. Try the best, then try the rest, she said, and the concept appealed to Ruth's perfectionism.

And so, over the next few weeks, they set about starving their bodies into bodies the Beatles could want: model bodies, twig-gish and ravishingly thin. Sometimes, at the end of a meal, Sunny would pick up her plate and lick it clean. She was so hungry!

"Zen cookery uses four yangizing factors to achieve change," Ruth said. She and Sunny were eating their usual dinner of brown rice with brown rice. "Heat, time, pressure, and/or salt."

"You girls need more variety in your diet," her mother remarked. "You need more color. 'A bright color on a brown gruel is like a song in the heart.' I made that up myself."

"Was Jay Blue anything like his image, Mrs. Livingston?" Sunny asked.

"No. In real life, he's dead timber. Not my type." She took another bite of Irish stew.

"Who's your type, Ma?"

"Tyrone Power. He had bedroom eyes. And Sam, your father, liked Kay Francis." Her mother set dishes of pink pudding before them.

"I don't want any," Ruth said.

"Sam was the only one who thought I was swell." Her mother sighed. "He was the only one who liked my cooking. Though when I was a visiting nurse, I had admirers. I once had a patient change her name to mine, you know."

Ruth rolled her eyes. "This patient changed her first name *and* her last name," she told Sunny.

"I know it!" crowed her mother. "She became Annie Garrahan. That was before I became Annie Livingston, of course."

"Did she change her name to Livingston when you did?" Ruth asked.

"Huh?" her mother's mind was back in the 1930s. "We'd lost touch by then. Who knows, she might have. She thought very highly of me, that's for dang sure."

"Well, I like your cooking, Mrs. L.," Sunny said.

Mrs. Livingston gave another martyred sigh. "I eat to live, I don't live to eat."

"The body is water, but the mind is sea," said Ruth. "The body—"

"The body is water, but the mind is at sea! What's that supposed to mean?" Mrs. Livingston interrupted.

Since earliest childhood, whenever Ruth tried to speak, her mother's voice had drowned her out. Rather than compete for conversational space, she had become a seriously silent person. Her father had mistaken her reticence for arrogance. He'd accused her of caring more for John Lennon than her parents. And what could she say? The Beatles are my Polynesia?

"The ripe raw breadfruit can be stored away in large underground receptacles for years on end," Ruth quoted from *Typee*. "It only improves with age." They were sitting at a card table in the cellar of her house. The cellar, fusty with oilcloth and light-absorbing knotty pine, reminded them of the Cavern, where the Fab Four had begun. Now that classes had ended for the summer, they spent much of their time there, playing the one folk song they knew over and over on their warped guitars. "Danger water's coming, baby, hold me tight," they sang in loud, flat voices.

"Were it not that the breadfruit is thus capable of being preserved for a length of time, the natives might be reduced to a state of starvation," Ruth continued.

"If I could get my hands on a breadfruit, I'd know what to do with it," Sunny said. But breadfruit was not available at the local supermarkets and when they asked after it, the produce managers became churlish and depressed.

"What was Jay Blue like?" Sunny asked.

"He was like—nothing. He seemed kind of lonely."

"Troy must be the loneliest place on earth. I bet we're one of the only places on earth without a sister city."

"One of the only! That's a redundancy," Ruth said.

"Wow!" Sunny dropped her guitar with a metallic boom. "Herman's first voyage was to Liverpool, right? And he was living in Lansingburgh then, right? Well, it's obvious. We'll start a petition to make Lansingburgh and Liverpool sister cities, and we'll ask the Beatles to sigh-sigh-"—her voice sounded as if she'd been breathing helium—"sign it!"

"We can't do that! It'll ruin our image. They'll think we're fans." Ruth fluffed her hair near the crown to give it more height. "Anyway, it's so—municipal."

"Your mother can do the embarrassing part, asking for their autographs." Since the girls were only fourteen, Mrs. Livingston insisted on accompanying them to New York. "We need more than one idea," Sunny said. "We shouldn't put all our begs in one ask-it."

"Wouldn't we have to get somebody's approval, like the Lord Mayor of Liverpool or at least the Mayor of Lansingburgh?"

"If the Beatles sign, do you think those guys will say no? They're politicians! They know which side their butt is breaded on!"

And Ruth didn't argue. "Do I dare to eat a peach?" she often asked herself. Lately, more often than not, the answer was yes.

On August 22, Ruth, Sunny, and Mrs. Livingston took the bus to New York City. The girls were using years of babysitting savings to pay for a room at the Warwick, where the Beatles were staying. They spent the hours before the junior press conference donning their Beatle girlfriend costumes: hiphugger skirts, net stockings, paisley shirts with white cuffs and collars, gillie shoes of golden suede. Do I look like a fan? No, do I? they asked each other.

The press conference was held on the second floor. Girls waited outside, trying to insinuate themselves to the front of the pack, and at last the doors swung open. As the crowd trampled past, Ruth was stabbed in the clavicle by someone's JOHN IS GOD button. She hugged her copy of *Typee*, which she planned to present at a suitable moment. An aide appeared and said, "The Beatles are about to enter. Would those in front please kneel?" All the girls sank like barn animals on Christmas Eve. "I mean," he amended, "so those in back can get their picture. Make room." Ruth and Sunny were pressed against an emergency exit when suddenly it opened, hurtling them back into the hall. A long navy-blue arm reached over their heads and slammed the door, stranding them outside.

"We won passes!" Ruth wailed.

"Win some, lose some," the policeman said.

"You're supposed to be a community helper," Sunny scolded.

"I'm helping those rich fairies stay alive." He patted his gun holster. "If you ask me, those guys are a little light in their loafers."

"Nobody asked you," Sunny snapped. Muffled munchkin squeals erupted from within the room, followed by deeper, foreign inflections that flipped up at the ends. Ruth and Sunny pulled their hair and groaned in frustration. When the doors opened, they rushed in, but the Beatles had been whisked away. We've been cheated! they told each other through disbelieving tears.

"Yes, they do that to your mother, too," Mrs. Livingston remarked when they returned to their hotel room. "But I don't let them get away with it."

The girls were prostrated in shock on the bed. "They're above us right now," Ruth said. "Just one floor up." And they listened to the footsteps on high, trying to guess their identities.

"C'mon," her mother said, putting on her pumps. "Let's meet the Beatles and get it over with. Then we can go out and have some fun."

As soon as the girls had repaired their eyeliner, Mrs. Livingston hustled them onto the elevator. When the doors opened at the eighth floor, a guard blocked their exit. Ruth peered into the corridor and spied the Beatles' road manager. "Neil As-As"—Sunny called as the elevator door slammed into her side—"Aspinall!" The road manager paused, and Ruth told him how they'd missed the press conference. He asked her age. Eighteen, she lied, and for once her mother didn't contradict her. Follow me, Neil said. When he saw Mrs. Livingston was with the girls, he hesitated. Then he unlocked a door, and with a sweeping gesture, bade them enter.

Four dove-gray suits with plum-red pinstripes lay draped across the bed, gleaming in the lunar light of the TV. Ruth reacted like a Geiger counter sensing uranium nearby. Her teeth began to chatter, and she had to suppress high-pitched trills of impending revelation. "If you wouldn't mind doing us a favor," Neil said. "These have to be ironed before the show tomorrow." He pointed to an ironing board in the corner. "I'll be back," he promised.

"Always leave the door ajar when you're in a strange man's hotel room," Mrs. Livingston instructed, propping it with the telephone book. She examined the suits. "What elegant tailoring! You have to take everything out of the pockets, or they won't lie flat. Oh, name tags."

The girls exchanged thrilled looks. "Which one do you want?" Ruth asked.

"Paul, of course," Sunny said. "Paul is All!"

"Is he the single one?" Mrs. Livingston inquired.

"He's The Cute One," Ruth said dismissively. "I want John, The Sexy One."

"Paul's had a very hard life, you know," Sunny told them. "His mother died when he was fourteen."

"John's mother died, too," said Ruth. "And his father deserted him. He's an orphan."

Mrs. Livingston sighed. She'd been born near an orphanage, and as a student nurse, she'd worked in the New York Foundling Hospital. "Poor motherless boys! At least they're young and healthy."

"Oh no," Ruth informed her. "Ringo had peritonitis as a child, and George had nephritis. They're actually kind of sickly." She knew her mother had sympathy for physical ills, though disturbances of the mind only made her irritable. Mrs. Livingston respected reality and those who kept in touch with its firm facts. Now she sat on the bed, watching TV, while Ruth and Sunny took turns ironing. John Lennon came on the screen, apologizing for saying the Beatles were more popular than Jesus. The report that followed said the group had been nearly crushed to death in Cleveland, picketed by the Ku Klux Klan in Washington, D.C., and almost electrocuted in St. Louis. They'd received death threats in Memphis, where someone tossed a bomb on stage, and today two fans had promised to leap from the ledge of a New York hotel unless they met the Beatles.

"Silly girls!" Mrs. Livingston frowned. Ruth and Sunny were caressing the suits as if they were alive. They ran the zippers up and down, unbuttoned the waistbands, rubbed their faces against the lapels. "Don't be getting lipstick on their outfits. And there's another thing I won't stand for."

Ruth held her breath.

"I won't have you throwing things at those boys while they're trying to play their music. They have enough trouble."

"The only thing I want to throw at them is myself," Ruth said. She ironed lasciviously, stopping to inhale the faint scents—shaving cream and sweat, patchouli and dry-cleaning fluid—liberated by steam and heat. She felt delirious. "How many pleats go in each leg?" she asked.

"Give me that iron," her mother said, pushing her aside. "I can't believe we came to New York for this. This is just like home."

At last the suits were finished, but there still was no sign of Neil Aspinall. "That dress manager of theirs. He has what are called 'craggy good looks.' Do you girls know what that means?"

"Like Frankenstein might have looked if Frankenstein had been good-looking?" Sunny suggested.

Suddenly fragments of song—"Summer in the City"—burst from a room at the end of the hall, a door slammed, and voices came lilting along the corridor. Ruth, Sunny, and Mrs. Livingston rushed to the threshold in time to see a fantasia of flowers and paisley, polka dots and stripes, mossy velvets and sunbright satins levitate down the hall. Then the mirage vanished in a Beatle-scented breeze. Ruth and Sunny grabbed each other. Did you see them? Did you see them?

" 'Had a glimpse of the gardens of Paradise been revealed to me, I could scarcely have been more ravished with the sight,' " Sunny quoted from *Typee*. "Didn't they look—mythical?"

Mystical, yes, Ruth said. She had expected the Beatles to sense their intimate bond with her and stop. How could they have mistaken her for a stranger?

"If you knew that was them, why didn't you speak up? You missed your chance," her mother said. "Here comes their handsome valet." Mrs. Livingston showed Neil the ironed suits. She pointed to a little heap of Beatle detritus on the dresser. "That was in their pockets."

"Oh, you can keep those things." The road manager's eyes looked dreamy and glazed. "As souvenirs."

"When do we meet the Beatles?" Mrs. Livingston asked.

"The boys are tired. They've had a hard week."

"Listen, we kept our part of the bargain." Mrs. Livingston folded her arms across her chest, preparing for battle. "These girls have come a long way. They've waited a long time."

"Okay," Neil said reluctantly. "All right." He extracted three red press passes from his wallet and handed them out. "Come by the suite tomorrow around four, and you'll meet the Beatles."

At the appointed hour the next day, they showed their passes and joined the line extending from the Beatles' suite. Ruth spotted Jay Blue just ahead of them, talking into a cassette recorder and punching the air for emphasis. She clutched *Typee* with clammy fingers. On this day of days, her bangs were wrinkled, her hair full of flyaway, her Beatle girlfriend ensemble disheveled from dress rehearsals. And how could she meet the Beatles with her mother tagging along? She wanted to be back in her room, copying their song lyrics with the patience of a scrivener. Last year she'd ordered some bromeliads from Florida, and when she opened the carton, the pots were swarming with centipedes. She had shrieked and thrown the shipment away before her mother, always disgusted by forays into the strange, could find out. Now she felt the same hysterical alarm. You go, I'll wait here, she said.

"The heck you will," her mother said, pulling her through the door.

The Beatles' suite was crawling with gifts. It's like Christmas morning in here, Ruth thought. *Your riches taught me poverty.* What she had to offer seemed shabby in comparison. By the time they'd edged near enough to see the group, everyone else had been ushered out except Jay Blue. The Beatles were holding court from the sofa. There was a gritty orb before them on the cocktail table, and they were staring at it as if it might hatch.

"Is that egg really one hundred years old?" Jay Blue asked.

"No," John Lennon said. "The Chinese only call it that so ignorant Westerners will think they'll eat anything."

"Say, that's a good idea!" said Jay Blue.

The Beatles seemed disgruntled, almost crotchety behind their granny glasses. Apathy poured off them, and joyless waterfalls of worry. Ruth yearned to make them happy, if only for an instant. Five minutes, their press agent called. There's no time like the present, her mother hissed, nudging the girls forward. Ruth knew Sunny would not speak for fear of stuttering. She wanted to be introduced as a mute painter who spoke only in watercolors of a halcyon refinement.

Hi, Ruth whispered.

The Beatles went on talking all at once and only with each other above the insect whir of the recorder. They seemed to be discussing the hundred-year-old egg. ". . . Looks like snot I suppose you could wear a blindfold whilst eating it my son please don't use the word 'snot' in my hearing snot nice I deplore having used it smells disgusting take it to the loo if you must burn incense," they said.

"Hey, fellas!" Mrs. Livingston interrupted. "These girls have brought you a special present."

The Beatles nodded and mumbled sleepily. George Harrison yawned. Ruth and Sunny had decided they must return everything they'd taken from the suits except one relic too precious to relinquish. Now they stepped forward and emptied their purses onto the table before the group. Out tumbled guitar picks, chewing gum, half a cigarette, a little box of perfumed incense papers, a ballpoint pen, and a sticker that said "I Still Love The Beatles."

"It's from your pockets," Ruth said.

"Are you thieves or magicians?" George Harrison asked. He lit one of the incense papers, and they began talking about the explosion during their Memphis show.

"You know how George is The Quiet One, I'm The Bigmouthed One, et cetera," John Lennon told Jay Blue. "We were looking around to see who was going to be The Dead One." And Jay Blue told them about a friend of his in the music business who'd been shot in the chest. Doctors had removed half the bullet and left the other half in his heart, and now he was fine. He just had some tear duct problems.

"Perhaps we shouldn't have called our record *Revolver*," George said, twiddling his thumbs.

"You know the old saying. Those who live by the song, die by the song," Mrs. Livingston put in.

John Lennon looked up, aware of her for the first time.

"My husband was musically inclined," Mrs. Livingston continued. "He was shot in the arm during Prohibition."

"Has Prohibition ended?" John asked.

Mrs. Livingston chose that moment to produce the Sister City petition. The quartet picked up pens, and John was about to sign when the TV began to report on anti-Beatle demonstrations in the South. "They're burning my book," he said.

"Shame on them!" Mrs. Livingston seized the "I Still Love The Beatles" sticker, licked it, and pressed it onto the petition folder. "There! That'll show them!"

John blinked slowly. Ruth thought it might have been the first time he'd blinked in several years. He said something to the others in a dialect that even she, with her scholarly knowledge of the Scouse language, could not translate. Then Paul McCartney hit the stop botton on Jay Blue's recorder, and they all started to speak in a rich mishmash of code that seemed to be their native tongue. Their press agent, sensing a change in atmosphere, came charging over. "Get Brian," John told him. And the Beatles fell silent.

"Well, a lot of people still love you," Mrs. Livingston assured them. "It's not just us."

George, Paul, and Ringo lowered their eyes demurely. John gnawed delicately at his index finger. At last Ringo spoke. "We're very fond of you, too," he said, and with his words, some hidden signal seemed to pass between the four, a vibration more enigmatic than a glance. Yes, we loove you too, they insisted. We loove you too!

"That's good," Mrs. Livingston said, grabbing the petition. "It was nice meeting you fellas, but we don't want to wear out our welcome—"

No! the Beatles shouted, and the force of their voices almost knocked Ruth's contacts off her eyes.

What's your name? Paul McCartney inquired gently of her mother. Yes, which one are you? John Lennon added.

"Annie. I'm the sensible one, and these two"—she nodded toward Ruth and Sunny—"are the dreamy ones."

"And what can the Beatles do for Annie and the Dreamers?" John asked with a pleasant smile. Yes, what can we do, would you like a cup of tea? the others echoed. And it was as if they'd morphed from petulant pop stars to solicitous male nurses, custodians of perfect love.

"Well, if we're staying, could somebody make these girls a peanut butter and jelly sandwich?" Mrs. Livingston said. "They haven't had a thing to eat all day." Ruth tried to kick her mother discreetly.

"Would you care for some macadamia nuts?" Paul McCartney said, tearing the cellophane from a gift basket piled high with exotic produce. Their manager, Brian Epstein, arrived then, looking impeccable yet flustered. He asked them to wait in the vestibule while he conferred with the boys.

"Gosh, Mrs. L., you've got the Beatles wrapped around your little finger," Sunny gasped as soon as they were alone.

"Listen to this," Ruth said, opening *Typee*. " 'The natives, actuated by some mysterious impulse . . . redoubled their attentions to us. Their manner towards us was unaccountable . . . Why this excess of deferential kindness, or what equivalent can they imagine us capable of rendering them for it?' " She gave them an astonished glance.

"I was kind of surprised myself," her mother admitted, "by how grateful they were that we still love them. I guess everyone needs a kind word. Then they all started speaking in Gaelic or Liverpuddle or something—"

Brian Epstein returned. His eyebrows met in a furrowed point. He cleared his throat and said there had been a slight mishap. Apparently some medicine of John's had been affixed to the back of the "I Still Love The Beatles" sticker that Mrs. Livingston had licked. This medicine, lysergic acid diethylamide, was used to enhance creativity. Thus, it could have disquieting effects. One could expect to feel rather odd. One could expect visions, hallucinations—

"You mean it's like someone put a Mickey in my drink?" Mrs. Livingston interrupted.

"Rather."

Nothing scared Ruth's mother more than an unquiet mind. "Listen, I'm not the creative type," she said. "I've never had a vision in my life! I don't believe in visions." Then all her bluster faded. She clutched her throat with a trembling hand. "I'm a registered nurse, and I never heard of any medicine being administered on a sticker."

"But you haven't practiced in thirty years," said Ruth. "Times change."

"Quite," said Brian Epstein. "This drug makes one highly suggestible. Whatever your companions suggest becomes your reality. But you musn't fret. You are amongst friends. The boys and I would like you to join our entourage tonight so that you might be in the safest, indeed the happiest, indeed the most—" he searched for the ideal hyperbole "—fabulous place on earth."

"Where is that, Mist-Mist-Mr. Epstein?" Sunny wondered.

"The Beatles' dressing room." And his eyes fluttered briefly, involuntarily, heavenwards. "Please." He adjusted his cravat. "I implore you. Do not share this with reporters."

"Don't be a snitch, that's my motto," Ruth's mother said. "Nobody likes a tattletale."

"Quite."

"Is this drug habit-forming?" she asked.

"On the contrary." And Brian Epstein smiled benignly, glad to be the bearer of good news at last. "You might wish never to take it again."

And so they had been driven by limo to Shea Stadium, escorted to the locker room, and abandoned in that windowless bunker. The lockers were painted gunmetal-gray, a few benches and folding metal chairs were the only furnishings. "Are we buried alive?" Mrs. Livingston asked.

Ruth was distraught. The Beatles had terrified her. Their god-like confidence brought out her awkwardness. She'd been crushed by their surliness, confused by their kindness. Worst of all, they'd been too busy doting on her mother to notice her existence. She missed the cell-like safety of her room. Yet she could not quit until she had given them her gift. This might be her only chance to achieve the metaphysical-physical contact of her dreams.

"Are you all right?" she asked her mother. Mrs. Livingston looked a little wild-eyed.

"This must be the dreariest place on earth," her mother said.

Ruth browsed through *Typee* in search of a soothing passage. " 'When I looked around the verdant recess in which I was buried, and gazed up to the summits of the lofty eminence that hemmed me in, I was well disposed to think that I was in the "Happy Valley," and that beyond those heights there was nought but a world of care and anxiety—' " Footsteps. Her pulse quickened. Her contacts were dirty. She was seeing everything through the oily shimmer her optometrist called spectacle blur. When the Beatles came sprinting in—day of daze!—each was haloed by his own greasy rainbow.

"How are you feeling, all right?" Paul asked her mother.

"I'm feeling kind of"—the Beatles leaned forward, attentive—"creative. I want to hold your—" She paused, distracted by their raised eyebrows.

"Hand?" Paul suggested.

"Guitar," her mother said, and he obligingly extended his

Hofner bass. "No, not that little one. I want to hold that big one," she said, pointing to a sunburst Epiphone Casino in the corner. George brought it over and began trying to teach her a chord. Are you the orphaned one? she asked. No, I'm The Lonely One, he told her. His guitar made an empty thunking sound when she strummed it. "Gee, this is harder than I thought. Don't you fellas have to practice?"

"All we have to practice is smiling," John said. He took a long drag on a hand-rolled cigarette.

"Are those roofers you're smoking?" The air was thick with rank, weedy fumes. Before he could answer she said, "Do you know these girls are your biggest fans?" Ruth froze, her shame revealed.

"No, but hum a few bars and I'll fake it," said John.

"That's an old one."

"We're old at heart." He rubbed his sideburn reflectively.

"You do seem kind of tired for young fellas."

"We had to perform twice on Sunday," Paul explained. "In Cincinnati and St. Louis. We had a contract." And he squinched his face into a frown.

"Well, don't be making any more contractions," Mrs. Livingston commanded. "Take a rest."

"Say, that's a good idea!" Paul said, in a fine imitation of Jay Blue. Once again, some unspoken agreement buzzed between the four, and they fell into a pensive silence.

"Cheer up, boys!" Mrs. Livingston said, springing to her feet. Then, to Ruth's horror, her mother began to do the dance they called her Routine: a high-spirited cancan with kicking Rockette variations performed to her own sung accompaniment. Ruth knew it well.

"Mom, stop," she pleaded. But the Beatles were yielding little ironic smiles. Ringo started clapping, and George began to play along. Julia, Paul said. Julia was John's mother, who'd died when he was a teenager. Every fan knew that. Ruth felt sullen with envy. She wanted to rise into the Beatles' consciousness, if only for a minute, but even in close proximity it seemed impossible. Her mother kept getting in her way.

At last Mrs. Livingston stopped prancing, out of breath. "Now why don't you sing to us?" she asked.

"They can't," Ruth said quickly. "They can't sing now."

"Course we can sing," said Paul. "Don't believe everything you read."

John wearily picked up an acoustic guitar. He strummed the first chords of "Anna," an oldie about a girl who'd come and asked him to set her free. He changed the name to Annie, in honor of Mrs. Livingston, and sang that all his life he'd been searching for a girl to love him, but every girl he ever had broke his heart and left him sad, what was he supposed to do? And the other Beatles chorused "like his mum," "I deplore," and "drink my sweat." After a verse or two, John forgot the words and the song broke down.

It's now or never, Sunny whispered. *Typee*. George was closest, so Ruth thrust the book at him. "It's about sailors held captive by a group of man-eating cannibals," she said.

"The fans would devour us if they could." He nibbled on his guitar pick. "It's because they love us. And it's the thought that counts."

"This is a first edition. It belonged to Herman Melville." She paused for effect. "You can have it."

"I don't want it," he said, handing it back. "It'll only get lost or left behind. It'll only get ruined." The room whirled. Her fears were realized, her gift rejected. "Try John," George added quickly. "His father was a sailor."

The walk across the room to John Lennon seemed long and fraught with obstacles. This book is set on a remote island where there's no religion or possessions, no greed or hunger, she began. He listened to her ragged exegesis with half-closed eyes, impassive as a Buddha. Then he opened *Typee* and read aloud.

"'Her manner convinced me that she deeply compassionated my situation, as being removed from my country and friends, and placed beyond the reach of all relief.'" He stopped and stared off into space.

"Can I ask you something? Ruth said. Everyone else was across the room, admiring her mother's earrings.

"Sure," he said. "Shoot."

"What would you do if you were in love with someone who didn't know you were alive?"

"Love really tears us up, doesn't it?" He paused. The pause was delicious, eloquent. "But we always get another chance."

The other Beatles were taking their stage suits out of the lockers. They called John over, then George spoke up. "We have to put out the lights so we can change," he said. For a second, Ruth imagined them assuming another identity, like Gregor Samsa turning into a bug. "You won't be upset now, will you? We won't be long. Just stay put." He asked her to work the lights, and she nodded, feeling a new sense of power.

The Beatles hummed and whistled like a human meadow as they dressed, and the darkness amplified their chirping and rustling. They shouted reassurances—We still loove you, Annie!—and in no time at all, they called for the lights. But Ruth must have lost her bearings because she could not find the switch. She stroked the cinderblocks and shuffled to the left, groping blindly. Then she tripped over a guitar cord and crashed against a texture she knew well. A suit of summer wool, now sculpted into three dimensions. Her previous experience of the Beatles had been so flat, so limited to pictures and screens, that the depth and breadth of this actual body felt almost wrong. She clung like a barnacle, nonetheless. Now that she had him, she would not let him go. And instead of pulling away, he stood patiently, perhaps resignedly, in an attitude of forbearance, emitting an aura of—was it possible?—understanding. His face felt gritty as a beach, and through his shirt she heard the rock-solid four-four of his heart and an ambient hum like damaged nerves. "Let there be light!" her mother called. "Quick, before I have a vision!" His hair sifted through her fingers then like salt dissolving, silky with escape. And she let him go.

She found the switch, and by the time her eyes adjusted, the Beatles looked perfectly composed. John, Paul, and George had assumed their guitars like shields. Only Ringo had nothing to hide behind. How do we look? he asked.

"Like stars," Mrs. Livingston said with satisfaction. "Like brothers. Like you should."

John, meanwhile, was searching his pockets. Now he held up an "I Still Love The Beatles" sticker for all to see.

"Mine is missing," Paul said. "And there was nothing funny about mine."

"You mean—she didn't take that drug?" said Ruth.

"Looks like your trip is over before it's begun," George told her mother.

Then Neil flung the door open, and a noise like a force of nature rushed in. John gave *Typee* to the road manager for safekeeping. The PA system boomed, "Now . . . the Beatles!" And they were gone. Ruth, Sunny, and Mrs. Livingston hurried out onto the field to watch them play. Flashbulbs splashed the night as John launched into "Twist and Shout," his legs braced like a sailor's on a tossing ship. Brian Epstein stood near second base, nervously chewing gum on the downbeat. Ruth was struck by how solitary the Beatles looked onstage, on their private island of fame. If a string broke or an amp exploded, if they needed a drink or felt unwell, there was no one to help them. They were at the mercy of the fans and police. For thirty minutes, the Beatles were the loneliest people on earth.

One of Mrs. Livingston's earrings fell off, and she pitched it at the stage. Sunny, meanwhile, was screaming Be-Be-Be-Beatles! Rah-rah-rah-Ringo! Ruth had kept one item from their pockets, a scrap from a cigarette pack. Now she dug this second-class relic from the depths of her purse. "Rich Choice" was printed on one side, a set list of songs handwritten on the other. She crushed it and tossed it toward the stage like an offering, a flower over a burial at sea.

"Those Beatles work a short shift, don't they?" Mrs. Livingston said. The parking lot was covered with tickets like fallen leaves. Sunny spotted a taxi with a model of a yellow submarine secured to its roof, and the driver said he'd take them to the city as soon as he had a full cab. He had one other passenger already, an older girl with a Beatle haircut, wearing a dress made from the Union Jack. A pin identified her as PaulMichelle, a stringer for *Teenbeat*. Enjoy yourselves, ladies? the cabbie asked.

"We had the time of our lives," Mrs. Livingston said. "The Beatles autographed our petition."

"No," Ruth corrected. "John never signed."

"Well, you gave him your book," her mother said proudly.

The driver checked the moorings of the yellow sub on his roof. "I want to shake the hand that shook the hand of John Lennon," he said to Ruth.

"Gosh, Ru, your hand's become a second-class relic," said Sunny.

"We didn't shake hands."

"But he sang to us. And George let me play his guitar," her mother boasted.

The *Teenbeat* stringer looked skeptical.

"It's true, PaulMichelle," Sunny said. "The Beatles really liked her. They thought she was—"

"Swell," Mrs. Livingston interrupted. "The Beatles thought I was swell. And they were nice, too. I felt like I'd known them forever."

"So what are those guys really like?" the driver asked.

"Not what you'd expect," Ruth's mother said. "They seemed

old as the hills. Believe me, those boys are century plants. Those boys were born old."

"But what were they *like*?" PaulMichelle persisted.

"Real regular and down-to-earth. They were so ordinary! That's what I loved about them."

"Ordinary!" Ruth scoffed. "Little do you know." Was it possible to love someone, with the love the Beatles sang in their close harmonies, without ever knowing that person?

"Well, I know one thing," her mother asserted. "Paul explained the hidden symbolicism of that Eleanor song to me."

" 'Eleanor Rigby'! What is it?" Sunny asked.

"I—uh—I can't remember. It was very hidden. But he told me, he explained it all."

"C'mon, Ma. Try to remember. It's important."

"It was something about lonely people. Where they come from, where they belong. There's a priest in it, a loner who never connects with Eleanor. They never get to know each other, then she dies, and it's too late. They're like two ships that pass in the night."

"That's not hidden," said Ruth. "That's really obvious."

Then PaulMichelle started talking about a relative of hers who had emigrated to Liverpool many moons ago and met the real Eleanor Rigby. This relative had revealed the secret meaning of the song to her. In fact, PaulMichelle considered herself an expert on the boys, for she had traveled with the tour since Boston, almost a week, and Neil had given her two of John's guitar picks, which she'd had made into earrings, see? And she shook her head to make them swing.

"Who was your favorite, Mrs. L.?" Sunny asked.

Ruth felt her mother weighing her answer. "George," she said finally. "I liked George Harrison best."

"But George is The Spiritual One," Ruth argued. "He's not your type at all. What about the two motherless boys? What about John and Paul?"

"George has a mind of his own. He calls a spade a spade, and I admire that. George was my favorite Beatle. But my favorite guy is Neil. Neil has dreamboat eyes."

"John, Paul, George, and Neil!" Ruth exclaimed in disgust.

"Who did you like the best, Hon?" Mrs. Livingston asked Sunny.

"Paul's her favorite," Ruth said quickly.

"Paul is All," agreed PaulMichelle.

But Sunny twirled a strand of her long dark hair. "There was something about Ringo."

"Paul," Ruth said firmly.

"Remember when the others put on their guitars, and Ringo had nothing but his drumsticks? He looked so unprotected. I guess that's when I fell for him. And now that I've met him," Sunny continued, "I think Jay Blue is kind of cute."

"I don't get you," Ruth said. Stars were easier to understand. Celebrities on elevated stages illuminated by giant lights, who could be resurrected anytime at will within your head.

"Who was *your* favorite, Ru?" Sunny asked.

Headlights from buses pierced the warm August darkness. Ruth saw Jay Blue standing alone by the WTRY Beatle Buggy, dabbing at his eyes under his sunglasses.

"I'm not sure," she said. Her favorite was the one who'd understood her wish for contact in the dark. But if she lived to be a hundred, she'd never know for certain who that was.

She felt her mother scrutinizing her. "Those fuzzy blond hairs under your chin," Mrs. Livingston said. "I never noticed them before. I have those, too. My own!"

And she seized Ruth in a bone-crushing hug. It was the first maternal embrace Ruth could remember, and she endured it stoically, amazed to be touched by this stranger, her mother.

CENTRALLY ISOLATED

Edna Garrahan Kelly O'Keefe

A S A GIRL, I decided to be happy. I took a vow of happiness, the way nuns take vows of chastity. Instead of Edna, my given name, Mother called me O-Be-Joyful, and I tried to live up to it. My first husband died in World War II and my second was a professional traveler, but I wouldn't let this get me down. I resolved to be glad, and a strong will was something my sister Charlotte understood.

Our little niece called her Girldedrawers and snapped her elastic while she did the dishes, and Charlotte was a good sport about this, same as she was about Miss Law, the owner of the Puritan Restaurant, who garnished her salary to stay in business, or Ray Northrup, the old flame who stole her heart and got away. It seemed she was forever taking buses to do for others, forever dragging on some errand of mercy. Yet there was no bitterness about her, only a slightly dazed graciousness, soothing as the churchy smell of a burning candle. It was hard to believe we were sisters, our dispositions were so different. Charlotte's was a life of sacrifice, while I was more dog in the manger. Take the time she borrowed my dress and I chased her around the kitchen table with an ice pick!

Her house was on my bus route, and I got in the habit of stopping by after work. She'd say Hi Stranger, and we'd talk about the Watergate cover-up or the new bridge that was supposed to lure people back to Troy. The first time I visited, we sat in the living room, and she served us ice cream and pie on blue willoware with divisions that kept the food from touching. I was working in the Troy High cafeteria, and it felt strange to be waited on after serving the kids all day. There was a ledger on the end table next to me, a little account book where my sister figured her relatives' taxes. It was held open by a glass paperweight that magnified her handwriting, the numbers delicate as seedlings. They were kindly-looking numbers somehow, tended with such awful care.

In her youth, Charlotte had been courted by a boy from a well-to-do family, but the romance fizzled after a trip to Connecticut to meet his people. Nobody knew exactly what happened. Don't say anything! someone would say when anything unmentionable was mentioned. *Speech is silver, but silence is golden.* That might have been our family motto. Shush was the family code, almost a form of courage, so she had to pretend the whole affair had been nothing serious. My sister Annie thought Ray Northrup's Protestant family wouldn't let him marry a Catholic, but my guess is Charlotte didn't want to live far away with strangers. She wanted to be with her own. She came home and worked as a waitress, and Ray always called on her birthday, till gradually his devotion became a source of pride, a little victory in my sister's life.

Otherwise, there's no denying, time took a lot out of her. A doctor performed a hysterectomy during her childbearing years, and a dentist pulled all her teeth. She developed arthritis and was almost forty when she married Ward Willoughby, a dead ringer for Popeye, except Ward did not dance hornpipes or sing chanteys. There was nothing jovial about him. He was as uncouth as my sister was refined. She said on their wedding night, he'd filled his mouth with peanut butter and squeezed it into hers when they kissed. He thought that was a scream. Ward had been sinfully abused as a child, and my sister always had a soft spot for a hard case. Instead of love, she must've had pitiful feelings for him. That's all I can think. She called him Itch, and he called her Girdledrawers, same as our little niece.

Ward lived to torment. Like, if he knew a kid was scared of spaceships, he'd say they go over so regular we set our watches by them, or if a child's pet turtle died, he'd say he'd cooked it into the soup she was eating. When our little niece, Ruth, was afraid to use the lavatory at school, Ward told her if she held it in too long, it would rise higher and higher, till it came out her eyes, ears, nose, and mouth. And once when his eighty-year-old sister visited, they argued and he gave her the bum's rush, knowing full well she'd be stranded at the end of his driveway with no way home to Pennsylvania. Charlotte had to call a cab to take her to the bus station. They had this marriage of inconvenience, you see, where my sister's part was drying tears and mopping up the blood.

Ward always had some messy project cooking in the cellar, in what Charlotte called the beatnik room. His hobbies got on her nerves, for she was neat as a hospital corner, but when he started the beeswax candle business, I noticed she liked to polish the tapers with a piece of old silk. She said the candles were so hard to make that she hated to see them burn, but burning was the best test of quality, and so she tried to give them the ideal conditions for this.

Her worries increased when Mother, on her deathbed, asked her to take care of our sister Dorothy, whose mind kept striking up a tune all its own. Charlotte spent her waitress savings to knock down walls and make Dorothy's living room bigger; she collected Green Stamps so Dorothy could trade them at the redemption center for a sunburst clock or pop-it pearls. But nothing worked, and she had to look on at a loss while her sister was put to sleep or shocked, and her promise to Mother crumbled. Then our brother Joe came down with cancer, and daily visits to intensive care added to Charlotte's discouragement. She said she only wished the nurses would not read Joe his get-well cards full of fakey bounce and brightness; she only hoped he would not kill himself.

One evening around this time she picked up the paper and learned her great friend Miriam had died in a terrible house fire, and thinking to buck herself up, Girdledrawers (for over time we all got used to this pet name) went out and bought a crushed velvet recliner she had admired. But after it was delivered, she found the fabric reminded her of nothing so much as a casket's lining, and from this, she recognized self-pity setting in and told herself to stop meowing and think of those who had it worse. Before Joe got sick, she'd recorded him whistling "Somewhere My Love," to capture his beautiful tone, and though she couldn't bear to listen to the tape after he died, she often hummed the tune, which seemed to give her hope.

You can understand why her old flame's annual phone call became a little oasis. And one year something extra happened. An unsigned birthday card arrived, bearing a Stamford, Connecticut postmark. My sister showed it to me shyly, trembling with pent-up pride. A dimestore card, with a little green bow. She said Ray must have recalled green was her favorite color, and she'd like to cook him dinner, just to thank him for all the wonderfulnesses over the years. Since the card was unsigned, she felt she shouldn't mention it when he called, and I agreed. Don't say anything! I said, and we laughed like conspirators, like old times, before hopes were dashed and heartaches began.

After this, an unsigned card arrived every year. Each time, I could feel my sister's anticipation followed by her little burst of hope fulfilled. She'd shake her head and wonder that Ray remembered and go over his thank you menu. It was to be her famous candlelit Christmas dinner, featuring plum pudding with genuine hard sauce she'd set on fire at the table.

Her husband Ward, meanwhile, had retired from his iron-working job in order to devote himself to the candle business full-time. He started using paraffin, a crude petroleum product, and concentrating on novelties—pillars made with ice cubes that left holes as they melted, or his special EKG tapers. For these, he'd copy your electrocardiograph on a candle that would burn at both ends while suspended horizontally by a loop. He thought it was a sure thing for Valentine's Day because of the heart connection. He even applied for a patent.

But my sister didn't like these newfangled candles. Over the years, she'd gotten to know the personality of beeswax, and now her learning had no use. She said beeswax, though costly, was the ideal candle material because of its ability to vaporize and burn with a bright, steady flame. Apparently there were people who could tell the history of a piece of beeswax from the texture of a break and the released fragrance, though this was a dying skill.

Ward didn't have much luck with his paraffin candles anyway, due to the hippie competition, and he had to try another livelihood. After many false assaults, he at last settled on the wrongest job possible. He decided to be a clown. Charlotte said he wanted to be a clown in the worst way, and so she gave up trying to wean him off it, even though it meant she had to listen to the legal implications of pie-throwing and splatting and sloshing techniques for hours on end. Worst of all, a famous, successful clown had created a character called Grandma, and from this, Ward got the idea of calling his clown Girdledrawers. Naturally, my sister hated to see her good name robbed and ridiculed. I told her nobody would hire a would-be miserable clown like Ward, but before you could say Bojangles, the Bloodmobile had asked him to get the show rolling, and soon he was booked for the Home School Association's Bake Sale, the BOCES Cosmetology Ball, and the Ding-a-Ling Bluebirds' Fly-up Ceremony. Charlotte didn't go to these events, but she must've gotten wind of them.

Then one morning while all this clowning was going on, Ward phoned to say he could not wake my sister up. She was remanded to the Good Samaritan, where they declared a coma of unknown origin, and though nothing scares me more than hospitals and sickness, I went to visit her posthaste. In the past I'd managed to keep my vow of happiness by accentuating the positive, but there wasn't much to go on in her semiprivate room. I looked through the bed bars at Girdledrawers, still in a doze, so thin she hardly disturbed the sheets. It was like finding something delicate, maybe a rose petal, wrapped up in butcher paper. Her homemade pantsuit ("sunburst-darted with a graceful fencer's look," according to the pattern—we'd laughed) was slumping on a hanger, her best blue nylon tricot pajamas were folded neatly on the dresser, and I felt the helplessness of these impersonal effects. My sister Annie must have brought these things over, along with Charlotte's birthday cards. She'd turned seventy last week.

I was looking at the biggest, sparkliest, most anonymous card of all when Ward appeared. I mentioned my sister's sad condition and ventured that she might not be getting enough of the sunshine vitamin, D, but he kept glaring at the card from who-knows-who and finally interrupted to say that after his clown show that evening, he would drive to Connecticut and tell Ray Northrup to get lost in person.

Well, the time to nip dangerous trends is in the bud. Thinking to talk him out of this awful plan, I said I'd like to see his act. He must have been flattered because he offered me a lift, and we set off in his Plymouth Fury. Ward talked about clown stuff—slow burns, pratfalls, blow-offs, how to give and take a slap—when he wasn't cussing at the other drivers. I said I felt bad about having a good time while my sister was so sick, and he said the show must go on. Honestly, you would have thought he was booked for Ed Sullivan instead of the Melrose Grange.

When we got there, the senior citizens' dinner was in full swing. Another man was performing a vocal number, "Beautiful Garden of Prayer," with a pantomime accompaniment. As soon as he quit singing, Ward appeared in his Girdledrawers regalia. He'd taken out his teeth and put on a pair of long johns topped by a rubber foundation garment with garters that flapped when he ran. This orange-pink girdle, meant to resemble flesh, reminded me of guts and trusses and made me think how much women's underwear had in common with medical restraints. A cheap plastic rain bonnet and an old pocketbook of my sister's completed his outfit. A pink dustpan, a glass of water, and a book of matches were the only props.

As I suspected, Ward was a cruel clown. He grabbed the wig right off one lady's head and mocked my sister's neat little housewife habits. I felt she was being ransacked while I stood by and was filled with dismay. At one point he said I bet you can't light a fire underwater and struck a match and held the drinking glass over it, and those old people must have been starved for laughs because they hee-hawed and applauded.

That was really something, I told him afterwards in the parking lot. I was mad as heck but still hoping to butter him up and talk him out of tracking down Ray Northrup. I mentioned the unsigned cards, saying how much they'd meant to my sister, but the more I stressed her pleasure, the wilder it made Ward. He said Ray Northrup thought he was a big shot just because he was a bank president. He called Ray a wiseguy and said he hated a wiseguy almost as much as he hated a buttinsky. I ignored this crack, but as he ranted, I realized my cause was lost, and with much reluctance and many a deep breath, I told a secret I had kept for nigh on sixteen years.

I sent them, I said. I went on to explain how long ago I'd asked my husband, a Trailways bus driver, to mail a birthday card to Charlotte, and in my hurry, I forgot to sign it, and as luck would have it, he mailed it in Stamford, Connecticut, which was on his route. When I saw how much that darn card meant, I didn't have the nerve to tell my sister the truth. She had been so wrapped up in the troubles of others—so busy paying for her niece's three-tiered graduation gown and college eduation—that her brow was perpetually creased with care. And that card made her happy. It made her so happy that I sent another one the same way the year after. And the year after that. Each time, I seemed to pick a mushier, fancier greeting. And so it went, for over a decade.

As soon as this confession left my lips I regretted it. I wanted to grab the words back out of the air. Ward looked bewildered for an instant, but he must have figured I was not the lying type. You don't say, he remarked, trying to be nonchalant. My bus showed up then (he had not offered me a ride home) and all I could do was ask him not to tell a soul.

When I visited my sister the next day, I found her awake but not out of the woods. They'd taken her false teeth, making her look like an old Granny. Her feet were a cold blue, but the blue of her eyes was warm as wax. The oxygen must have made her giddy, for she kept saying she'd been the best in her class at sums. Then she imagined she was in the basement, making candles. A broken taper cannot be mended, our supplies are limited, she said. She seemed to think there were people in the corner, putting things into boxes on an assembly line. They aren't our family, and they aren't our friends, she whispered. This was followed by words I couldn't catch, and when I asked, she said, Edna, you know who Itch is. There's only one Itch.

Ward arrived a minute later and started in about Watergate,

calling Nixon a great statesman. You haven't been right in thirty years, my sister told him, don't just stand there, make her a Tom Collins. I had to laugh, though I was feeling terrible about the truth I'd shared with him. I kept thinking what a disappointment it would be for Girldedrawers to learn her secret admirer was me. As I was leaving, her mind returned to candles. "Three wicks braided will give a great flame," she said. "Slap honey over the burn and it will heal with no scar."

She was released shortly after, but every so often from then on she'd go to sleep and not wake up. The doctor said it might be something to do with the carotid artery and arthritis and smoking. Whatever it was, it scared the daylights out of us. To add to the awfulness, Ward's mental makeup started flaking and his crankiness increased. He told my sister Annie she could not turn around in his driveway when she dropped Charlotte off. Then he sent her a mean letter that began "Dear Boss Lady" and ended by saying he would not allow her to come to his funeral. Of course, we all laughed at this. Only Ward would suppose that being barred from his funeral was the worst possible punishment.

In between calamities I'd retired, and so I didn't happen by my sister's house as often. One humid, heavy afternoon, I decided to pay her a visit on my way home from the city. I found her more low-key than usual. Instead of busying around, dusting or making us a lunch, she sat staring at the new curio cabinet where she stored her birthday cards. She'd told me how Ward had wanted the cabinet in Traditional Toledo Gold, while she'd wanted an Early American Nutmeg finish. Now I saw Toledo Gold had won. I tried talking about the returning POWs and the high cost of meat, but she didn't seem interested. Next I tried the wicked hot weather. Still, I could not rouse her.

You don't know who to believe, she finally mumbled. You don't know who your friends are. Since we both were students of the less-said-the-better school, I had to piece what happened from dropped hints. It seemed like Ward had caught her fussing over her old birthday cards, and she'd mentioned her idea of inviting Ray Northrup for Christmas dinner. I could imagine Ward's scowl at this. Like his hero Richard Nixon, my sister's husband got up in the morning just to confound his enemies. It scared me to think of the secret I'd shared with him. By telling him about the cards, I'd given him the power to spoil her little happiness. And any havoc he didn't wreak right now would be put on layaway, I was sure. Mostly, I was ashamed of how I'd misled my sister, and I dreaded what was coming.

But whatever Charlotte knew and felt, she would not say. She only said Ward had told her he was going to do his Girdledrawers act on community TV that afternoon. Naturally, she did not want this. She had demanded back the things he'd taken from her: the plastic rain bonnet, rubber girdle, pocketbook, and dustpan. Oh no, Lady Jane, he'd said. You bought that stuff with my money, and I'm entitled. I could picture him lording it over her while she tried to hold her ground. As the fight got worse, she said maybe they should split up, and he said no, they had to stay together to see whether they really hated each other. Finally, she'd stood in the doorway, trying to block his way, and that's when he'd claimed I'd seen his clown act and liked it.

"I was just trying to stay on his good side, palsy-walsy," I interrupted. "I wanted to part friends." I thought I could encourage her by laughing it off. I might have even winked. Then I remembered the macaroons I'd brought, her favorites, from Nelligan's Bakery. I gave her the bag and followed her into the kitchen, where somebody's half-eaten breakfast was laid out on the table—Wheaties, toast with jelly, an ashtray full of ash. These cookies need to be hospitalized, she said, putting them in the icebox. Her hand shook as she lit a cigarette and said she was all mixed up. She said she'd tried to do the Test Your Wits puzzle in the newspaper that morning only to find she couldn't understand one of the questions. It was "Intelligent people try to avoid (POISONS or PRISONS)." She then made the mistake of asking Ward's opinion. Now my sister had always had the upper hand because she was the smarter of the pair. I knew Ward would enjoy the chance to make her feel small. He must have enjoyed telling her that the doctor said her blackouts could cause brain damage.

"Oh, that's just big talk," I said, waving it away. But I was recalling how she'd barged in the neighbor's back door one day, mistaking this stranger's house for our sister Annie's. The neighbor had told Annie, and Annie told me. Charlotte never mentioned it. She had been visiting Annie on a weekly basis for more than thirty years, so it was an embarrassing faux pas. For some reason, I thought of her underwear made into a clown suit, the way Ward had turned her into a laughingstock in front of strangers. And I remembered the birthday cards I'd sent, the sly way I'd let her cherish a deceit. All our lives my sister and I had trusted one another. Our trust had been unspoken; that was the beauty of it. Now it seemed Charlotte, who'd only wanted our respect, had been dishonored in return for her good works. As this feeling hit me, the carefreeness I'd guarded for so long tottered on the brink of choked emotions my voice could not get past. And so my lips stayed sealed.

Words once spoken cannot be withdrawn, and that is why our entire family would say nothing about anything important. We never stopped to think that silence also can't be taken back. Silence smolders. The time that was supposed to heal all wounds never came. Instead, there came a phone call. I was eating Freihofer's golden molasses cookies at the kitchen table when it came. It's Girdledrawers, Ward said, and for a second I thought he meant his clown. She's all burned, he said. She's gone. I heard the tears in his voice, and the horrible dawning on me began.

What had happened? It seemed he'd gone out on an errand, and when he got back, he found her in the cellar. I'd talked to her only that morning; she'd told me she was going to wash her hair. Now she was all burned, now she was gone. I'd never heard of such a thing. In shock, I called a taxi and rushed outside to wait.

As an RN, my sister Annie was the obvious choice in any health crisis, but she hadn't been home when Ward called. There was only squeamish me. My cab pulled in the driveway behind the ambulance, and I sat on the retaining wall, next to him. Neither of us said much. Tears oozed from his little blue eyes, but I was too agog and aghast to weep. The coroner talked privately with Ward, then asked to speak with me alone. We sat at the picnic table out back. It was a lovely April day. He asked about my sister's state of mind and health, and I waited for him to ask about her marriage, but he only wanted to know what kind of hose she wore, whether her stockings were nylon or cotton. He told me all about how nylon melts while cotton burns, like this was important.

When he stopped talking, I asked point-blank what happened. Suicide, he said. Well, I could not believe it. I can't believe it, I said. Are you sure? It would not sink in. It was so unlike my sister to do anything untidy, let alone violent. I'd heard of Buddhist nuns turning themselves into human torches, but not my sister. I'd been thinking someone murdered her. I even suspected Ward, though I wouldn't say this. I stayed in back, at the picnic table, till the ambulance left. I didn't want to go anywhere near my sister. It was like she'd suddenly changed into something contaminated, inhuman and fearsome.

I dreaded the job of telling others. My niece Ruth, a college student, argued with me about the cause of death. You don't have to believe it, I told her. I wasn't going to try to convince anybody. Let them spare themselves.

The undertaker encouraged us to have an open casket. He

probably thought seeing my sister peaceful would ease our terrible imaginings; he wanted us to reap the benefit of his skills,
get our money's worth. But we decided on closed and bought
a coffin massive and shiny as a new car. I pictured it hovering
above the open grave, suspended on machinery that would
lower it with a sound like wheels spinning in snow once the
mourners had gone home. The Church did not allow suicides
to be buried in consecrated ground, so our only hope was to
cover up what she had done and pray the priest would not be
nosy or a stickler.

We were in the windowless back room of the funeral parlor
when my niece asked to see the coroner's report. It held another
shock. Evidently, my sister had tried fire, and when that failed,
she'd taken poison. The autopsy had shown it. The report
described an old toiletry kit with arsenic in it, and I remembered Mother saying Aunt Kitty, who'd lived with us on the
farm when we were kids, ate a little ratsbane every day to
improve her complexion. It was an old beauty secret. Her ratty
heirloom must have fallen into my sister's hands somehow. After
she read the report, my niece apologized for arguing, and I felt
a petty sense of triumph, though I could not believe the findings myself.

They all offered me a ride home, but I insisted on taking the
bus. I usually looked forward to meeting old cronies, but tonight
I wanted to be alone. The route went over the Hudson River,
past the Puritan Restaurant where my sister had worked and
Lord & Tann where she'd bought her beautiful suits. All her old
haunts. Downtown Troy was mostly empty storefronts and
going-out-of-business signs. The Sweet Shoppe where she'd
met Ray Northrup was now a vacant lot.

I thought how the world had gone on, heedless, while she
was in her last agonies—the traffic had zoomed by, the sun went
on shining, the backyard birds kept twittering and tweetling,
and all of a sudden, I wanted to break those birds' necks. I didn't

know who to be mad at most or first. I talked to Charlotte in my head, saying *Why did you, how could you?* That she'd struggled so to die increased my appallment. Old, I felt, and heavy, as if my heart had gained weight. And not just my heart but my lungs and stomach, nerves and brain. As soon as I got home, I threw out the golden molasses cookies I'd been eating when Ward called. They'd had a bitter, baking soda taste under their sweetness.

The wake was a daze of handshakes and evasions in close, flowery air. Afterwards, my sister Annie's house was full of relatives and funeral food. I slept over so we all could go to the cemetery together in the morning, and it must have been around three a.m. when I was awoken by a scream ripping from my chest, up my neck and out my mouth—for I had seen her, seen my sister in the air above me, an arm's-length away, her chest and face alive in flames. I must have been sleeping with my eyes open. They were open when I saw her, that I know. The worst part was the hallucination had not been set in some never-never-nightmare-land. The setting was reality, the bedroom. Annie's house was small and everyone was very close, so I expected some family members to rush in, but after a minute, I realized no one was coming.

Had she looked wrathful? Stern? I wasn't sure. The impression was of massive suffering. Poor tormented soul! She had died without knowing that everyone her whole life through had felt nothing for her but stupid, tongue-tied love. I dwelled upon the unsigned birthday cards, thinking Ward could have told her I'd sent them to mock her. He could have said I was in cahoots with him, that we'd laughed behind her back these many years. I called her Dear Heart then, as I never had before, and the bed shook with my dumb sobs.

How would I ever sleep again? Or smile truly, without a ghost of remorse behind my smile? I tried to see her side. She'd witnessed our sister Dorothy's helpless breakdowns and would have done anything to avoid that fate. To be of no use, feeble-minded, ailing, unable to drive or take a bus, cooped up with Ward, at his mercy in solitary confinement in her centrally isolated home—the prospect must have been too much.

In the morning, I wondered whether I'd dreamt everything, including the scream, but Annie settled the matter by saying that she'd heard me. "I thought you yelled in your sleep, and I didn't want to wake you," she said, and I thanked her.

Fearing a stink from the Church, we'd decided to bury Charlotte in the Protestant cemetery. It was out in the back of beyond, far from our Catholic graveyard, which is why the hearse got lost and some of us missed the funeral. Afterwards, I wrote Ray Northrup. I didn't go into detail. I wanted him to assume she'd gone to sleep, like with her spells, and had not awoken.

Three months went by before I found the strength to sort through Charlotte's belongings. I decided to face this sad music on what would have been her seventy-second birthday. The mail came as I was leaving my house, so I brought it with me. Ward was out, but he'd left the door unlocked. I sat in the living room, half expecting my sister to appear and say Hi Stranger. As I glanced at my mail, I was surprised to see an envelope with a Stamford, Connecticut, postmark. More than surprised. It chilled me to the soul. I opened it carefully, with a kitchen knife, and found a sympathy card, "The End of the Road is But a Bend in the Road." Those words were printed on a bright yellow sky, and the poem went on for five pages. There also was a four-page note from Ray Northrup, saying how much he'd enjoyed calling my sister every year, and though he missed the chance to do so, it helped to share his feelings with me.

"Now, we must find that comfort we so deeply need to carry on throughout this life experience in knowing that we were Blessed in having had the privilege of having had a relative or friend of such a beautiful personality," he wrote. "The Love,

Happiness, Helpfulness, and Kindness she bestowed upon us in her lifetime can only be repaid to her memory by trying to live our lives as she did hers. I appreciate your communication to me which I re-read many times when I think about the fact"—and here his blue handwriting staggered and sank—"that nevermore can I look forward to her sincere good wishes for my welfare and future being. Fondly, Raymond."

I took the unsigned birthday cards from the curio cabinet and worked this new one under their rubber band. Then I set about packing my sister's few possessions away in boxes. I found some lovely lady things in an old hope chest: a blue silk kimono, an elegant cloche hat, an old fan covered with dance cards. And when I opened the linen closet to look for a dustrag, I discovered her candlemaking manual. Some passages had been underlined in pencil pale as a moth's wing: *the wick is the soul of the candle; a pillar must burn in peaceful air.*

I knew my sister's death had changed the future, the rest of my life, to be exact. Now I considered how, more mysteriously, her final act reached back and changed the past—since all her good deeds must be seen in its severe, remodeling light. As I sorted through her belongings, I half-hoped to find some word of explanation. But when I imagined what she might have said, I began to feel grateful that she hadn't left a note. I've come to think of it as her last gift to us. By not saying anything, she let us dream up our own consolations and forgiveness over time. Silence is so steadfast, you know. It is so ample, after all.

If It's Not Too Much to Ask

Ruth Livingston

FTER ARI LIECHENAUER ran his chastity belt through her dishwasher, Ruth Livingston told him he would have to find another place to live. Graduate students, she explained, did not camp out in their teachers' garages and use their appliances. Ari and his animals would have to go. After issuing this ultimatum, Ruth spent two days researching land-lords who allowed pets, while the melancholy student walked the bluebird trail behind her farmhouse. Sometimes, on her breaks, she'd happen upon him fast asleep in the meadow or gazing dreamily at the farmer's wheat fields tossing like a golden sea. In this setting, it was hard to disagree when Ari said the housing options she'd found were soulless enclaves of garish geranium landscaping and hollow core doors. What sort of place do you have in mind? Ruth asked. The student's glance took in a monarch feeding on the milkweed, a dragonfly shimmering on the cinquefoil. "Something like this would be fine," he said.

Over drinks at the picnic table, Ruth tried again to teach thirty-seven-year-old Ari the facts of student life. His lips, like those of certain purebred cats, curved in a perpetual smile that did not signal happiness. "You've been awarded our best fellowship," she began. He nodded. "You'll have money and time to write."

They were sitting near the old silo that presided over the grounds. Ruth thought she glimpsed a hunter's blaze-orange by the woodlot, but the bright blur stabilized into a stand of tiger lilies.

"Isn't that"—she searched for a neutral yet heartening word—"something?"

"I just feel so tired."

"Have you tried vitamins?"

"I've tried St. John's wort. Natural remedies." He glanced around. "Ideally, I'd like a place with no artificial fibers. I'm sensitive to outgassing."

She'd noticed that Ari liked to dress in costume. Today he was wearing a black scarf tied in a blousey bow, a Romantic affectation that reminded her of someone. Lord Byron?

"Ari, graduate students sometimes have to live in houses with—well, vinyl siding."

"Vinyl." His eyes filled.

"There are compensations," she said gently. "You'll have excellent health insurance. It even covers therapy."

"When I climbed the silo, I thought I saw some St. John's wort growing—over there." He pointed to the far side of the meadow.

"When did you climb—"

"The view was intoxicating." He grabbed a leaf from a nearby maple and wiped his nose on it.

"The silo is old. It can't support your weight."

"Geese flew over, close enough to touch. That's how I fell, trying to touch a goose."

"You fell from the silo? But your health insurance hasn't started yet—"

"I landed on my feet. At most I sprained an ankle."

Ruth grabbed her drink, and the coaster hit the table with a thud. "When did this happen?"

"It must have been after I almost drowned in the pond. I'm an excellent swimmer, but"—he yanked his jeans below his waist, revealing a metal dial fixed to a substantial leather belt— "This succubus"—he rattled the fittings—"pulled me down." Spikes of sun jumped from a lock that resembled a bank vault wheel in small. Ruth covered her eyes. The list of rental possibilities slipped from her grasp and scampered across the wildflowers. "It was an accident. Though to be perfectly honest, snuffing myself sometimes seems the best solution."

"No, Ari, no!" Ruth recognized the voice she used when her cat stuck his foot in the toaster. She softened her tone. "Think of Tristan and Isolde. Think of Robert Burns." These were his lovebirds and ferret, currently homesteading in her garage. "Consider your fish."

"This morning the ammonia levels in the water were alarmingly high. I can only guess that Robert Burns has been peeing in the tanks again."

"If I get you some vitamins, will you take them?"

"I can't swallow pills," he said wistfully, "unless they're very, very small. And then I tend to lose them. Like a child really."

"Then take children's vitamins. The chewable kind, shaped like zoo animals. Or we could pill you, like a cat." She pictured herself pushing his head back, prying his jaws open, tossing in the vitamins, closing his mouth, and stroking his throat till he swallowed. It made her laugh.

"I'm sorry, Ruth. You've been very patient."

"Ari, if you feel that way again, promise you'll talk to me."

"What way? Excuse me, Ruth, I'm having trouble hearing you."

The neighbors were decimating the farmer's crops with their dirt bikes, a B17 bomber droned by on its way to an air show, and Mr. Rubbish, the local garbage collection syndicate controlled by organized crime, purred and thrashed at the end of the driveway.

"Depressed," she said. "Suicidal."

He nodded. "Ruth, I keep forgetting. How long do I have?"

"It's a two-year program, but some students stay on as lecturers." She'd meant to present him with a nonnegotiable deadline by which he must be out, but this script was displaced by the image of him smiling from the bottom of the pond. She noticed that the weeping cherry had withered to a brown fountain overnight. Paper wasps floated around the silo's decaying mortar, and a sour smell drifted from its innards. The psychosis of the natural world oppressed her. Last year she'd placed one of the bluebird nesting boxes too close to the woodlot and their cerulean eggs had been ravaged by a flying squirrel. Now she saw a house sparrow perching on the barbed wire by one of the boxes. It clutched something—a used condom?—in its beak. A sparrow like that would peck a bluebird's skull apart. It would pluck out the fledglings' eyes and replace the bluebird's nest of fine grasses with its own slovenly odds and ends. The drab little bird flew in the box as she watched.

As a third-year tenure track assistant professor of American Literature and Imaginative Writing, Ruth Livingston spent each spring convincing twenty people to quit their jobs, give up their homes, forsake their loved ones, and travel hundreds of miles in hopes of improving their poetry.

When she first called Ari with the news of his fellowship, he said he'd like to accept, but his animals constituted a relocation hardship. A cousin could put him up once he arrived, but this relative had a fish allergy. Where could he leave the tanks and cages while he searched for an apartment? How about my garage? Ruth said.

"An offer like that / is some welcome mat," Ari rhymed.

"Is that a yes?"

"It isn't a yes and it isn't a no. It's a yo / it's a nes / it's a firm / more or less. I'd like to consult my keyholder."

Keyholder. That must be the latest slang for lover.

"One more question, Ruth. Do the MFA students have personal assistants?"

"They have faculty advisors. Close readers. They have time to write." She could think of no more comforting fact to impart to an almost-young almost-poet.

"An offer like that / makes my ego fat."

"Is that an acceptance?"

Her cat, Bartleby, was scratching at the door. As she inched around her desk to let him in, the phone cord snagged her unfinished book on Herman Melville, and the manuscript tumbled, piecemeal, to the floor.

" 'Look for me under your boot-soles,' " Ari said. "Whitman."

Bartleby curled up on the title page and began to drool.

"I worry about you out there alone," her mother said when Ruth called. "With those roughnecks across the road. It'd be okay if you had some company."

Virjinia, Ruth's partner, worked as an editorial supervisor in New York City. Once when Jinny was visiting, they'd seen a flag flying from the neighbor's garage. I think it's the Woodstock Nation banner. I think I see a peace sign, Ruth said, handing Jin the birdwatching binoculars. It says SKINHEAD MILITIA, Jinny pronounced at last. That peace sign is a skull and crossbones.

"Well, I won't be alone much longer," she told her mother. "A student will be keeping his pets in my garage." She wanted to hear that she'd done the right thing.

"People take advantage of you. You let them."

"It's my job."

"Job, phooey! It's your downfall. I thought you moved to that farm to get some peace. It's turning into a—a—"

"Animal shelter?" Ruth suggested. "Zoo?" Every year she spent hundreds of dollars on Havahart traps for kittens abandoned by students and delousing medicine for sweet-tempered beagles discarded by hunters. She'd tried to find homes for the kittens among her colleagues, but they wanted perfect specimens in rare colors—dilute calicos and chocolate points. They would not accept a tailless cat or one with extra toes. The craven beagles also were impossible to place. Her office mate explained that they were considered stupid, declassé dogs, and that these days everyone wanted a golden retriever.

"—A funny farm," her mother said.

"I think bees are nesting in the bedroom wall. Listen." Ruth pressed the receiver against the humming plaster while her mother's voice continued, tiny and distant, trapped inside the phone. Bartleby, meanwhile, began a rhythmic calling, craving attention. He spoke in chords rather than single tones. Ruth thought he sounded like two cats joined at the larynx.

A week later, she returned home from teaching to find Ari unloading his black mollies in her driveway. That day she'd taken her remedial summer session poetry writing class on a field trip to the State Prison Craft Fair. Her limited social resources were depleted from hours of smiling at felons. She drove by her farmhouse several times before she had the strength to face the new arrival. At last she pulled in and parked behind his hatchback. Mosquitoes whined outside the closed windows of her car, making her nostalgic for the insecticides of her childhood: environmentally hostile aerosols called Swat or White Flag. At the craft fair, she'd purchased a landscape by an inmate convicted of second-degree manslaughter. Now she placed her lesser acquisitions—hand-carved wooden roses, T-shirts that said 2 HOTS & A COT—on top of the painting and held it before her like a loaded tray as she approached the student.

"I think my biological filter just died," Ari greeted her. "And I might need to kick start the bacteria colony again."

"Oh," said Ruth. "I'm sorry."

"And I have a bad outbreak of whitespot in the planted tank." Ari was dressed as a health care professional. He tucked his long braid into the waistband of his seafoam-colored hospital scrubs.

"What is whitespot?"

"A parasite. I lost five pentazona barbs to it. Gods, I feel so guilty about all this. I really don't know what has gone wrong." He removed a gallon jug from his hatchback and set it on the ground.

"I once bought an angelfish because it looked so distraught in the pet store aquarium . . . ," Ruth said. She paused, arrested by the harness he was removing from the car. "Do you also have horses?"

Ari chuckled. "You refer to this, I think?" He held the appliance at arm's length. Its metal hoop and chains twinkled in the fading light. "My keyholder calls it 'stainless steel underwear.'"

Ruth cast about for another topic. The sensual high point of her day was the removal of her contact lenses. A tug at the lid, a blink, the little irritant gone. How she looked forward to it! "When did you become interested in—fish?"

"They were part of my decorating business. I placed aquariums in offices. Once I was asked to furnish the office of a certain hot scholarly commodity who required a personal meditation room in any color but blue, two air purifiers, fresh boxer shorts, cauliflower-free veggie trays, a director's chair, twelve bath-size towels, and bendy straws. He was a medievalist, so I added an ancient chastity belt as my own touch."

"Is this one old?"

"Verily. For everyday use, I prefer the modern ones, with no rough edges. What happened to your angelfish?"

"I put it in a goldfish bowl, and it committed suicide by jumping out."

Ari removed a cat carrier. "The angels are notoriously inbred. My advice is don't buy the sickly-looking ones out of pity. They will break your heart, guaranteed."

He left around midnight, and Ruth grabbed a flashlight and went out to inspect her garage. Aquariums gurgled against the walls, pet carriers stirred on the shelves, hooded birdcages dangled from the ceiling like ghostly chandeliers. An open book rested on an old church pew. Her beam lit up the words *Live Rock* next to a squirmy drawing and a diary entry: *Today it exploded with life. Worms, I think. An anemone and some creature that is very fast and maybe an inch long. Also, as I looked into the center through a little gap I saw pinsized critters swimming. I will ask Giselle. Of course, I was thrilled to find life in there after all of my disasters.*

"I'm worried about Bartleby," Ruth told Virjinia during their daily phone call. The cat wasn't eating, and his brown fur had taken on a khaki-green cast. "He's looking kind of moldy."

Jin was kind and methodical. Do you have your utensils? she'd ask before they ate. Would you like more grains, another starch? Now she said she'd research Bartleby's symptoms.

"When will you be at the library?"

Jin sighed. Her lunch hours were lost to her current editing project—a textbook on sexually transmitted diseases by Dr. Horace Gerkovski, pronounced Jerkoffski. "Says it all, doesn't it?"

Ruth laughed. Bartleby crawled into her lap, purring, and began kneading her green Victoria's Secret robe. She'd read that purring was a way of welcoming company or asking for help. She stroked his fur, which had become rough and foul-smelling, trying, distractedly, to comfort.

Every day, Ari ate a pizza on the tailgate of his car before disappearing into the garage to care for his animals. At the end of the first week, Ruth found seven bright plastic spiders scattered about the gravel driveway. It took her a minute to recognize them as the gizmos that held the pizza lid off the pizza cheese. That night she invited Ari to join her for dinner. He was wearing overalls and a broad-brimmed straw hat. Mennonite chic.

"How's the apartment search going?"

"Giselle is helping." A strand of linguine slithered into his mouth.

"And who is Giselle?"

"My keyholder. A true artist."

"How can you tell?" She tried to keep the edge out of her voice.

"Giselle was my teacher. She's highly principled, that's the thing. If her work is going well and she has an appointment, she'll just break it. Her recommendations consist of one perfect sentence worth more than a hundred sentences from anyone else. Her students have collected her sayings in a privately published volume, *The Book of Gee.*"

A blurry blob suddenly obscured Ruth's sight. She swatted at her eye, and a box elder bug tumbled from her lashes onto her plate. When the seasons changed, thousands of these big, dopey insects clustered on the warm aluminum siding. They crawled across the inside windows, buzzing like zippers. Jinny had given her a small appliance called a bugsucker for her birthday. For Christmas, she'd given Ruth a Shop-Vac.

Ari eyed her plate. "Do you want that piece of bread?" he asked.

After he'd left, Ruth went out to retrieve her mail. She found a black-edged postcard slinking between the catalogues and read it before she realized it was for Ari. Then she called Jinny and read it to her." '*What does the little fast thing look like? Is it a man-tis? I'd isolate and identify it while you don't have too much rock for it to hide in.*' "

"Creepy," Jin said.

"Listen. '*Is the anemone quite small and gray? If so it's an aiptasia, which will spread and kill any fish over time by stinging them to death.*'"

"Nasty."

"It gets worse. '*I had two and I destroyed them immediately with an injection of boiling calcium. Don't chop it up as every piece will develop into a new one. Giselle.*' "

"Wow," said Virjinia. "Parthenogenesis."

"You said it. It's like a horror movie out here." She sniffed the card. It smelled of a high school biology lab, a sickly sweet fra-grance of formaldehyde and dissected frogs.

Ruth taught at a small midwestern college known as the "Princeton of the Prairie." Whenever she mentioned her farm-house on Crucible Road, someone would say, Isn't that where people go to dump old appliances? Isn't that where the bodies were found? It first happened at a compulsory spooky lunch given by *Stroke,* the college literary magazine, where everyone wore black and discussed the ethics of double submission and reviewing your ex.

Ruth turned to the colleague on her right. "Sally," she whis-pered. "What do they mean?"

Sally Windemire-Whittington, editor and graduate advisor, sniffed her wine judiciously before answering. "Rex Robert Stacey," she said, with a guarded little smile.

"The garage band?" Ruth asked. Or was he the latest darling of academe, the scholar du jour?

Sally Windemire-Whittington laughed. She explained that twenty years ago, in 1966, Rex Robert Stacey had murdered several hitchhikers and dumped their bodies on Crucible Road, where Ruth lived. Rex Robert Stacey was the area's most infamous serial killer.

"Oh," said Ruth. "I thought you meant my neighbors." The house across the road—the only house for a half mile in either direction—had been rented by a heavy metal band who called themselves Rex Robert Stacey. Their thrashing often kept her awake till dawn. Once when she'd phoned to protest, they'd blasted parodic lyrics based on her plaint into the pastoral darkness, and the next morning she saw they'd driven the farmer's tractor over her bonica rosebushes. "When I reported the crime, the deputy said the lead vocalist was the sheriff's son," Ruth told Miles Mannish, vice chair, seated to her left.

Miles Mannish empathized. He was deeply annoyed by the windchimes his neighbors had hung on their porch, their miniature clanging, day and night. "It's astonishing how disturbing that sound can be, like—" He tapped his knife against his glass to illustrate.

"—Tinkerbell in heat," Ruth suggested, and her words fell into the quiet that precedes an announcement.

"False alarm," the vice chair told the group. He kissed his napkin discreetly.

When she got home, Ruth found silky puddles of lingerie extending from the garage to the back door. There was no sign of forced entry. Unless . . . Could someone have crawled through the cat's tiny door? The path extended like satin stepping stones through the kitchen into the dining room. As she was dialing 911, Bartleby loped in, gripping something lacy in his mouth. Ruth followed the trail of underthings to her bedroom. She'd left the bottom dresser drawer open, and its contents frothed onto the floor. Weird kitty, she said. Sick kitty.

Every Wednesday at four, Ruth watched her favorite TV show, *Homebody Aerobics.* The music, a public domain disco strummed on acoustic guitars, sounded like a folk Mass trying to go glitzy, and the instructors all wore the same austere ensemble: dark culottes, sneakers, and a little white bonnet. She was fascinated by the production's monastic earnestness, so at odds with the hedonistic vigor of the 1980s. Were they latter-day pilgrims? Time travelers? One day as she was exercising and contemplating, a knock came at the door.

"Am I interrupting?" Ari sidled in. "Oh, Amish aerobics." He fluttered his hand over his mouth, masking a yawn.

Ruth laughed appreciatively.

"Now clap and shoo and swat and roll and roll!" the instructor ordered.

"She's doing the Shoo Fly Pie routine. I wonder if she'll do Horse and Buggy Jog or Butter Churn Hop or Grain Mill Twist." Ari sounded nostalgic.

"You're familiar with this program?"

"Only because Giselle and I spent last winter in Lancaster, Pennsylvania. The Old Order guys call these youngsters the Disco Amish. They're a radical splinter group."

Ruth laughed. "Very funny, Ari. But the Amish would never be on television. It's against their religion."

"This marginal faction believes being on TV is less contaminating than working at tourist stands. There's less contact with outsiders."

"You mean these people are heretics? They're—shunned?"

"More like barely tolerated." He yawned again.

Ruth studied the instructor's face for signs of strain. "No," she said, shaking her head. "The Amish are unworldly. They don't use electricity."

"Those are just English stereotypes. Today's Amish have gas-powered Cuisinarts."

"I don't believe you!" Ruth put her hands over her ears. "Don't tell me this!"

"Sorry. I didn't mean to upset you." He sank onto Ruth's gray velvet couch and curled his long legs to one side, adorable as a snail. "Of course," he said, "it's hard to exercise when fettered by love."

"Ari, these are the best years of your life." When she was in high school, her mother had given her the same depressing news. She longed for fresher home truths. "Take those chains from your heart," she improvised.

He fingered the dark edge of his hidden belt "It might be possible to get at the hasp with a high speed disc grinder. But a cutting torch would never work, and I can say with certainty that your pruning shears had no effect." He helped himself to a Hershey kiss from a bag on the end table. "Do you happen to have a wet saw?"

Ruth quickly got into the habit of sneaking into her garage for the purpose of reading the latest entry in Ari's diary, a trespass she regarded as a form of self-defense. One day, when she crept in on this mission, she heard a rhythmic brushing noise, as though the ferret were sweeping its cage with a little broom. Suddenly, a figure rose up from a dark corner.

"Did I scare you?" Ari asked. He was wearing a beekeeper's hat, and he threw back the veil with the triumphant flourish of a bride. Ruth's gaze fell on a futon with a hot plate beside it. "I've been sleeping with the animals," he admitted. "My cousin's house is full of teddy bears in football uniforms. It's too depressing."

"Oh, how horrible." She paused. "But Ari, you can't live here."

"Ruth, if money is an issue, I'd be glad to work." He affected an air of quiet reasonability. "I could rip out those invasive foreign weeds and plant the meadow with native species. I could decorate your office. I'm handier than you might think. I also cut hair."

Ruth's last haircut had been administered by someone called Jimmy Snips, who'd learned to style hair by grooming Persian cats for shows. It's what I call a peekaboo look, he'd said, handing her a mirror.

"Can you get bees out of a wall?" she asked Ari.

"A bee in a wall / is a creature so small / that no one can find / a bee in a wall." He laughed.

Muhammad Ali in negative—that was who he reminded her of with his silly rhymes. Tall but spindly. So white he almost glowed in the dark.

"Believe it or not, I wasn't always such a together person," he confessed.

"Oh," she said. "Really?"

"Even after I stopped drinking, I'd wash my hands with Jack Daniel's, just for the smell. And there's one habit I still haven't been able to kick." He jiggled the pinch lock on the ferret's cage. "I thought the chastity belt would help, but it's more effective than a wedding ring in attracting women, let me tell you. It has a prowess all its own." He smiled rakishly. "Celibacy is a great aphrodisiac. Ask any priest. There's nothing sexier in a man."

"Ari, you're foaming at the mouth," Ruth said, backing away. She glanced around. She wanted a witness. She wanted to open the door.

"Oh, no," he said. He scooped some water from one of the aquariums and gulped it down. "No, I was brushing my teeth when you came in.

An hour later, he drove off in a cloud of burning oil to search for an apartment. As soon as he'd left, Ruth helped herself to his diary. She suspected he was putting messages in it just for her. Last week he'd written *Ruth is a mensch.* Today's entry began *Ruth is a saint.* Then the aquatic melodrama continued: *I awoke to more life in the tank. Flea-sized creatures skittering around on the sand, and a coiled beastie that looks like a tiny snail, maybe 1mm across. I also have little white spotted things on the glass with tiny arms*

sprouting from them. Maybe Giselle can help. I don't want to kill some-
thing that might be nice. Next to the word *nice,* he'd drawn a smi-
ley face with a slash across it.

What would Herman Melville do? Ruth wondered.

"Evict him!" her mother said. "I evicted a tenant once," she
added proudly.

Ruth pried at the tight curls of the phone cord. She sighed.
"You didn't evict him. You paid him a thousand dollars to get
out."

"Well, it worked, didn't it? He got out, didn't he?"

"Remember La Raine?" La Raine, another student, had kept
her cats in Ruth's garage between apartments, and after she'd
left, she sent a bouquet of white flowers with an appreciative
note.

"Remember the Alamo!" Mrs. Livingston scoffed. "Tell it to
the Marines! Once when my sister Edna needed an apartment
we scouted around and found one in a single day. One day! Tell
this freeloader he has to scout around. Tell him to take a leak."

"Don't you mean take a hike?"

"Take a slow boat to China," her mother said. "Get lost!"

I have a sort of sea-feeling here in the country . . . Melville had loved
a slow boat.

Ruth lay awake, listening. The downstairs study had sunk
under the weight of her books. She was having the foundation
replaced under that wing, which was up on screw jacks. It
caught the wind like a sail, and the whole house swayed and
moaned. She was mad at Herman Melville, so mad she fairly
twirled above the mattress as she turned. Why was she writing
about his poetry rather than writing her own poems? Melville
had been cosseted by women all his life. Women, those enablers!

She got up and went to the window. The old silo looked like a negative lighthouse, issuing darkness rather than radiance. Melville would have loved it here, beyond the reach of sewer lines and pizza delivery. He'd loved his Pittsfield farmstead, yet he'd begged Hawthorne to go vagabondizing with him. *Let's get lost.*

When Ruth was a child, she and her Aunt Charlotte had played that game, boarding the first bus that came along, not knowing where they'd end up. A few years later, Charlotte's husband, a man she called Itch, dragged her West to live in the desert. *Let's get lost.* All her aunts had been reluctant travelers. Aunt Edna had moved from rental to rental, and Aunt Dorothy, her godmother, had taken long, mad, amnesiac strolls. *Letsgetlostletsgetlost.*

Now Bartleby began calling, rhythmically, plaintively—rah-rah-OW, rah-rah-OW. The cat was lonely. When Jinny visited, they sometimes went to open houses, and at one transitional colonial, the seller had been playing a tape on sexual responsibility for her cat. Playing it softly, to keep the cat company, they thought. They'd laughed about it. Later they learned that the seller's husband, a psychologist who counseled adolescents, had died recently, and the voice on the tape was his. Ruth wondered how his wife could come home to that almost subliminal mutter, the beloved voice like a buried heartbeat or the white noise of a neighboring sea. *I almost fancy there is too much sail on the house, and I had better go on the roof and rig in the chimney.*

The trees creaked and groaned in the gale. Rah-rah-OW. A storm was brewing.

The next morning, Ruth phoned Jinny. "What should I do?"

Jin was thoughtful, deliberate. By the time she answered, Ruth often had forgotten her question. Now she heard Jin take another sloshing sip of herbal tea. This was followed by the silence of the grave, into which one could read anything. "Well?" Ruth said impatiently. "Well?"

"I think you should make the garage so unpleasant that he doesn't want to stay."

"How can I make it more unpleasant than it already is?"

"Decorate it with teddy bears in football uniforms?" Jin laughed. "I have some good news. I think I've discovered how to move the bees out of the bedroom wall without harming them. All the entrances have to be caulked, except one funnel-shaped door. The bees can crawl out, but they can't get back in."

"Why can't they get back in?"

Dead air. Ruth shook the phone receiver as if to wake it up. Then she began talking just to fill the silence. "I myself come from a family of displaced persons, homebodies forced to wander. I'd ask their advice, but none of them are alive."

"They're hovering outside," Jinny said. "They have to keep their wings going in order to stay afloat, and their spread wings won't fit through the trap door."

"What?" Ruth snagged a box elder bug in a tissue and snapped its exoskeleton with practiced skill. "Oh, the bees. What happens to the queen?"

"The queen dies in the wall."

"Edgar Allan Poe would love it here," Ruth said.

A week later, she drove to a nearby strip mall for a consultation with a psychic whose speciality was talking with the dead. In her purple shorts and purple T-shirt, Georgia Glazier looked more like a New Age golfer than a person who made her living by consorting with ghosts. Her office was an aggressively sterile space, free of whimsical, otherworldly props. A small fan whirred at her sneakered feet, which were planted firmly on the floor. "They've got you surrounded. What a gang . . . they won't shut up."

"They can go first." She wanted to make things easy for the dead.

" 'Being a saint is for the birds.' Somebody's saying that. Name starts with a C. She's real antsy."

"Auntsy. That must be my Aunt Charlotte." Ruth wanted to know whether it was less lonely on the other side, whether being dead was restful, whether Charlotte wanted to come back. Will I ever see you again? She wanted to know that.

Georgia Glazier closed her eyes, concentrating. "'Better a saint than a farmer,' somebody else is saying."

"I'd like to know why Charlotte killed herself."

The fan swiveled, a rise and fall of white noise.

"She says stop worrying. They're just totally intact over there. She says there had been problems for years."

"She kept losing consciousness."

"That was the best part, she says, being unconscious. She has a sense of humor. Ho-ho!" Georgia Glazier's laughter was croupy, harsh. "Do you have a cat that's dead?"

"No."

"There's a cat by your side. This cat is your familiar. He belongs to you," she said warmly.

"What can I do about problems at work?" Time was running out.

"Your co-workers get in your aura. You're very porous. You have to sweep them out. You need to learn protective techniques. Cover your power center. And remember to take your own personal putting green with you wherever you go, or you'll get stuck in the rough."

"Right." Golf metaphors were Greek to her. "Will my partner and I ever live together?"

"You could handle that. You both are kind of real unique. You both are kind of nature people." Georgia Glazier paused. "But this cat." Her voice oozed warmth. "This cat *really* belongs to you."

Back on Crucible Road, the meadowlarks were larking, and the
neighbor's boomboxes were booming. Ruth found a note from
Ari on the kitchen table. *My erotic hardware and I took advantage
of your dishwasher whilst you were away. Cheers, A.* Ruth imagined
his terrible belt—an instrument of oppression—in the rack
beside her grandmother's handpainted china. She would turn
the water heater up to scalding. Better yet, she'd dump the dishwasher out on Crucible Road, with all the other tainted
appliances.

Of course, he'd had to remove the belt to wash it. Ari
untrussed, Ari sprung—it was a whole new prospect. She
tracked him down at the far northern fence line where he loi-
tered, scribbling in a notebook. "Giselle returned the key. I'm
afraid she's lost interest." His eyes filled. "I took it off, then I put
it right back on. You can fall in love with a prison, you know."

Ruth glanced at his notebook. The page was covered with
sketches of fanged ribbons, each snippet neatly labeled.

"My life list," he said, handing it to her.

" 'Factory Freak, Briers Flop Over Bob, Devil's Rope, Brass Bawdy
House Token.' Life list?"

"Of barbed wire. I'm adding your fence to my collection."

"Ari, you must find a place to live." She noticed a festering
triangle in the groin of the apple tree. Tent caterpillars. She
could hardly wait to get the propane torch and burn them alive.
"Winter is coming," she told him. "Winter! Just think."

"I'm a feeling person in a thinking world." He pointed to a
white pine in the woodlot. "Is that a hemlock?" His mouth
drooped downwards. "All the apartment complexes have"—his
chest began to heave—"vinyl pickets or chainlink."

"What sort of place do you have in mind?"

Ari glanced to the north and glanced to the south.
"Something like this would be fine," he said.

That night Ruth drove in to pick up some student work at the university. She saw a light in Sally Windemire-Whittington's office and decided to pay a friendly visit.

"I'm thinking of moving into town. Into Scab Hills." This charming older section of the city was popular with faculty members.

The graduate advisor guffawed. "You'll never leave your farm. It's perfect for you." Sally was wearing kneesocks, penny loafers, and an ID bracelet; her chignon was secured by a nail file. Are you part of the Groton School's work-release program? Ruth wanted to ask. Instead, she began babbling about Ari. What would you do? she said finally.

"My dear, the next time a student threatens to kill himself in your meadow, call 911, and take the animals to the Humane Society."

Ruth was shocked. "Those animals are his family. If I take them to the Humane Society, they'll be euthanized."

"Don't be sentimental, Ruth." Sally smiled. "Might I suggest that you have boundary issues?"

"Did you ever play field hockey?" Ruth asked.

The drive home was long and lonesome. By living in the country, she'd hoped to find the solitude that fed her writing. But lately, the moth larvae hatching in the carpet, the dismembered deer by the roadside, the coyotes' weird yapping in the night, the mice in the cupboards and snakes in the basement, the spiders big as cookies, the weekly visits from Jehovah's Witnesses, the lovers with drained batteries pounding on the door at three a.m., the desperate souls who jumped in her car when she paused at the end of the road, the tear-streaked sufferers—children, victims, criminals, prostitutes, she couldn't tell one from another—who turned up begging for help, they needed her help!—made her almost want to sell her quaint farmhouse and move into the faculty ghetto with the other professors.

But Sally Windemire-Whittington was right. She'd never leave her farm. She'd be buried under the silo.

Bartleby crouched on top of the bookcase, his eyes open yet focused inward, as if he had swallowed a riveting puzzle. His wakefulness frightened Ruth; an insomniac cat was an aberration.

"No animal should suffer like that," said Dr. Pamela Kleigstone, DVM. She'd done tests and found a tumor. "We have an opening at noon. It's time."

As soon as Ruth hung up, Bartleby jumped into her lap and began to purr, and an hour later he was eating his Feline Diet Gourmet Buffet with real appetite.

She called back. "I'd like to wait a little longer."

"Fine," said the receptionist, "but we're closed over the weekend."

If the cat got worse, she'd have to bring him to the emergency hospital, a bedlam of howling dogs. Most of all, she wanted him to die peacefully.

It was time. But there was no ritual. She'd have to improvise.

Bartleby entered his cage willingly and was silent on the way to the vet's. In the examining room, Ruth spread her green Victoria's Secret robe on the steel table, and he basked in her attention, melting under her gaze as if she were the sun. She fed him margarine with a tiny blue baby spoon, and his eyes never left hers.

"He's in heaven, Mom," Dr. Kleigstone said.

No, Ruth thought, this cat is not my child. I never had to drive him to soccer practice or playdates; he needed no expensive toys, clothes, or schooling.

"As soon as I do this, he's gone," the vet said, poising her hypodermic. "It's instantaneous. Are you ready, Mom?"

Ruth did not believe in instant death. Death was a process. Death took time. Yes, she said. And Bartleby looked surprised. His eyes briefly glimmered with a new bad understanding, a look that said what is this new not-good thing—

"That wasn't so bad," Ruth said. "I'd like to go that way myself."

"He's gone," said the vet.

Ruth kept stroking his head. "I think I hear him purring." Her mother, a registered nurse, believed it took a few minutes for the soul to leave the body.

"He couldn't be purring."

"Funny, I still hear him." It sounded crazy, so she added, "Yes, I see his pupils are dilated," but that sounded strangely clinical. Bartleby used to bound out to greet her when she got home, his tail raised like an exclamation point. She stroked his whiskers, remembering. Then the vet scooped him up, a helpless length of fur.

Wizard-looking creature, why not throw him in the pond?

Ruth believed postcards were a form of exhibitionism: anyone who cared about privacy would use an envelope. So when she found another black-edged card in her mailbox, she didn't hesitate, though reading it made her break out in hives and warts, and the last sentence, in particular, made her feel defiled. A shower, she decided, a purge. And that was when she saw them—loathsome, repulsive!—brown freckles at the base of each pubic hair. She threw some clothes on and rushed out to find Ari sitting in a half-lotus on the roof of his hatchback. He wore the saffron robes of a renunciate, and his head was shaved.

"Come inside," she beckoned sweetly. "We'll talk." As soon as she had him in the kitchen, her demeanor changed. "Disrobe!" she screamed.

Ari wasn't modest. Once she'd come upon him sitting naked, or *skyclad*, as he called it, in the living room, while his clothes were in the dryer. But now he balked. "Ruth, you're scaring me," he said.

"Strip or I'll call 911," she hissed, reaching for the phone. A vestigial part of her was stunned at her own behavior, while some fresher consciousness was vividly unconcerned. He began squirming out of his toga, keeping his eyes on her, as if she might produce an assault weapon from the pie safe. As the drapery fell away, she saw he was not wearing his hideous belt.

"There!" she said triumphantly, pointing. "I knew it!"

He looked down. "Oh," he said, "crabs. Is that all? You just have to boil all your sheets and towels and underwear and use an insecticide called A-200 on yourself. No problem."

"I wouldn't use that stuff on Astroturf."

"Is your scalp infested or just—"

She whipped out the postcard from Giselle. "Read this."

He seized the card and read aloud: " '*They are isopods that form the food chain. I tried to get rid of mine with cocktail shrimp, but they fell foul of the killer in my tank. If yours is a mantis, I would not hesitate. They are lethal to anything and very clever. Every day he will evade you better. Wizard-looking creature, why not throw him in the pond?*' " Ari brightened. "I must say I'm happy to hear from her."

"How dare she tell you to throw your nasty sea monkeys in my pond?" He'd given her crabs, transmitted them via the towels he'd borrowed. "You're a leech, a poetaster, be out of here by Monday or—" she cast about for an effective threat "—I'll take the animals to the Humane Society."

Ari gathered his robes and began backing toward the door. "As it happens, I've found another place. Problem solved." He gave his head a proud little jerk. "I must say I object to being called a poetaster."

She raised her arms like a witch casting a spell. "Scat!" she cried.

She sprayed the phone with Lysol. Then she called Jinny. "I can't believe I did it. I can't believe he's gone."

"You did the right thing."

"I should have waited."

"You did the right thing."

"If I'd asked, 'Would you rather I kill you now or see how you do over the weekend,' what do you think he would have said?

Jin sighed. They'd been over this before. "'Rah-rah-OW?'" she suggested.

She called her mother. "I can't believe I did it. I can't believe he's gone."

"You did the right thing."

"Why did I wait so long?"

"Shhh, don't say anything. He might come back."

"What do you mean? He said he had another place."

"Change your phone number," her mother suggested. "Change your locks."

The next day, as she was boiling her underwear in the pasta pot, a young man materialized through the steam, playing air guitar. The washer's bump and grind must have overwhelmed his knocking. Rex Robert Stacey! he shouted. Which Rex Robert Stacey? she yelled, turning off the appliances. The serial killer? The scholar? The garage band?

"We're recording our first album, *Breathalyzer*, tonight." He wore a leather vest and epaulets of chains. "I thought I'd tell you so you wouldn't freak."

"Listen, Rex, your telling me does not make it all right. If you told me you were going to kill someone, would that make it all right?"

"Okay, bitch. I tried." He seized a kiwi from the bowl and bit through its hairy rind. "Don't call me if somebody blows snot rockets all over your rosebushes. It's your funeral, know what I mean?" And he banged the back door so hard that the crimson dimity shade fell off and rolled across the tile like a bloody carpet.

On October 31, her colleagues tried to have a Halloween costume party. "Why is everyone dressed as an English professor?" Ruth asked Miles Mannish, vice chair. The department lounge was crowded, and her voice blended into the ambient decibel level. The table centerpiece, a cunning graveyard designed by the Disaffected Teaching Assistants Subconcentration Committee, featured headstones with the names of tenured faculty. Ruth offered the vice chair a toothpicked hors d'oeuvre. "Stigmata appetizer?"

"Thank you, no," said Miles Mannish. "They taste like sweaty feet."

"Nice graveyard," she said, at a loss.

"It's a serenity garden, in point of fact." He was trolling the room for better conversational bets. "Oh, there's a costume." It was Ari, clad only in a towel. "Gandhi," Miles Mannish said, moving off. "Prepostcolonial."

She'd seen Ari just once since he'd moved out. He'd arrived late for orientation day, and finding the only vacant seat was beside Ruth, he'd seized the empty chair, elevated it above his head, and ostentatiously carried it to the far side of the room. After this, Ruth invented a spiritual exercise to transform rage to cosmic sympathy. It involved imagining his funeral in some detail, and practice had made her adept at the visualizations. Out of the corner of her eye, she noticed Sally Windemire-Whittington and Sigmund Merchkin confabbing by the door. Then Sally came over and plucked her aside.

"Siggy says Ari's been performing his ablutions in the men's room. Siggy thinks he's living here." Sally smiled gleefully. "We've arranged an intervention at five in the white conference room. Please join us." And she swanned away.

The English department was a labyrinth of blazing white walls that turned and twisted back on themselves so that navigating was, as Ruth often noted, like being lost in a Borges story. By the time she found the white conference room, the key players were assembled, and the grim formality of crime and punishment hung in the air. Miles Mannish and Sigmund Merchkin looked at ease in their crepuscular suits, while Ari—he'd donned a tuxedo shirt and red bow tie—was visibly trembling. It seemed he was being asked to leave the program as well as the premises. "If I could only have another day." He smiled helplessly. "One day / one delay / one execution stay." She envisioned him in a casket, wearing a striped top hat, his white-gloved hands crossed on his chest, grinning his goofy grin for perpetuity. The funeral of the Cat in the Hat.

"Leave him alone!" Ruth commanded, and a hush fell over the room. "You've heard of the Federal Witness Protection Program?"

That got their attention. Even Sigmund Merchkin nodded encouragingly.

"Well," she continued, "there should be an Academic Poet Protection Program." The interest faded from her colleagues' faces. "Poets are very porous. People get in their auras. As educators, we should" she hesitated, fumbling—"teach them to cover their power centers . . . and take their personal putting greens with them everywhere. . . ." Her voice faltered.

"That's special pleading," Sigmund Merchkin grumbled. "No special pleading."

Sally Windemire-Whittington took the floor. "Ari, your behavior seems somewhat passive-aggressive to us."

"Indeed," said Miles Mannish. "We can't expect the house fairy to come down the chimney with the perfect abode, now can we?" He chortled at his mixed metaphor, then added, "What sort of place are you seeking, if I may ask?"

Ari glanced around the white conference room. "Something like this would be fine," he said.

Over the next few weeks, Ruth heard that Ari had become a captive animal specialist. Then she heard he'd taken a day job as a deboner in a meatpacking plant so he could study marine biology at night.

One December morning, the phone rang, waking her from a dream italicized with meaning, *a heavy dream,* about a psychic called Black Bottomed Pool who wore a swimming suit and gold chains but otherwise looked like her partner Jinny. What should I do? Ruth kept asking, but the psychic didn't seem to hear. At last she made a pronouncement: *Black Bottomed Pool answers only one question.* She said it grudgingly, and waves of mortification washed over Ruth, for she understood that she had asked too much of the oracle. She'd asked too much! Then—hell's bells—the phone rang, dragging her from the depths of negative epiphany.

"Have you heard the terrible news?" It was Sally Windemire-Whittington.

Ruth's first thought was that Ari had been stoned to death or severely beaten with a trailer hitch. He brought that out in people. But Sally explained that he'd been bitten by a raccoon. Rabies was suspected; the prognosis was dire. He was asking for Ruth. He wanted her to visit. Of course, she said, of course.

Ari's hospital room was murky, dim. He was lying on his back, sleeping so quietly that Ruth was frightened till she saw his chest flutter gently. It looked as if he'd grown big white paws, his hands were so thickly bandaged. *Where's my ex?* his roomate called from behind a screen.

Ari opened his eyes. "Ruth." He seemed suprised.

"I brought you some new tapes." Her voice sounded wrong, too cheerful.

"Don't let them kill the raccoon," Ari said.

"If you like Deadbeat Dad and Desire Maggots, you'll enjoy StreetCreature and Lawyering Up. At least that's what the sales guy told me."

"I haven't had a perfect life," Ari confessed. "It's been bruised."

Excuse ME! his roommate roared above the gurgle of his life-support systems. *Excuse ME!*

"The only good I've done has been for animals."

I was never fully thrilled! the roommate cried. Or did he say *killed*? She wasn't sure.

"If they observe the raccoon for ten days, they'll know whether it has rabies. I'm already taking the shots; killing it won't help me. Ruth, please save the raccoon."

"I'll call when I get home."

"Thank you." He sighed with relief. "Now if you could help me to the bathroom . . ."

He leaned on her; they staggered in, and she steadied him by the toilet. "I'll be outside—"

"Wait!"

"Yes?"

"You have to hold it."

"What?"

"I can't, with these bandages on my hands. They're sterile—"

"I'll get the nurse." She moved toward the door.

"No, Ruth, no!" He swayed in place. "The day nurse is a major creepette, a fascist. She'll put a catheter in if I call her again." It was suffocating in the tiny room, yet Ari's teeth were chattering. He looked so helpless standing there, unable to pee by himself. A tsunami of compassion swept through her.

It was hard to aim the stream correctly, and afterwards she felt weak, as if her blood sugar had plummeted.

She'd never wanted to be a nurse. That was her mother's vocation.

"One more thing," Ari said as she fluffed his pillow. "Rabies is an excruciating way to go. It's a foaming, choking, drooling, convulsing way to go. Gods, I'm scared."

They have no fridge, so they put us in the freezer! his roomate yelled.

"You're not going anywhere," Ruth said. "You're being treated—"

"It's too late once the virus reaches the brain." He looked at her beseechingly. "For pity's sake, if I get worse—" He fell back, exhausted.

"Nobody dies of rabies anymore." But she wasn't sure. "Really, you don't seem that sick."

"The virus moves from the wound toward the brain at three millimeters per hour. It's only a matter of time. I have the needle and drugs. You'd just have to give me an injection before the horror begins. Please, Ruth, if it's not too much to ask . . ."

"This," she said, "is an impossible conversation."

"You'd just have to put me out," he sniffled. She handed him a tissue, and helped him blow. "Of my misery."

"Should I call—" she searched her mind for that ballet name "—Giselle?"

He shuddered with repressed sobs. "I'm all alone." He looked panicked, bewildered. The used tissue floated to the floor.

So cold! his roommate yelled. *So cold your brains hurt!*

"It's okay," she said helplessly, trying to soothe. "Okay, okay."

"Then you promise?" Ari said.

No, she thought, she would not bestow that dubious gift again. She would not. She'd let him suffer first. She would.

"I promise you'll get better, and all your dreams will come true." What was it about deathbeds that brought out the cliché in people?

On her way through the lobby, she passed a Christmas tree surrounded by brightly wrapped gifts. Those festive, empty boxes were her least favorite Christmas decorations, she decided. They looked so sad somehow. Her shoulder bag weighed on her, dragging her down like a sack of rocks. By the time she reached the car, her entire arm was asleep.

What is this ugly thing? she wondered. Tomorrow was her birthday, and she'd received two packages in the mail, one from Jinny and one from an unknown address. The mystery gift was an ugly beige plastic box that rattled when she shook it, like a jigsaw puzzle. At last, she turned it over and saw Bartleby's name.

Oh.

Jin's gift turned out to be a bird tape Ruth had wanted, *Begging Calls of the Young at the Nest*. "Clever girl," Ruth said when Jin phoned. "Now I'll be able to tell who's cheeping in the bluebird house. If they're sparrows, I'll—" What would she do? Drown them? Even sparrows needed a place to live.

"You'll ask me to build more birdhouses. And I will."

They'd be together very soon. Ruth sensed it. She would move to New York for the summer, and after that Jin could freelance and live with her on Crucible Road. They'd do fun couple things together, like visit the remaindered food at Odd Lots, pack a basket with pomegranate trail mix, poppyseed wine, and have a unique picnic in the meadow. They'd visit the death row pets at the Humane Society, and when insomnia struck, she'd list their markings and names to put herself to sleep.

They'd be together at last. Finally, fully thrilled.

"Sounds good to me," Jinny said. It was time.

After ten days of observation, the raccoon proved to be a healthy wild animal who simply did not like Ari. Ruth heard the good news on her thirty-fifth birthday, the same day that a professional beekeeper, Wilbur Lindquest, came to install the bee escape in her bedroom wall. He told her honeybees were endangered; a parasite was killing them. "You should keep bees," he said.

"I prefer not to," said Ruth.

The queen dies in the wall.

After Wilbur Lindquest left, her mother called. "We threw you a great christening party," she reminisced. "All my sisters were there, Charlotte, Edna, Dorothy, everybody! I ordered a big sheet cake that said WELCOME HOME. When it arrived, Charlotte answered the door and turned pale. 'My God,' she said, 'I thought it was a casket, it was such a big long box, I thought it'd say REST IN PEACE.' " Mrs. Livingston laughed, and Ruth marveled at the humor on her mother's side of the family. Time and again, they failed to see the ominous.

"We were dying, it was so funny," Mrs. Livingston recalled fondly.

One Sunday, about five months later, Ruth heard a car pull in the driveway, and going out to investigate, found a gang of elderly women posing for photos by the silo. "Are you Witnesses?" she asked. She'd had it with Jehovah.

"We're sisters," said the one with the camera. Her ironed shirtwaist looked familiar. Was it Miss Ryan, Ruth's eighth-grade homeroom teacher? "I'm Clara," the old woman said. "And these gals are Evie and Daisy. We were born here."

"You were born in my house?"

Clara nodded. "We're having a family reunion. We haven't seen each other for seventy-seven years."

"Oh! Well. In that case—would you like to come in?"

It was a small house; a tour wouldn't take long.

"Our mother died here in 1909, right after Daisy was born," Clara said. They were standing in Ruth's bedroom. "Papa had to sell the farm and send us to relatives in different parts of the country, anybody who'd take us." She glanced around. "Nothing has changed, right Evie? Of course, Daisy won't remember."

After she'd shown them the house, Ruth put the kettle on. While she was in the kitchen, the phone rang, and a male voice began droning into the machine. She strained to hear. *Blahblah International Press . . . a slim volume of my blabblah . . .*

Was it Miles Mannish?

I now enjoy a blahblahblah in Ireland, Poland, Finland, Newfoundland, Greenland, Swaziland, Zululand, Blahblahland, and the Marquesas.

Sigmund Merchkin?

The central blahblah about the Ethiopian diaspora is especially important to me, as I was breeding Somali cats at the time.

"Is that your hubby?" Clara called. Or maybe she said "hobby."

"No!" Ruth had liked Ari better when he spoke in silly rhymes.

Now the University of Blahblahland has invited me to blah for them, and my animals need a home.

"Blah, humbug!" Ruth said.

When I asked to be allowed to go to Blahblahland for a countrywide blah tour, my employers said no.

"No!" she echoed.

When I asked for a leave, they said, show up or be blahed. So, I was forced to resign. Any ideas?

"No!"

I'm only sorry that John Berryman, Elizabeth Bishop, James Wright, et cetera, are now blah and can't really blahblahblah on my behalf. I'm sorry I have only you to ask.

"Need help, hon?" Clara said, coming in.

"No, no, no!" Ruth paused. "I mean, yes, thank you." She handed Clara a plate of cookies. Then she stomped into the living room, where her guests had settled, and plunked down a tray, splashing tea onto Melville's *Collected Poems*.

"We thank you kindly for letting us see our home," Clara said. "If there's anything we can do in return, don't be shy."

Oh, Ruth started to say, it's nothing. Then her gaze fell on the box of Bartleby's ashes. "Well, there might be one thing," she said slowly.

They nodded politely.

"I was about to hold a small memorial service in the meadow when you arrived. I wonder—if it's not too much to ask— would you have time for a funeral before you leave?"

"Why, surely," said Clara, grabbing her pocketbook. "All the time in the world."

It was a sweet summer evening. The sunlight was thickening, and the ground near the pond smelled richly alive. Ruth was glad the sisters had worn sensible shoes. She started the cassette, *Begging Calls of the Young at the Nest*. His name was Bartleby, she began. Then she paused, self-conscious. Cheep-cheep-EEP, the tape twittered, cheep-cheep-EEP . . .

Evie spoke up. "Bart must have liked the birds. I bet you and him had some swell times. Was he musical?"

"He had a beautiful voice."

"Athletical?"

"He could jump from the floor to the top of the TV cabinet."

"He must've been a sketch," Evie said.

"A real card," Clara added. "I bet he made you laugh."

"He made me laugh!"

"How old was Bart when he passed?" Clara asked.

"Eighteen."

Clara's eyes filled. "And you're all he had."

"Well, he's danged lucky," said Daisy, "he had you."

"I bet you was like a mother to him," Evie said.

"I bet he was well mannered, too, like you," Clara added.

"He never stole from the table or drank from the toilet," Ruth told them.

"You mean he didn't tomcat around." Clara fluffed her hair.

My meadow has never been so crowded, Ruth thought. She opened Melville's *Collected* and read: "*The ghost is yielded in the gloom. . . . Now save thyself*—" She paused. The baby birds called faintly from the tape. "*Now save thyself who wouldst rebuild the world in bloom.*"

She felt inspired.

She felt inspired to throw the book in the pond.

It hit the water with a leaden *plonk*. "Jiminy!" Daisy cried, as waves sniped at their shoes. "She shouldn't have chucked her Bible like that." Evie jabbed her sister in the ribs. "That's pitching the baby with the bathwater," Daisy insisted.

"Must be some religious custom," Clara said, crossing herself. "Tell Bart you'll miss him, hon, then we'll say goodbye." The sun was setting, her guests were eager to be on their way.

"I'll miss you," Ruth said.

"Sure you will," Clara said. "He was your pal."

"You were my pal," Ruth said. "Oh, shit, I don't know if I can do this." She struggled with the ugly plastic clasp. She'd heard ashes were not what you'd expect but varicolored, with coral inclusions, heavenly-lurid, like a fuchsia-striped sunset. She was afraid to look.

"Pretend like you're planting seeds and give him the heave-ho," Daisy instructed.

How light he was. Was there anything in the box at all? "You were the best cat," Ruth said. "Goodbye." And she flung the ashes over the water, like throwing emptiness away, a Zen koan, and they must have been a fine dust, almost nothing, because she didn't see them rise or fall.

Amen! the sisters chorused.

Ruth brushed a thistle from her skirt.

"You gave him a nice send-off," Clara said.

"Thank you." Ruth hit the stop botton, and the baby birds abruptly ceased. "I couldn't have done it without you. You were good company."

"I don't like a fancy funeral," Clara said as they turned to go. "Far as I'm concerned, when my time comes"—she paused and surveyed the rough brown grass—"something like this would be fine."

L'Air du Temps

Ruth Livingston, Annie Garrahan Livingston

S HE WAS HAVING a bad year and longed for amnesia, if not oblivion, but she didn't do drugs and when her old friend Sunny offered her Ecstasy, she accepted only because the blue smurfs and pink diamonds looked interesting, like something she could make into jewelry. She'd make an Ecstasy bracelet and wear it to faculty meetings. That would be daring. Not as daring as the colleague who brought a puppet to a meeting, or the lecturer who taught in her Burger King uniform. But they had taken fun too far. They'd crashed and burned, and now no one was allowed to speak of them for legal reasons.

Last year, another professor had cornered her to complain about colleagues who'd stopped publishing. These people have *hobbies*, he said disdainfully. They *garden*. Ruth pictured her nerves as small snarling uprooted things. When her brain went into negative labor at three a.m., she colored miniature mandalas with very sharp pencils, pressing hard. I'm having hobbies, she thought. Once, she gathered every perfume in the house and inhaled the fumes, hyperventiling till she nearly fainted.

That was selfish. Because if Ruth lost consciousness, who would take care of her mother?

Her mother was losing her memory, and she preferred to lose it at home. "There are too many Hollows where you live," she said. "I don't want to be anywhere called Hollow." So the mountain must go to Mohammad, the department chair remarked when Ruth applied for a leave. Now her mother was always nearby. She followed Ruth from room to room, a symptom called shadowing, according to dementia.com. It drove Ruth crazy.

She'd first noticed a change during phone conversations. *Those long skinny green vegetables*, her mother would say, instead of *asparagus*. Last summer when she visited Ruth and Virjinia, she brought winter clothing and kept getting lost on the way to her bedroom. The tall trees scared her, and when they sat in the rock garden, she said, "Those rocks won't get any bigger, will they?" Before she left, Ruth begged her to live with them. Let us help you, she said. "I can help myself!" her mother snapped, applying antiperspirant to her ankle.

So Ruth and Virjinia had moved to Troy, and now it was almost New Year's. Not just any New Year's. The century was turning. Ruth thought they should celebrate. "My celebrating days are over," her mother said dismally. Then she added, "Do something you young people enjoy. Play Beatle songs." She tried to think of Ruth, though the Ruth she thought of was fourteen.

Her high school graduation dress was still in the attic. Her mother had let her design it and taken her to fittings, and when dreamy Ruth forgot to attend the French exam she needed to graduate, her mother had defended her. She'd never said a recriminating word, though Ruth had to go to summer school, and the white dress was never worn. Maybe she'd wear it this New Year's for a laugh—her cautionary gown, her frock of failure. They could use a laugh.

Her mother's pleasures were few. She liked to go to the bank where the tellers knew her name—Hi, Annie!—and she liked to push the supermarket cart. Every night, Ruth heard her talking to herself before she fell asleep. Sometimes she sang—*dee-dee-dee*—but sometimes she asked herself terrible questions: *What's going to happen, Annie? I don't know, do you?* Then Ruth felt obliged to turn the baby monitor up and listen, though it filled her with anxiety. *Help me, dear God, help me go angel rest. Help Ruth and Jin.* It broke her heart.

Time was in the air. They looked at photos of Ruth's mother and father, taken the day they'd met at Lake George. "I fell in and started yelling, I can't swim, and they roared laughing, remember?" Annie said. She thought Ruth had been around forever. "Finally, somebody said, Stand up, Annie, it's only three feet deep. Since that day, I've never wanted to be near water."

Everyone was wondering where to be for the millennium. At first, it had seemed a fun concept, but as it drew closer, people worried their computers would lose their memories at the stroke of twelve. They regretted tombstones pre-engraved with 19 and feared they'd have no one to kiss when the ball dropped. The paper said stock up on batteries, blankets, flashlights, bottled water. Have enough cash for a long weekend.

"I'm glad this happens only once in a million years," Annie said. Because things were unraveling. The basement flooded, and they put down a musty compost of old newspapers. Ruth stopped coloring her hair, and her part turned silver, as if her head had a zipper. Jin was lost in thought. "Where's Jin?" Annie asked.

She hated Jinny's mess on her dining room table. Ruth said Jin had joined the silent service, become a bubblehead. It was her new hobby. She was making a model submarine. To Annie, it looked spooky. Sometimes she thought—why is Jin building a little coffin in my dining room?

"Remember how Jin used to cook with plaster of Paris?" she
said. "I told her, this would be delicious if it had any taste."
Annie's husband had never known their daughter's friend
Virjinia. He was long gone. Sometimes she couldn't remember
his name. They said time healed all wounds, but it shouldn't have
healed this much. Time had gone too far.

She couldn't think. Maybe she should make a list.

She used to rely on lists. She used to be so independent she'd
wrapped Christmas presents for herself, even tagging them, *For
Annie*. She used to be able to change the channel, but now she
had to watch what they watched.

They watched a submarine movie. Dark, sealed-off rooms.
Everybody trapped, suffocating. And she was so afraid of water!
Fires kept breaking out, even though they were deep in the
ocean. Was that possible? And no matter what movie the sailors
requested, they were always shown *The Sound of Music*.

Afterwards, Annie dreamed of a bird that sang underwater. It
was a dull bird, and it came out of a dull shell to sing. She woke
up gasping. The alarm clock said one a.m., the dead of night, yet
a real bird was chirping its heart out. She lay smothered in
nightness, an inside night, smaller than the outside one. Had
they locked the back door? She tiptoed down. There was something on her dining room table. She could not think how it got
there or what it was, but she was afraid to walk past it. Whatever
it was, she hated it.

She went back to bed and dreamed about a bird of glassy fire.
It looked like a perfume bottle she'd had. The perfume was
flowery, but not like funeral flowers. It smelled the way a flower
still growing on the earth would smell.

When Ruth heard about the dream, she said the perfume was
L'Air du Temps. The Lalique bottle was famous. That perfume
was still available, though they'd reformulated it. Ruth thought

smelling the original might help her mother remember the era when she wore it. It was known as cued recall: if you memorized a list underwater, you'd remember it better underwater. She'd learned that from a colleague whose work on mnemonics had been dismissed as maudlin by the tenure committee.

But when she mentioned it, Annie said, "That's a weird idea." She frowned at the blue candy bracelet Ruth was making. "A roomer left a case of that perfume in the Phoenix Hotel. Nobody wanted it, so my husband put it in the cellar." Her daughter had one foot in the past. Even as a child, she'd wanted old-fashioned dresses. There was something wrong with her.

"Could you visit the Phoenix and see if it's still there?" Ruth asked Jinny. She thought her mother had regressed to the terrible twos, the age when a child says no to everything. "We could smell it on New Year's. Smell the past."

Jinny nodded.

But she couldn't make it happen. "Your father's hotel isn't what it used to be," she said when she returned. "It's like Père Lachaise up there. Dark. *Really* dark. With bottles, syringes, and graffitti everywhere. There was nobody at the desk, and somebody yelled down, Who are youse looking for? Then a big burly guy appeared. He opened a drawer full of guns and knives. I was thinking, if we get to choose our weapons, I'll choose grammar."

"Right!" Ruth's eyes widened.

"He asked what I wanted, and I said vintage L'Air du Temps perfume in the original Lalique bottle. Follow me, he said, and that's when I lost my nerve."

"Now *he'll* find it," Ruth said. "And he won't appreciate it."

"I'm sorry," Jin said. But she gave Ruth a sour look. "What could I have done? You want me to get murdered?"

"Right!" Ruth said. "My plan exactly."

"You don't have a plan," Annie said, eyeing the mess of jewelry fittings and candy on the kitchen table. "When you have to ask your mother to dig the blue M&Ms out of the other colors, something's wrong with you."

The next day, Jin took Annie along on her errands. Ruth was alone in the house. Snow drifted down, muffling the noise of Route 7, skiers in SUVs rushing through gritty Troy to quaint Vermont. She wanted to make some resolutions. She found a yellow legal pad and sat across from Jinny's submarine. A sub like that would be powered by nuclear fission, radioactive uranium that took 760 million years to decay. That makes it approximately eternal, Ruth thought with a shudder. For humans, time was a constriction, a funnel: the possibilities kept narrowing.

"Troy is where love comes to die," her old friend Sunny had remarked, and Ruth laughed. But was it true? Jinny hadn't worked in over ten years. Whenever they talked about it, they quarreled and Jin sulked. Sometimes Ruth fantasized about pushing her down the stairs and stomping on her when she hit the bottom. Overpressure, crush depth—Ruth had learned those terms from her. Jinny's submarine was black. Why not yellow? Why couldn't they all live in a yellow submarine?

"You must change your life," she scribbled on the legal pad, then shook her head. Quoting Rilke! You must leave your lover, she thought. But if they broke up, who'd take her mother on walks? Who'd cook her mother's oatmeal? For much of her life, Ruth had doted on Jinny. Now she felt as if a delicate infrastructure were crumbling under her ribs, a fragile edifice she needed to survive. "Treasure!" she exclaimed, pressing her hand to her chest.

When Jin got home, she'd heat stuff up. They ate a lot of vaguely ethnic food that seemed to have been premasticated and flavored with frankincense and myrrh. They were vegetarians, the options were limited. The last time Jinny tried a recipe, Ruth said it tasted like something scraped from the sink drain.

When Jin got home, she made smoothies with soy milk, soy yogurt, frozen peaches, frozen mangoes, organic bananas, flaxseed oil, and an acidophilus pill. She loved her own cooking and ate with devotion, in total silence. Afterwards, Ruth felt stronger. Had she been unfair to Jin? It was no picnic, living here in Troy.

"Any interesting news?" she asked her mother. Annie was staring at the local paper. It was mostly ads for bankruptcy lawyers, taxi services, fish fries, and dentures. Sometimes there was a tiny plea for the Clothe-a-Child Program.

Jin said, "An ornithologist thinks he saw a nightingale in Frear Park. Or maybe he just heard one."

"Oh, I hear them all the time," Annie said.

"Where do you hear them?" Ruth demanded. "They're English birds."

"You hear them right in the backyard." Annie folded and unfolded a distressed Kleenex. "You see them in Lansingburgh." Her daughter was such a know-it-all!

"You need new glasses," Ruth said. "You can't see well enough to read. I'll make an appointment."

"There's nothing wrong with my glasses!"

"And today is shower day. I'll help."

Annie looked tragic.

"Oh, please!" Ruth yanked the elastic from her ponytail. She dreaded shower day. Jinny cleared her throat.

"What is it? What?" Annie said.

"Showers are fun," Ruth coaxed. Her mother didn't even like to wash her hands. They had to force her to eat, drink, and bathe. At the end of Ruth's leave, she and Jinny would go back to the Midwest. Then what would become of her mother? Her funny, exuberant mother. . . . "Maybe we'll see a nightingale on the way to the eye doctor's."

Annie gripped her glasses. When her daughter got her first pair in the fourth grade, the doctor said they'd open up a whole new world for her. Annie didn't want a whole new world. She didn't want to see any nightingales.

" 'It singeth of summer,' " Ruth quoted. Summer, not winter! Last year, an ornithologist found a bird long thought to be extinct living in a remote area of Arkansas. He said it was like a funeral shroud being pulled back to glimpse it rising, Lazarus-like, from the dark woods. The lines about sinking Lethe-wards were Ruth's favorite part of Keats's Ode. What were those lines? She could not remember.

Ruth directed Annie's shower through a crack in the curtain. Afterwards, she styled her hair and handed her a mirror.

"Don't you look great? So young!"

"I'm ninety," Annie said, "and now I look eighty-nine."

Next, Ruth tried to find Jinny. Maybe she'd dozed off somewhere. Wake up! she wanted to yell. When they first moved here, she'd asked Jin to whistle in the morning. She was a gifted whistler; it would be cheerful. I can't unless I feel it, Jin said. I asked you to whistle, not compose a sonota, Ruth thought. Jinny was foundering, blindsided by time. Ruth understood. She found her in the cellar, detailing her submarine.

Annie's shower had taken two hours. It would be dark soon. Ruth wanted to talk with Jin in a place where her mother couldn't overhear.

"New Year's," Ruth began. "We have to decide."

"I thought we were staying home. It's the worst night to go anywhere."

"We need a plan!" Ruth hissed.

"Jin and I are going for a ride," she told her mother. "We'll be back soon." Annie coughed in protest as Ruth handed Jinny the car keys.

They drove to Frear Park. Ruth looked for the gargoyles around the big white fountain at the entrance. As a child, she'd wondered why calm, classical faces spewing water were considered attractive. Now the faces were rust-stained, gaping. They got out and and walked into a snowy field. "We have to talk," Ruth said.

"Don't you want to hear the nightingale?" Jinny said, turning away.

Ruth grabbed her wrist. "There is no nightingale!" Nightingales were in West Africa this time of year. She'd looked into it. Legend said the bird sang with its breast pressed against a thorn to stay awake.

Jinny stared at the heavens. "What are you thinking?" Ruth asked.

"I was thinking about glo—"

"You were thinking about global warming, weren't you? Why can't you think about the coldness between us? Think about finding work!"

Ruth earned a living, and Virjinia looked after their domestic life. But things got away from Jin. She'd start a bathroom remodel, lose interest, and the naked subfloor would give them splinters for a decade. She'd shock the well with too much chlorine, so their hair turned brassy and their pasta tasted like a swimming pool. For years, Ruth had complained of a sulfurous stench in their farmhouse, and Jinny insisted nothing was wrong. Right before they moved to Troy, a workman accidentally discovered a serious gas leak.

"It's a wonder we survived," Ruth said. She felt drowsy, her toes were numb.

"I'm sorry." Jin's face looked stony in the moonlight.

"You say you're sorry when you mean you're angry," Ruth said angrily. She shivered. No nightingale could survive in this bitter place. It was the perfect place for them to finally scream at each other.

Her mother was at the window when they returned. "I thought you got lost," she complained. "I didn't know where you went."

Jinny made white rice with bottled ginger sauce for them and microwaved a Banquet frozen entrée for Annie. She poked at it tentatively. At last, she said, "Did you have a good time on your outing?"

Ruth nodded. "Jin's going to New Hampshire for a while. To work with a friend."

Annie put down her fork. "I don't think she should."

"Well, she has to. It's an opportunity."

"Do you have to, Jin?" Annie asked. "I don't want you to go."

"This friend wants me to be his business partner." Jinny scraped one chopstick against the other. "We're going to see a loan officer. I guess I'll need some kind of outfit." She'd have to buy an outfit. She set down her chopsticks, sobered by the thought.

The next morning, Jinny called a cab and left for the airport. She took only a small suitcase and a smoked tempeh sandwich.

"Jin forgot part of her ship," Annie said. She put a dark piece on the table between them.

Ruth was reading. What an oddball, Annie thought. Her friend's gone, and all she cares about is books.

"I'm the last of my family," Annie said. "I don't have any close relatives."

Ruth turned a page. "What am I?"

"I've lived too long."

"I'm a nineteenth-century Americanist, " Ruth said, "but I should have been a poet."

"You know what I think?" her mother said. "You're a snob." She crossed her arms in judgment. "You're helpless. You need someone to take care of you."

"That's not fair," Ruth said. "I'm not a snob." Her eyes filled.

"All right, all right," Annie said.

Ruth stared at her journal. That morning, while thinking about ambergris, she'd burned the oatmeal. Ambergris! She knew the components of laudanum, but she couldn't make coffee. Instead of *Be Here Now*, her maxim was *Be There Then*.

"I'm worried about Jin," Annie said. "She must be in a different time zone."

"Time is nothing but the relationships between different clocks. David Mermin said that, a physicist."

Her mother looked blank.

"Did you know radioactive rain fell on Troy in 1953?" Ruth asked. She'd thought of a bracelet she could make. The beads would be amphoras filled with time-sensitive liquids, legacy fluids with different half-lives and decay rates. "Let's go for a ride, do a little sightseeing," she said.

Annie would go anywhere rather than be left alone. Ruth helped her into her favorite red coat. Then she drove them toward Lansingburgh, 109th Street and the Hudson River, where her father's nightclub, the Ship of Joy, had docked in the 1930s. Off-track betting was there now. Perfect. Ruth parked in their lot. I'll be right back, she said.

The Hudson was a drowned river. It smelled of mildew and polycyclic aromatic hydrocarbons. Ruth squatted on the bank, took a jar from her pocket, and captured some rank, pewter-colored water. Then she hurried back.

Annie glared at her. "Where were you? I couldn't see you."

"I didn't go anywhere." Ruth searched for the jar lid.

"You left me!"

Ruth held out the specimen. "The river."

Annie shoved her arm away, and the water spilled on her red coat.

"Oh!" Ruth cried.

"Now look what you made me do!" Annie searched for a tissue. "That was mean."

To Ruth, the specimen had seemed sacramental. It had given her hope. But her mother was rigid with fury.

"Take me home," Annie demanded.

"First let's visit the Phoenix and ask about the perfume. L'Air du Temps."

"Take me home!" Annie stamped her foot. "You're getting us lost! What's wrong with you? You're . . . an oddball. You're . . . a lost soul."

Ruth scrutinized her mother. She set the map on the seat between them. "Would you like to go for a walk in the mall? The way you did with Jinny?"

"You should call her," Annie said. "We don't even know what state she's in!"

"She's in the Republic of Jinny." Ruth made an illegal U-turn. "This is life without Virjinia, the Post-Jin era. Get used to it!"

That evening, Annie found herself in a dumb yet scary predica-ment. As she was pulling off her turtleneck, the neckband lodged under her nose, and the shirt turned to swaddling. It was a pretty turtleneck, ivory with little pink flowers coming up on it like spring. But it had no give. Her arms were bound, she was blindfolded, smothering. She couldn't free herself, and the effort left her breathless.

"Ru!" she said. Ruth's bedroom was across the hall. She was in there doing her artwork, knee-deep in her findings and clasps.

"Get me out," her mother called.

"Let's think." Ruth sat down on Annie's bed.

"Never mind thinking! Get the scissors." As a registered nurse, Annie had performed emergency tracheotomies on choking victims, she'd ripped shirts from the dying.

"Where are they?" Ruth said. She sounded uncertain.

"I don't know." Annie struggled, gasping. Then Ruth started

pulling. She pulled so hard Annie thought her neck would snap. It was like being born, but instead of being pushed into the world, she stayed still while a narrow tunnel inched away. When she emerged, her face was chapped, and she fully understood why babies scream at birth.

Her daughter's glasses were askew, her hair piebald and ragged. Worst of all, there was a scabby brown choker around her neck and matching bracelets on her wrists. "Bird's-nest jewelry," Ruth said. "Work in progress."

As soon as she was alone, Annie tried to twist off her wedding band. If she gave her ring to Ruth, her daughter wouldn't have to make ugly junk jewelry. Annie's hands were clawlike, the nails yellow and terrible. She couldn't get it past her knuckle.

"'I'll See You in My Dreams,'" Annie said. "Remember that one?" They were sorting beads in the kitchen.

"That's orange, not yellow," Ruth said. "Today you're getting new glasses."

"I don't need new glasses!"

"You need to see. We have an appointment with Dr. McFarney."

"She's way over in Green Island," Annie said. "And Jin isn't here to drive us."

"I can drive," Ruth said. "I'm not helpless, you know. We have to be independent." She shifted uneasily. Life without Jinny was hard. Self-reliance was overrated. She added, "I want you to read and see the world."

"I don't want to see the world!" Annie cried.

"Would you rather stay home alone?" Ruth said.

Annie didn't trust the Green Island Bridge. She closed her eyes as they drove over it.

"I'm here to have my head examined," she told the receptionist.

"Her eyes," Ruth said. "She's here for an eye exam."

They sat and stared at the fish tank. There were a few other patients, paging through magazines. Every so often a technician called a name and someone was led away. Annie worried she'd get lost when her turn came. She'd lose track of Ruth, Ruth would think she'd left and go home. Then where would she be? Lately, Annie missed her mother. Her mother always stuck up for her. She never felt alone in the world while her mother was alive.

She focused on another patient's T-shirt to test her vision. *St Cieran's Home Survivor*, it read. The woman wore hair scrunchies like little clown ruffs on her wrists. "I was raised there," she told Annie.

"Did they treat you good?" Annie had been born on a farm across from that orphanage.

"I used to escape and kneel in the middle of the road, praying someone would kidnap me," the survivor said. She snapped one of her fluffy bright handcuffs. "Let's just say I've got marks that will never tan."

Ruth went in with Annie when her name was called. The assistant had her peer through instruments and answer questions. Then Dr. McFarney made her entrance. HEL-lo, she said, smiling and jerking her head back as if to acknowledge a round of applause.

"My daughter says I can't read." Annie wore her glasses on a chain around her neck. She gave the doctor a look of appeal.

"Hooked on Phonics worked for me," Dr. McFarney said brightly.

Ruth sometimes called her Dr. McBlarney, and Annie was afraid her daughter would make that faux pas now, but she just said her mother couldn't sort the orange beads from the yellow ones.

"Bad puppy!" McFarney said. "Look what happens when you give a girl a woman's job." She tested Annie's eyes, put in dilation drops, and sent them to the waiting room while the drops were working.

"Ever been to the Thousand Islands?" the doctor asked when they returned. "I'll be there New Year's Eve."

"Oh, yes," Annie said. "When I was a kid, my sister Charlotte's boyfriend said he'd take us to the Thousand Islands. He said somebody built an island there shaped like a heart."

"No heart is an island!" McFarney burbled.

"He drove us out to the country, muddy hollow, and every time we passed a vacant lot, he'd say, There's island number one, there's island number two. By the time we got to island number twenty, it was getting dark, and I was thinking how long it would take to visit the Thousand Islands. It would take the rest of my life!"

"There are more than a thousand islands in the Thousand Islands," the doctor agreed.

"Later I realized we were only out by St. Cieran's Home, but at the time I thought we were lost. I thought we were being kidnapped, and I started bawling, saying my mother needs me home. 'Well, little Annie,' he said, 'you'll just have to call and tell her you'll be gone a long, long time.'"

"Did Aunt Charlotte confront him about child abuse?" Ruth demanded. Her mother's eyes had dilated into huge black orbs. "Did she dump him?"

"Dump him! She married him. He became my brother-in-law. And then he became a clown. Uncle Ward, remember?" Annie tapped her toes delightedly.

"Happy New Year!" Dr. McFarney held the door open. "See you next century!"

In the parking lot, Annie jerked away when Ruth tried to take her arm. She wanted to look vigorous, in case she met any old friends. "The Thousand Islands," she murmured. The air felt sharp as cutlery. The concrete was dazzling. People living on that heart-shaped island couldn't see it. That's why they went looking for it and got lost. The thought seemed solid, Annie wanted to hold on to it. But by the time she got home, it was gone.

That evening, Annie watched TV with her eyes closed. Ruth said, "The drops make everything blurry, but once you get your new glasses you'll see better."

The drops had been a mistake. Her mother's eyes looked like negatives of Orphan Annie's. Old pupils might not be ready for such shape-shifting.

"It's called the graveyard spiral," the TV was saying. "You feel like you're on a level course when you're actually in a dive."

Ruth shivered. Wasn't it taking too long for those drops to wear off?

After dinner, she assembled her perfumes on the cocktail table. They'd have a sniffing. Guerlain perfumes evoked the past most powerfully. L'Heure Bleue, composed in 1913, was the first Guerlain to use aldehydes, and aldehydes were the start of olfactory modernism. L'Heure Bleue evoked indigo kimonos, cobalt runway lights. The head notes hinted at licorice, Earl Grey tea. The stopper was a hollow heart.

"This stuff smells like mothballs," Annie said. "It smells like an old tintype." Her head throbbed. Ruth was swooning in the blue TV light. Why did they call it toilet water? Annie wondered. Why did they make it yellow? This perfume smelled the way hospitals smelled in her day. Like ether. Stagnant cut flower water. Sick roses. "Where's Jinny?" she said. "I don't know why she went away, do you?"

Ruth held out a smelling strip. "Just breathe."

"I know there isn't much action here, but you two aren't real livewires anyway."

"She's coming back tomorrow night," Ruth said. "It's New Year's Eve, you know."

"You know what real livewires call New Year's Eve?" Annie

touched the corner of her mouth briefly, reflectively. "Amateur night."

"At this moment, Jinny's probably finding reasons why her job prospect won't work." Ruth said.

"She does her best, poor soul. You'd be lost without her. I see it in the offing."

The offing. Where was that, Ruth wondered. Near the gloaming? Or was it temporal, like L'Heure Bleue? Maybe it was metaphorical, near the slippery slope, the skids.

"I'm lost *with* her," Ruth said. "Why can't you ever take my side?" She was annoyed. "My job is killing me, but if my life depended on it—and it does—Jinny wouldn't find work."

"Can't you retire?"

"No," Ruth said darkly. She adjusted her Zen back support cushion. She shouldn't argue with her mother, a person who didn't know enough to pull up the blankets on a cold night, a person who'd mutter—I'm *cold*, it's *cold* here—till Ruth appeared and covered her.

"You don't know," Ruth said, "how cold academe can be. Listen. I had a friend who was in the hospital, and I went to visit her. That's what friends do, right? I called her partner first to make sure it was okay, then I went with magazines, flowers. She had two other visitors, people I didn't know. It was a little awkward, but I tried to be upbeat, friendly—"

"Sociable," Annie said approvingly.

"About a year later, this friend asked me to read her memoir and suggest publishers. The last chapter was about her hospital stay, and she described an *accomplished* Melville scholar who'd visited and *held court*. That's how she put it. She said she couldn't stand being part of the audience, so she made an excuse and used the bathroom just to get away. She described specific honors I've received, so everyone would know who she meant. She'd circulated this manuscript, shown it to people I considered friends, and no one told her to change it. No one spoke up for me. I felt so"—Ruth tried to see Annie's vast pupils in the dimness—"betrayed. And that's the world I'm in. The wrong world. A bad place."

"Shh," Annie said. "Don't say anything."

"You're right. It's smarter to blue-sky it and sabotage your enemies. But I confronted her. She cried and said she hadn't intended for me to see that part. She'd forgotten it was there."

"Did she make it up to you?"

"Are you kidding? When the book appeared, there it was. There I was." Ruth paused. "She wasn't well liked. People said she was nasty and her work unreadable. But I always defended her. I really thought she was my friend."

Annie rubbed her eyes. Her head hurt.

They fell silent. The TV shed its trashy sapphire glow. "During the test, student pilots must demonstrate their ability to pull out of an extreme dive," the aviation expert was saying. "It's called Recovery from Unusual Attitudes."

Ruth sighed. "There's a notice on airplanes, *The closest exit may be behind you.* There isn't enough time to recover from some things. Physics probably has a term for it—monkeys-typing-Shakespeare, I don't know. Einstein said time exists so everything won't happen at once. But there isn't enough of it. I wish he'd spoken to that."

Annie hooked her finger to her lip like a pensive child. "Memory makes everything happen at once."

"That's good, Ma. 'Memory exists so everything will happen at once.' I like that." Really, Ruth thought, she was an adorable mother.

That night, Ruth lay awake, obsessing. They were entering the last day of the century, and she had no plan. *You must change your life!*

A friend who'd lost her spouse had told Ruth that her heart literally ached, it wasn't just a figure of speech. She'd even seen a cardiologist about it. Now Ruth felt something straining, giving, near her breastbone. When they last talked, Jinny offered to come back and cook a millennial dinner for them with thyme in every dish. Time! She pictured Jin leaning away as she spoke, actually bending over backwards. "I miss you," Ruth had whispered.

"If only my presence could live up to my absence," Jin said.

Ruth sometimes composed imaginary perfumes to put herself to sleep. Now she thought of a fragrance that smelled only of water, a perfume that had forgotten its flowers. Lethe. That's what she'd name it. It would have an industrial note, a trace of something evil, just as the classic perfumes had their cruel residues of civet and of musk. Perfumers called their creations juice, but Ruth thought of hers as ink. Lethe would be navy, like the deep-sea zone that fascinated Jinny, a place of intense pressure and low oxygen, black smokers and marine snow. It was cold there and utterly dark. Whatever lived in that place had to produce its own light. Bioluminescence. That was the term for it. Ruth got up and groped in the desk for the flight schedule Jin had sent. There was something in the drawer. Something like shrapnel. A submarine part. A periscope.

Annie's headache didn't go away. In the middle of the night, she got up to wait on it, do for it. She toddled to her bedside chair. Earlier, they'd lit a candle made by her sister Charlotte. It had burned with a pure and steady flame. Charlotte's candle! Its waxy sweet breath was still in the air. The alarm clock said December 31. The children would be coming soon, she thought, the trick-or-treaters, and she didn't have any candy for them. This was a serious spell. Her face was frozen, her side paralyzed, she couldn't move or speak. She looked out at her backyard through the blinds. The light was blue as deep-sea light on her silver fence and clothesline. On her snow.

The emergency waiting room was decorated with Happy Millennium balloons. Ruth was hungry, but she would not leave her mother. Her stomach growled. She found a cough drop in her pocket.

"I'm better," Annie said. "Let's go home."

"You're having an MRI tonight," Ruth reminded. "It's easy, not invasive." Her ears popped. She yawned to relieve the pressure.

"You're tired," Annie said. "Did you eat? Eat or you'll faint. They must have a—" she searched for the word "—food place. You look kind of peaked. Too bad Jin's not here. Jin was a good cook."

"She's flying in tonight," Ruth said. "I'm meeting her."

"Tonight!" Annie frowned at the dark windows. "This is the worst night to go anywhere. Tell her to come tomorrow."

The cough drop looked like dry ice. Ruth held it to her nose, sniffing.

"For God's sake, eat it!" her mother said. "You're not supposed to smell your food."

Ruth glanced around to see if anyone had noticed. She was losing a sense of social context. Sniffing like an animal! It even embarrassed her mother. She'd gotten distracted by the century turning and Jinny's arrival. There'd be no taxis, the airport would close, Jin would be out in the cold. Ruth had to be there. She put the cough drop in her mouth and offered one to Annie.

"I'm scared," Annie said. "The airport's far away. It's dark. I'll get lost if you leave."

All Ruth's colleagues knew she was her mother's caregiver. Many were sympathetic. The department chair told her he also took care of his mother, who lived near Paris, France.

"I promised I'd be there," Ruth said.

"Then I'll go with you."

Ruth closed her eyes. She lowered her head so the blood could reach her brain.

"You'll get lost," Annie said. "I know the way, I can help." She squirmed in the hospital wheelchair, and her pocketbook slid to the floor. "What's that?" she said, pointing. Water was trickling from an adjoining wall. "Should we say something?"

The front desk was deserted. Ruth pushed her mother's chair toward radiology. Annie worried about finding the right words. I'm a registered nurse, she'd say, and I noticed something. What? Something pertaining to water. Something important. She would help.

As they neared the MRI room, a technician came flying out. "Stop!" she yelled. They retreated, and she followed, scolding. "The machine is a powerful magnet. It pulls things into itself. You could be seriously hurt!"

By the time the janitors arrived, the water had formed a slender moat around them. They were on their own little island in the waiting room. "It's time to go," Ruth said.

"Don't be going yet," Annie begged. She rummaged in her purse and came up with a dollar. "Get a bite to eat, will you?"

"I'll be back soon, Ma."

"I'll be back soon, too," Annie said. As the orderly wheeled her away, she tried to see Ruth out the windows. All she saw was an old woman floating through darkness. Snow was falling. It was a bad night.

On the car radio, a homeopathic doctor said, "The active ingredient is completely removed from the remedy. Only a vibration remains. It works because water has a memory."

Ruth adjusted the rearview mirror. She'd heard that someone had built a snow labyrinth in Frear Park. She and Jinny would walk it. They'd concentrate on their breathing, listen to the snow crunch, sniff its eternal ozone, and remember all they'd lived. They'd remember all they'd loved and pardon each other.

The radio host grunted. "That sounds like baloney, if you'll pardon my French."

The department chair had described his mother's move to a nursing home. He'd assured her she was going on holiday with him in the south of France, so she was delighted to cooperate. Everything went smoothly till they arrived at the home and his mother refused to leave the car, actually locked him out. Two male nurses had to force a window and inject her with a sedative cocktail while she wept and clung to the steering wheel. The department chair had intended to visit her on his way back from Provence, but—and here his eyes inexplicably filled—he was so dismayed by her performative outburst that he had not seen her since her admittance.

Ruth's high beams tunneled through the darkness.

Her old friend Sunny had warned her about a movie she must not see. It took place a hundred years ago in an impoverished Japanese village. There were dire food shortages. In order for the community to survive, sons and daughters had to abandon their elderly parents on a snowy mountain where they'd die of exposure. This was the cultural law. Those who didn't enforce it could be buried alive. The movie showed a son's agonizing struggle up the mountain with his mother on his back. "Not many feel-good moments," Sunny warned.

And recently, a student in Asian Studies sent her a link to a new Japanese product for the elderly called a Cuddling Robot. It could tell the time and inquire after their health in a friendly, respectful tone. It looked like a hard resin model of the Pillsbury Doughboy.

The MRI technician took Annie's watch, earrings, glasses, coins, and bridge. Then she slid her into the white tube. Annie had expected total darkness, but it was lit up inside like Grand Central Station. Did people still meet there under the clock? she wondered.

First the machine chirped like a mechanical bird. Then it roared like a vacuum. Ping-ping-ping it went, and bong-bong-bong. At last, it played a drumroll, followed by knocking. This is it, Annie thought, the century's turning. The big ball in Times Square is sinking, the sun of a hundred years is going down. You've lived too long, she told herself. You've outlived your sisters, brother, husband, father, and mother.

"You okay in there?" a voice asked, out of the blue.

She gave a little jump, it was so close. It didn't sound familiar, but she might not remember the tone after all this time.

"It's almost over," the voice said.

There was something in the air.

Something like a bakery. Like the vanilla extract her mother wore for perfume.

"Get some rest now, will you?" Annie said, closing her eyes.

She took a deep breath.

That was the thing about time, the past. Once you'd breathed enough of it, you could smell the world's deliciousness even when it was no longer there.

ACKNOWLEDGMENTS

"Happy Dust" appeared in *Missouri Review* and received the Editor's Prize in Fiction. It was reprinted in *Peculiar Pilgrims: Stories from the Left Hand of God*. "Queen Wintergreen," originally published in *TriQuarterly*, was reprinted in *The Best American Short Stories* and in *Cabbage and Bones: An Anthology of Irish American Women's Fiction*. "A Shadow Table" appeared in *Tin House*. Aspects of that story were informed by and are indebted to Etsu Inagaki Sugimoto's *A Daughter of the Samurai*. "The Glorious Mysteries" was included in *Writers Harvest II*. "The Real Eleanor Rigby" appeared in *Gettysburg Review* and was reprinted in *The Pushcart Prize XXIX* and in *Peculiar Pilgrims: Stories from the Left Hand of God*. "Centrally Isolated" was published in *Epoch*. "If It's Not Too Much to Ask" appeared in *Georgia Review* and was reprinted in *The Long Meanwhile: Stories of Departure and Arrival*.

THANKS

Hank De Leo gave maximum sustenance. I'm also warmly grateful to Mary Callahan Fulton and Maureen Murphy for indispensable memories and insights.

Jill Bialosky, Emily Forland, and Wendy Weil were true advocates of this book. I couldn't wish for more dedicated or perceptive close readers. I deeply appreciate their astute suggestions and wise counsel.

Emma Patterson and Paul Whitlatch also provided timely, valuable assistance.

For crucial critiques and/or enthusiasm, I thank Charles Baxter, Ethan Canin, Martha Collins, Louise Erdrich, Edward Falco, Susan Hahn, T. R. Hummer, Caledonia Kearns, Katrina Kenison, Michael Koch, Molly McQuade, Greg Michalson, Speer Morgan, Rob Spillman, Peter Stitt, and Linda Wendling.

I'm grateful to Huda Akil, Alton Becker, Kenneth DeWoskin, Sabine MacCormack, Bruce Mannheim, Joseph Vining, James Boyd White, and Christina Brooks Whitman for their helpful readings.

Various stories were aided and abetted by Andrea Beauchamp, Gorman Beauchamp, Erin Bednarczyk, Sandra Carpenter, Lynn Connally, Ida De Leo, Bonnie Fucci, Amanda Hoenigman, Jim Hoffman, John Holland, Maurita Holland, Tom Louden, Margaret McDonald, Marian McDonald, Ed O'Connell, Pat O'Connell, Christina Owens, and Jon Randel.

My thanks to Cornell University; The National Endowment for the Arts; The University of Michigan; The John D. and Catherine T. MacArthur Foundation; and The Ingram Merrill Foundation for the gifts of time.

FICTION CATALOG
2012